WRANGLING A GROOM

DJ JAMISON

AUTHOR'S NOTE

Marital Bliss is a series that explores marriage themes, from marriage of convenience to fake fiancé to marriage pact, arranged marriage, runaway groom, or whatever else my brain devises. Some of these tropes are light and funny. Some are more serious. Wrangling a Groom falls into the latter category. I hope you enjoy the journey Wyatt and Diego take to find an HEA they thought they'd lost.

Sometimes love takes detours.

PROLOGUE

Two six-year-old boys sat in a tree together, very much *not* k-i-s-s-i-n-g. Not like Grandad, who was kissing that horrible Ms. Fletcher beneath the sprawling oak's branches. Grandad was going to *marry* her, and then she'd be Wyatt's grandmother, and she didn't like kids or horses or anything about ranching. It didn't make any sense at all, but Wyatt overheard Mama saying that men lost all good sense around a pretty face.

Wyatt looked over at Diego. He wasn't a girl, but his face was pretty — and he didn't make Wyatt do stupid things.

"Is Grandad *really* going to marry her?" Diego asked.

Grandad was really Wyatt's grandfather, but all the kids around the ranch called him that. Diego's father was a foreman on the crew, and Grandad said he was the kind of man you could count on to get things done. Wyatt and Diego had been best friends since they could crawl.

"Dunno," Wyatt said. "Think maybe we should get married?"

Diego's eyes widened to a comical degree. "*Us?* But we're boys."

"So?" Wyatt said. "At least you're not horrible. If we make a

I

pact to get married when we're older, then we won't have to worry about some awful pretty face coming around."

"I guess." Diego sounded skeptical.

"Come on, let's make a pact. It'll be fun!"

Wyatt scrambled down the tree, and Diego followed him, just like he always did. They ran past the smooching couple, Ms. Fletcher exclaiming about rude little boys as they flew past. Laughing, Diego shouted, "Race ya to the barn!"

Dust kicked up under their feet as they poured on speed. Wyatt skidded around a corner, Diego on his heels, and they both raced for the spot behind the barn where they hid out to avoid notice and the chores that always seemed needing done.

Diego was gaining on him, and Wyatt threw out an arm to block him. They went down in a tumble, skidding into the building.

"You made me fall," Diego accused sharply, eyes glassy. "I'm bleeding, see?"

He pointed to his knee, scraped and oozing a hint of blood. Wyatt checked himself over, but he was in one piece.

"Sorry."

"It hurts."

"Hey, we can use it in our pact. You need blood for a pact; everybody knows that."

Diego looked at him dubiously. "Really?"

Wyatt nodded his head. Looking around for something sharp, he spotted a nail bent and poking out sharply from a plank of wood. He raked his hand over it. The skin split open, blood rushing to the surface. He held his hand up proudly.

Diego looked awed. "Didn't that hurt?"

"Nuh-uh," Wyatt lied.

It *really* hurt, but he didn't want to show it. Grandad was always telling him to toughen up; ranch life was hard. Ignoring the pain, he focused on the pact they were about to make. "Get some of your blood on your hand, then we'll shake on it."

Diego dabbed at his knee, then lifted his hand, and Wyatt pressed his bloody palm against it, wincing at the sting.

"There, it's done. Now we can marry each other when we're older."

"How much older?" Diego asked.

Wyatt thought about that. "Not as old as Grandad. But still, we need to be old. Not like teenagers."

Diego brightened. "My parents got married when they were twenty." Then he frowned. "But they got divorced, and they said it was 'cause they were too young."

"Twenty-five then," Wyatt announced. "I, Wyatt Jones, make a pact to marry you, Diego Flores, when we're twenty-five years old."

After Diego repeated the vow, he asked, "Don't you need a wife to have kids? You'll need kids to take over the ranch for you, like you're gonna take it over for Grandad."

Wyatt pondered that. "Mama can just have more for me. Come on, I'm hungry. Let's get a snack."

Mama stopped them before they'd made it three steps into the kitchen from the back door. "Hold up, there," she said sternly. "What happened to you two?"

"Diego fell and skinned his knee," Wyatt said. "And we decided to get married."

She laughed. "Is that so? A busy day then." She grabbed a cloth and wet it, instructing Diego to take a seat so she could clean him up. "And what about you? Is all that blood from Diego's knee?"

"No, it was for our pact. I cut my hand so I would bleed too."

"Cut it on what?"

"A nail on the barn," Diego said.

"A nail on the— Oh, for heaven's sake, you'll have to get a tetanus shot!"

"A shot?" Wyatt looked down at his throbbing hand regretfully. "I don't want a shot."

"Too late for that now," she said. "Let's get you clean and bandaged, then we'll run you into town to see the doctor."

Wyatt's lip wobbled. "I just wanted to make a marriage pact with Diego."

Her lips twitched as she pushed him into a chair. "Well, baby, sometimes love hurts."

1

―――――――

"Where the heck is that address book..."

Wyatt Jones sifted through his grandfather's papers in his antique oak desk, trying to make sense of his hodge-podge file-keeping, his eyes gritty from exhaustion. The old man had been sick for a long time, lung cancer finally getting the better of him. All that tobacco and pipe smoke, Wyatt reckoned. The sweet, smoky scent lingered in the office, a tangible reminder of the man who had always sat behind this desk.

Wyatt squeezed his eyes shut as his sinuses burned. "Shit. Not now."

The ranch stopped for no man, not even the one who'd kept it going for so many years. *Kept it going with an iron fist and no shits to give about anyone else.*

But that wasn't fair. Grandad was a hard bastard at times, but he was family. And it wasn't as if he hadn't loved Wyatt. These past few months, he'd softened some, age and illness sanding down his rougher edges. He even went so far as to say that maybe Wyatt couldn't help the way he was, just like Grandad couldn't help being sick.

Comparing homosexuality to an illness wasn't ideal, but considering where they'd started, Wyatt would take it.

Ranch life ain't got no room for unnatural perversions, Wyatt! You need a wife, a family. That's what will keep you going. This isn't an easy life, and you can't do it alone.

Grandad's attempt at acceptance, however misguided, meant peace between them when he died. Not to say that Grandad wasn't disappointed. He'd wanted Wyatt to carry on the family name and create the next rancher for the Triple J. But that wasn't happening. Wyatt might have spent most of his life closeted, but he'd put his foot down when it came to marrying a country girl and having babies.

Eventually, he'd put his foot down about living a lie too. Too little too late, though. Wyatt might be openly gay now, but he was still alone. He'd taken too long to find the guts to stand up to Grandad.

He pulled out a handful of handwritten receipts, swearing to himself, as he fanned them out on the blocky desk that had been in the ranch house since it was built in the late 1800s. Squinting, he struggled to decipher his grandfather's writing, a headache starting up behind his eyes. He had no idea where these had come from, but he'd need them come tax time. Grandad's system had worked for him, and Wyatt knew where some things were — having taken over most of the management of the ranch when Grandad's illness began to worsen — but he was still finding things in odd places.

Setting aside the receipts, he sorted through a few more papers before finding the old address book. "Aha, there we go."

He flipped it open. Ranchers from around the county, suppliers, former ranch hands. They were all jotted down, with last known address and phone number. He had a lot of calls to make, and Wyatt didn't look forward to it, exactly, but it felt necessary. Like making the calls might make it feel true.

Grandad is gone, and he's not coming back to save the ranch. It's all up to you now...

"Knock-knock." Mama stood in the doorway. She'd come to help with funeral arrangements, but Wyatt knew she wouldn't stay long. The ranch hadn't been her home for years now. "Rosie has lunch ready."

Wyatt held up the address book for her to see. "Grandad never did get on with smartphones."

She chuckled, moving in to take a closer look. "You should have seen his face when we got our first microwave. He wanted nothing to do with that monstrosity."

"How'd you ever convince him to get one? He was always so stubborn."

"Rosie told him that if he didn't like it, he could cook the meals. After that, he thought it was a mighty fine idea. He still scowled at the damn thing each time he entered the kitchen."

They laughed until Mama's eyes filled with tears. "I'm gonna miss that old fool," she said, dabbing at her eyes, "even if he was the most bullheaded man I ever met. Sometimes I just wanted to —" she held out her hands to demonstrate "—wring his neck."

Grandad had only been her father-in-law, and Mama hadn't seen eye to eye with him on many occasions, but she'd stayed so that her children could be raised on the Triple J, like their father had been, before he'd been killed by a horse kick to the chest. That was before Grandad sold off most of their horses and invested in ATVs.

Wyatt stood and drew Mama into his arms, inhaling the comforting scent of the rose-petal perfume she'd worn his whole life. She was a good six inches shorter than his six-foot-two, but he could still remember when he hugged her waist as a little boy.

"Grandad's always been larger than life," Wyatt murmured. "We'll all miss him."

Grandad had made mistakes, but then hadn't they all? Wyatt knew he lived with regrets. He liked to think he wasn't alone in that. But Grandad *was* the Triple J. How did a ranch keep functioning without its heart — even a hard-edged one like William C. Jones?

———————

Diego listened to his voicemail a third time as he watched Matias spray stringy cheese onto crackers. He didn't even know they still made that fake crap, but the way Matias was going to town, you'd think it was nectar of the gods.

Breakups sucked. Diego knew firsthand. But damn, he'd never seen Matias looking so ... *un*sexy. Gone was the smoky eyeliner, the sultry smiles he shot his adoring audience at Caliente nightclub, where he commanded the dance platform. There was no sashay in the poor jerk who lounged on Diego's sofa, though he still wore clingy pants and a long tank top that slipped off one shoulder, so there was hope yet.

The slow, honeyed drawl of Diego's own ex slid into his ear from the phone speaker. "Diego, this is Wyatt. I got your number from Roberto. I know you probably don't want to hear from me, and I wasn't sure I should even leave this message. It doesn't feel right not to tell you in person, but... you're a long way away, and for some crazy reason, I need to be the one to tell you. Grandad died. Lung cancer. He was sick a long time, lasted longer than the doctors said he would."

No doubt he was a hard bastard right up to the end.

Grandad Jones had been the quintessential cowboy, with a steel core and a no-nonsense approach to life. Unfortunately, Diego's relationship with Wyatt had fallen into the nonsense category in Grandad's world.

Wyatt continued. "The funeral is on Sunday, after church services. I know your father would like it if you were here. Josefina too. I can't—"

Beep.

Diego would never know what Wyatt couldn't do. The message cut him off mid-sentence, and he didn't call back to finish. Diego played the guessing game, finishing out Wyatt's comment in his mind:

I can't wait to see you?

I can't apologize enough?

I can't turn back time, but I wish I could.

Diego would like that last one too. But time had a way of stubbornly marching forward. Diego thought of the letter, folded and faded in his wallet. He could almost feel it, burning through the leather, through his jeans, branding his skin. Wyatt's last attempt to reach out to him, but not the first.

He had the words memorized, but as he hit replay on his voicemail and Wyatt's voice washed over him once more, he pulled the wallet from his back pocket and slipped that bit of stationery free to read Wyatt's pretty, cursive handwriting.

Diego,

I never thought the day you left that I would go so long without a word from you. I hurt you. I own that, and I'm sorry for it.

I don't know if you're reading these words, if you've read any of the words I've sent your way. I feel like I'm shouting into the abyss. But if you do hear me... please come home. Come home for a day, for a week, forever. We made so many promises. I'd like to keep them all, but short of that, I'd like to keep at least one, to always be your friend.

Sincerely,

Wyatt

Diego had never replied, just like he'd never replied to any of Wyatt's earlier attempts. But this letter — which arrived just before his closest friend went to Maine to marry the man he loved and confront his past — had struck a chord in Diego. He hadn't been ready to fly off to Texas and take his past by the horns, but he hadn't been able to ignore the letter, either. He'd kept it, read it time and again, and wondered if he might be ready to revisit that chapter of his life.

Grandad Jones was no small part of Diego's falling out with Wyatt, but he'd been a strong influence in Diego's life. Diego grew up on Grandad's ranch, ate dinner at his table at least a hundred times, had sleepovers in his house, and received his share of back slaps and *atta boy's* as he learned the ropes of ranching.

Diego had loved Grandad Jones, and as furious as he was that the man hadn't accepted him and Wyatt together — had out and out forbidden it — he also knew that if he'd been dating Wyatt's sister, instead, Grandad would have welcomed him into the family.

Because that's what they were. Dysfunctional and not blood-related, but family. When it came down to it, the Triple J Ranch had been Diego's home, and William Jones had been his grandfather too.

Matias's voice jarred him from his thoughts.

"Good news or bad news? I can't tell from that face you're making."

Diego glanced up, realizing he still held the phone to his ear even though the recording had ended. He resisted the urge to hit replay one more time. Wyatt's voice was compelling, that was for damn sure. If he closed his eyes, he could picture Wyatt as he'd last seen him, and yet, his voice sounded deeper than he remembered, more graveled.

Had it really changed over the six years he'd been gone, or had he forgotten Wyatt's voice? He couldn't be sure, and that made his finger itch to hit the button again, until he'd memorized the exact cadence and pitch, until that honey drawl was fixed in his mind.

"It's not good news," he said finally. "My... grandfather died."

Matias paused, cracker topped with a precarious pile of

jiggling fake cheese — an incongruous bit of ridiculousness that made Diego want to laugh despite the serious turn of conversation, or maybe *because* of it.

"I'm so sorry," Matias said. "Were you close with your abuelo?"

"Once, maybe," Diego said. "Not recently, but ..."

"What?"

"I think I want to go to his funeral," he said, surprising himself. "I think... maybe ..."

"Maybe what?"

"Maybe it's time to go home."

2

Diego arrived just as the memorial service began at the small cemetery on the grounds of the Triple J Ranch. He'd driven from Miami — twenty-two hours on the road — because his credit cards were still maxed out from his trip to Bliss Island the spring before. He'd barely made it in time, stopping at a gas station outside Cow Creek to wash up in a grimy sink and change into his suit.

The ranch cemetery held generations of Jones men, women, and children. Old gravestones, decaying wood crosses, and simple markers sprouted from the ground like wildflowers. He'd never given it much thought back when he'd lived at the ranch, but now it sent a shiver down his spine, thinking of all the souls here within its boundaries.

Wyatt was at the front of the small gathering of people who'd come to pay their respects to Grandad Jones. He stood out like a beacon to Diego, his bright hair shining the sunlight, empty of the cowboy hat that usually sat there, almost as much a part of his features as his eye color or jawline.

If hearing Wyatt's voice had rattled him, seeing him in the flesh was the equivalent of a minor earthquake. Diego's feet were still beneath him, but he felt the tremors shift his insides as he stared at the man he'd once loved.

Wyatt looked strong—but also brittle. His jaw was clenched, lips pressed tight, as if he was fighting to keep up the stoic façade, but his bloodshot eyes gave away the truth. Wyatt wasn't unmoved by his grandfather's death; he was just well-trained to contain his feelings.

Unhealthy masculine bullshit, and a lesson Grandad had ingrained in them both from a young age, though Diego had never been able to live by it. He was too hot-tempered, his emotions taking him from irritated to furious in sixty seconds. Not Wyatt, though. He was easy-going, so much so that it came as a shock when you did piss him off.

Wyatt looked the same as he remembered, sparking sensory memories of exploring the long, lean lines of his body, but he looked different too. They'd been lanky, more boys than men, when they last saw one another. Wyatt's shoulders had since broadened, and his posture straightened. His expression had grown more serious too—or maybe that was the grief.

Diego's cousin, Josefina, smoothed a hand over his shoulder. "You look fine. Good." Her gaze darted to Wyatt. "He looks good too. Sad, but handsome."

Diego shot her a look. "I hadn't noticed."

She smiled knowingly but didn't comment, brushing a hand down his sleeve, then straightening his tie. He felt like a five-year-old getting fussed over by his mama. Josefina had always been like that, trying to mother him.

He pushed her hands away. "Stop, Fina," he muttered, casting a look around them. "I'm not a child."

"I'm aware," she said, patting her rounded stomach. "I've got some experience."

Standing to her right, her husband, Leon Carpenter, held their small son, Lakin. And beyond him, Wyatt's sister, Ella, her husband, Tucker Dalton, and their two sons looked on. Ella should be up front with the family. The fact she wasn't told Diego that Grandad Jones had never relented on his insistence that she couldn't be a Jones *and* a Dalton, thanks to a stupid feud that had begun long before he'd died.

Ella had chosen love. Unlike Wyatt ... who'd chosen his inheritance.

Diego wondered idly if Grandad Jones was spinning in his grave, having a whole household of Daltons at his funeral.

Good thing they'd come, though, Diego thought as he let his eyes skim over the sparse group of people. Not a whole lot of *friends* had turned out to say goodbye to William C. Jones. A few ranchers from the county were in attendance, but there were twenty people at most.

In the front row, Wyatt stood with his mama, as well as Diego's father, Roberto, and the household manager, Rosie.

Not a whole lot of friends here for Wyatt either, then.

Behind Wyatt and Roberto, a young, coltish guy leaned forward, whispering into Wyatt's ear. His hair fell forward, brushing Wyatt's for a moment, intermingling blond and brown strands, and Diego's body tightened with tension.

"That's Colby," Josefina murmured. "The man next to him, the big one, is his uncle. They both work on the Triple J now."

Diego breathed easier when Colby stepped back. He cast his eyes over the crowd for any of the other ranch hands he remembered. Some came and went, others stayed for years. But there were always more than a handful.

"Where are the other ranch hands?" he asked, speaking under his breath. "I hauled my ass all the way from Miami. Seems like the least they could do is be here too."

"There aren't any," she said. "This is everyone."

Everyone? Diego scanned the group again. Counting Wyatt and Roberto, that made four men to work the ranch. That couldn't be right.

Before he could question Josefina further, the preacher

wrapped up his prayer — shit, Diego hadn't even bowed his head, too distracted to listen — and the memorial ceremony concluded. Wyatt shifted on his feet, turning his head. He froze when their eyes met.

For a second, Diego felt like an insect pinned to a board, so piercing was Wyatt's gaze. Then the preacher stepped forward, gripping his hand, and he looked away.

"Come on," Josefina said. "Let's give our condolences."

Roberto looked over his shoulder, eyes crinkling with a smile when he spotted Diego, though his lips didn't so much as twitch.

"You made it," his father said, clapping Diego's shoulder when he reached them. Diego had to fight to keep his eyes off Wyatt. Not because he was stunning, though Diego couldn't deny that he was. It was just that he hadn't ever thought he'd see him again, and even though that was his choice, it was a little overwhelming to be in his presence. The living, breathing man was more *real* than the memory he'd spent so much time resenting.

"Yeah, just barely," Diego said. "It was a long drive."

Wyatt turned then, a paltry attempt at a smile on his face. "Thanks for coming."

"Sure."

They looked at one another, but words seemed to escape them both.

Then Rosie stepped forward, breaking the awkward moment. "Diego Flores, it's good to see you!" She dragged him into a tight hug, rocking him side to side. "It's been too long. Come on up to the house. I've got some cold cuts laid out."

Diego's eyes automatically sought out Wyatt over her shoulder. His polite expression had morphed to one of amusement, a familiar twinkle in his eye. Diego rolled his eyes, and Wyatt coughed to disguise a small laugh.

It shouldn't have pleased Diego to draw that out of him. Wyatt had made his choice a long time ago, and it hadn't been Diego. He'd broken his heart, but ... Hell, today, Wyatt looked like the one who was heartbroken, and something in Diego responded to that.

"Thanks, Rosie," he said, pulling out of the boisterous hug. "That sounds nice."

———

Wyatt wasn't hungry. Hadn't been hungry for days. Rosie kept looking at him with big, sad eyes and tsking about not letting the grief keep him from eating. Wyatt almost wished it was grief, because whenever someone offered him condolences, he felt guilty. Grandad had died, but it had been a long time coming, and Wyatt had plenty of time to say his goodbyes.

It wasn't grief that kept his appetite away. It was stress. It was the realization that everything rested on his shoulders now: the Triple J Ranch operation, centuries of Jones legacy, a lifetime of expectations. It all came down to him. He held people's livelihoods in his hands. If he failed, he wouldn't fail just himself or Grandad's memory, he'd fail Rosie and Roberto and Hank and Colby.

It was a lot of pressure. The ranch had been running lean for the past few years, but it'd only gotten worse as Grandad got older. He'd refused to loosen his grasp on the ranch's management until he got too ill to keep up, and by then, the damage had been done. Of course, Wyatt had done his own share of damage simply by existing. Men in these parts didn't want to work for the gay rancher. *The gay rancher,* because as far as Wyatt knew, he was the only one—or, at least the only one foolish enough to let it be known.

When he'd insisted to Grandad that he accept Wyatt—and help others accept him, too—it had felt essential. As if he'd disintegrate into dust and ash if he continued to live a lie. Grandad hadn't been pleased, and it'd taken some talking around, but he'd eventually backed Wyatt's decision, standing up for him when word got out that he was dating a museum curator in nearby Cow Creek. Hadn't lasted, that relationship, but the fallout had.

While Grandad had his back, most folks fell in line. But as word got out that he was sick, attitudes changed. A few deliveries from local vendors got lost. Ranch hands began to leave, one by one. And then there'd been the vandalism: Wyatt had woken one morning to a spray-painted message on the side of the barn: *This ain't fag country. It's GUN country.*

If that wasn't a threat, Wyatt didn't know what was.

"You should eat," Mama said, coming to stand beside him. "Rosie prepared a nice spread."

Wyatt looked sidelong at her, guilt bubbling up once again. Rosie had worked hard to prepare this luncheon, and he was squandering her efforts. Picking up a slice of sharp cheddar, he nibbled. "Rosie works hard. I appreciate it."

Mama sighed, smiling at him. "I know you do, and so does she. I just want you to take care of yourself. You work too hard, and you're too hard on yourself."

"I'll work on it," he murmured, gaze straying.

People milled through the house, though most of them had congregated around the kitchen table once they'd offered their condolences, staying close to the cold cuts, cheeses, and fruit Rosie had laid out. Diego stood apart from everyone else, leaning against the kitchen counter near the sink, his eyes on the view out the window.

He'd bulked up. Diego had always been more muscular than Wyatt, but now his shoulders were rounded with muscle, and the shape of his biceps could be seen even through the sleeves of his suit. A layer of stubble shaded his jaw, transforming the boyish cuteness he'd always had into raw, masculine sex appeal.

Mama followed his gaze. "I'm surprised to see him here. Did you know he was coming?"

"No. I only got his voicemail, and he never called back, so... I'm as surprised as you are."

She nodded. Mama knew as well as he did why Diego left six years ago. She'd had words with Grandad, for all the good it did. She'd had a few words with Wyatt too. But Mama was a forgiving woman. She loved harder than anyone he knew, and she never held a grudge.

Unlike Diego.

"I wonder how long he's staying," she mused.

"I don't know."

She hummed thoughtfully. "Maybe you should go find out?"

Wyatt reckoned he'd be safer asking a coyote why he was trying to eat a chicken, but he nodded anyway, happy for an excuse to set down his untouched plate. He ladled up two cups of punch, wishing they were beer. Barbecue and beer had seemed too irreverent for a funeral, but it might have fit Grandad's personality better. He wasn't one to stand on ceremony, though he did like tradition.

Traditional values, his voice echoed in Wyatt's mind. *Family. Religion. The world has forgotten what matters. That's what's wrong these days.*

Grandad never directly brought up gay people, but Wyatt always felt it like a little dart to his skin anyhow. He'd been a glowing, neon sign for everything wrong with the world in Grandad's eyes.

He accepted you. He said so. Sort of.

After years of hearing those little comments, knowing what Grandad thought, it was hard to dismiss them, even if he'd changed his tune near the end. The damage had been done. Wyatt had done a fair amount of damage himself, too, especially when it came to the man standing across the kitchen.

The man who looked more like a stranger than a lifelong friend. Well, almost lifelong. Wyatt hoped they'd be friends again. He hoped they'd be more than friends, but that was probably just wishful thinking.

Wyatt carried a cup of punch to him. "Thirsty?"

Diego turned, eyes dropping to the drink in his hand, and for one awful moment, Wyatt thought he was going to refuse his offering — or worse, throw it in his face.

"Sure. It's a hot one today."

"Especially in these monkey suits," Wyatt agreed, handing Diego one cup and lifting his own to sip the punch, grimacing at the too-sweet fruity flavor.

Diego opened his mouth. "I'm—"

"Don't," Wyatt said quickly. He didn't know how he knew, but he was certain Diego was about to offer more condolences. "You're the only one who hasn't given me his sympathies. I'd like to keep it that way."

Diego glanced toward the cluster of folks around the table, then back to the window. "I'm in the mood for some fresh air. What do you say?"

"God, yes."

They slipped out the back door, and Diego shrugged off his suit jacket as soon as they cleared the yard. As Diego rolled up his shirt sleeves, exposing forearms dusted with dark hair, Wyatt stared a few beats, until he realized what he was doing, then jerked his eyes away.

He removed his own suit jacket and pulled at his tie, loosening the knot enough he could pull it over his head. Then he took a deep breath, so deep it raised his chest. "That's better. I can finally breathe."

When he looked over, Diego was staring at him. "What?"

Diego shook his head. "Just thinking."

Wyatt wanted to ask what he was thinking about, but he was also afraid of the answer. If Diego was thinking of the past, it wouldn't bode well for him. If he thought too much about that now, he'd never have the guts to say what he needed to while Diego was here.

Clearing his throat, and shaking away memories of the argument that had broken them, Wyatt asked, "How long you here for?"

Diego squinted into the distance, taking in the view drenched in golden sunshine. "Not sure yet. Not long."

Wyatt tried to see the ranch through his eyes, then wished he hadn't. The place looked... worn down. The large barn, the bright red of a fire engine in his childhood, had faded to a rusty color, a mix of red and the brown of the wood coming together, he reckoned, except for one bright splotch of paint that reminded him of the vandals' threat every time he looked at it.

The little cabin where Diego had grown up with his father fared a little better, though the roof leaked and the porch sagged. The stables to the south were a newer structure; the Triple J was a cattle ranch, but even with the ATVs, they'd always had a few working horses on hand.

Off in the distance, too far away to see, a defunct bunkhouse sat abandoned. In the ranch's heyday, it'd once housed up to a dozen ranch hands. Now, the only one to live on site was Roberto. The rest of the crew, which used to be significantly larger, drove in from Cow Creek or nearby country homes, though Rosie still fed them most of the time.

But the land still undulated in endless waves, mostly flat but with a few hills in the far reaches of the nine-thousand-acre ranch, and the sky was as vast as ever above, bright with sunshine and white, fluffy clouds. That was far more valuable than faded paint and loose boards. Those were just materials, but the grass, the trees, the animals? That was life itself.

"Is it everything you remember?" he asked Diego.

"No, not everything."

Wyatt glanced back to Diego to see his eyes firmly fixed on his face. "The buildings are in need of a touchup, especially the barn." He felt embarrassed that Diego could see the disrepair that had set in. "I guess time caught up with us."

"It has a way of doing that."

Diego started walking toward the barn, and Wyatt fell into

step with him. "What's with the paint there?" he asked, pointing to the fresher paint that had covered the vandals' message as they came around the corner, facing the back wall.

The worst part? That vandals had tainted their special place. Wyatt and Diego had hidden out here behind the barn more times than Wyatt could count. They'd played games, snuck cigarettes and the odd beer, shared dozens of kisses.

"Had to cover up some graffiti," Wyatt said as his skin heated.

"Ah. Little punks."

Wyatt snorted. "Yup."

He stared at the nail, now pounded flat, where he'd once raked open the skin of his hand to make a blood pact.

He reached out, brushing a finger over it. "Do you remember?"

Diego leaned closer. "A nail? Is that...where you cut yourself for that ridiculous pact?"

Wyatt smiled faintly. "It wasn't ridiculous."

"We were six years old," Diego said. "We didn't even know what love or marriage meant, not really."

Wyatt's stomach tightened at Diego's dismissive tone. But he remembered, that was the important thing. As much as he disparaged it, he'd never forgotten, had he?

"We're twenty-five now," Wyatt said. "That was the age we chose."

"Huh." Diego tilted his head, as if to think. "I guess it was."

"You got anyone special?" he blurted.

Diego looked taken aback, but he answered. "Nope."

"Me either."

Saliva pooled in Wyatt's mouth as nerves took over. This was the moment. He took a deep breath, dredging up every bit of courage he had. Courage that had failed him six years ago.

"I think we should do it."

Diego looked lost. "Huh?"

"The marriage pact—"

"*What?*"

"Just hear me out," Wyatt said quickly. "I don't know how long you're gonna stay, and I don't want to go another six years without seeing you. We made a promise—"

"When we were kids!"

Wyatt talked faster. "*Still.* You're here, and at the exact right time. That has to mean something, right? We were good together once. We loved each other. That's more than a lot of people have. I don't know about you, but I'm tired of being alone. I'm tired of nothing but regrets. Let's keep the promise we made, D! Why not? What do we have to lose—"

"Stop," Diego cut in. "Just stop."

Wyatt gasped for breath, feeling as if he'd run a sprint. His heart pounded, and nausea hit him so hard he had to clamp his teeth against the urge to spew at Diego's feet.

Fuck, he wanted this so much. And Diego was going to say no, he was going to say—

"I can't listen to this."

He turned away, and Wyatt reached for him before he could stop himself. He grabbed at his shirt, and Diego turned on him so quickly he fell back against the barn wall, the window sill digging into his back. He barely felt it as Diego leaned in, eyes snapping with fury.

"You're out of your damn mind," he said. "You have no right to ask me this. No right to touch me. You threw it all away." Stepping back, he threw out an arm. "Now, you've got all this. It's everything you wanted."

"It's not everything I wanted," Wyatt protested.

"Then it's what you wanted most," Diego said. He shrugged, as if he didn't care, but Wyatt could see through the casual gesture. Diego was tense, his jaw muscle jumping. "You made your deal with the devil, Wy. Now you have to live with it."

"This isn't what I wanted," Wyatt insisted.

But Diego was already backing away. Wyatt almost missed the

fury when Diego's expression turned coolly neutral. Anger was something familiar. This distance, though? This wall between them? That felt wrong.

But then again, everything had felt wrong since that day six years ago, when Wyatt said the wrong thing and Diego left him.

"It's too late, Wy. I don't want to talk about this."

"Okay," Wyatt ground out, his throat so tight it hurt to speak as all his hopes turned to ash. "I'm sorry."

"I need to go check in at my hotel," Diego said. "I've had enough reminiscing for one afternoon."

"You can stay here," Wyatt said. "We've got plenty of room."

Too much room, a sprawling ranch house with room for several generations, and just one Jones man to fill it. Grandad's second wife, Rachel, hadn't taken to ranch life, and had moved on years before he died. Ella got married. Mama moved to town.

"I've already booked a room in town," Diego said. "I'll stay a couple of days. It's a long drive, and I'm not eager to make it all over again."

Wyatt's heart sank, though he was relieved he hadn't pushed Diego to leave town right away. He'd rushed things. He'd known it was too soon, but he was terrified Diego would leave and he'd never get this chance again. If there was one thing Wyatt had learned from his mistake six years ago, it was to never let fear hold him back from something he wanted.

And Wyatt wanted Diego more than anything else in the world.

He'd learned that truth the hard way, when he'd let him walk away.

3

The Old Hotel at Cow Creek had been beautifully restored. Diego was surprised, considering how faded the rest of the town looked, as if it was a handful of people away from joining the thousand-plus ghost towns in Texas.

Panels covered with textured, cream-colored wallpaper, lush carpet, and a chandelier suspended three stories above gave the old building elegance, while brick pillars and wrought-iron balconies attached to suites on each of the floors above evoked the feeling of an outdoor courtyard. Small sconces inset into the walls, designed to look like outdoor lanterns, added to the effect.

The beds were nice too, not that it had helped Diego. He hadn't slept well, plagued by the desperate look on Wyatt's face when he'd proposed the afternoon before.

Was that really a proposal? It'd sounded more like a plea for forgiveness, maybe even rescue. *What have we got to lose?* Diego snorted. Now that Wyatt had nothing to lose, he wanted Diego back in his life. But when he had things at risk? He'd broken it off with Diego, said he couldn't risk his grandfather making good on his threats to disinherit Wyatt.

Diego knew exactly where Wyatt's priority had lain, and it wasn't with him.

Checking the time, Diego grabbed a cup of complimentary coffee and hit the road to the ranch. It was going on ten, the men already working, but Rosie came out the front door as he arrived, beaming a wide smile and holding her arms open, fairly demanding a hug. Diego gave it to her happily, squeezing her and lifting her off her feet, making her squeal and laugh.

"Stop showing off," she said, smacking his arm as he put her down. "I know you're stronger than an ox."

"Better-looking too, I hope," he said with a grin.

"You missed breakfast. The men are already out in the southeast pasture today," she said. "I was fixing to run them out some lunch before long." She brightened. "Maybe you could do it for me? I've still got cleaning up to do from yesterday's stampede through the house."

Diego smelled a setup but didn't fight the suggestion. "As long as you feed me first. I'm starving."

"Well, come on. I might have a few pancakes I can warm up," she said, turning and leading him toward the kitchen.

Rosie was petite but sturdy, with long curls she wore piled on her head and eyes always full of love for everyone around her. It was a wonder she'd put up with Grandad Jones for all those years. It was an even greater wonder she'd put up with Rachel for the two years she'd lasted before filing for divorce. They'd butted heads several times, with Wyatt's mother working overtime as the peacekeeper. Once Grandad Jones exiled Ella, Mama was through with him too. She'd remained the couple of years until Wyatt was of age, then moved to town.

Grandad Jones had sure burned a lot of bridges, and each time, Wyatt had stayed by his side. All for the sake of the ranch.

"Sit down." Rosie urged him into a chair at the square kitchen table. "This will only take a minute."

He felt a little guilty, letting her wait on him, but nostalgia washed away the feeling. He'd sat in this very chair while Rosie bustled around the kitchen more times than he could count. It was familiar and comforting.

Before long, she sat a plate before him stacked with pancakes, and a small bowl of strawberries too. A jar of dark, molasses syrup made his mouth water. He'd been eating his pancakes with maple syrup for a long time, nearly forgetting how much he liked the richness of the molasses.

"This is great, Rosie. Thank you."

"You're welcome, hon," she said, taking a seat near him and watching him eat. "After you finish eating, you can run some sandwiches out to the boys. But first, tell me all about your life. You're a bartender, I hear?"

"Yeah," Diego said thickly between bites. "It pays the bills."

"Do you love it?" she asked. "Is it what you hope to do for the rest of your life?"

He paused, sipping the last of the coffee from his take-out cup from the hotel. "I don't know about the rest of my life. Pretty sure my tips would suffer once I went gray and saggy."

She laughed heartily, smacking his arm again, before asking him about his apartment, his friends, his city. By the time he'd cleaned his plate, Rosie had pulled six years' worth of life story out of him, all so effortlessly that Diego wasn't quite sure how it'd happened. He wasn't usually this much of a talker.

"Now, then, it's time you know a thing or two about the ranch," she said matter-of-factly as she picked up his plate to rinse it.

"What's what?"

She looked him in the eye. "It's faltering. When you take these sandwiches out, you'll see. Four men to do six men's work." She clucked. "That's just the daily chores. The bigger projects, the upkeep around the ranch, it's all suffering. Heaven forbid when spring rolls back around and we're dealing with calving. I'll probably have to join the men out there unless they get some new blood by then."

"What happened around here?"

She smiled sadly. "Just life, I s'pose. Wyatt can explain it best. Or Roberto. Isn't my place."

"Then why are you telling me?"

Rosie busied herself packing up a stack of sandwiches into a bag, while Diego burned with curiosity. Turning, she handed him the bag. "I guess I'm just tryin' to tell you in my roundabout way that if you were to give the men a bit of help while you're here, we'd all be grateful."

She looked him over, head to toe, taking in his T-shirt, faded jeans, and boots. "Then again, given the way you're dressed, maybe I don't have to ask." She dimpled as she smiled. "You look prepared to get dirty."

He laughed, rolling his eyes. So much for getting the guest treatment. Diego was almost relieved to be asked for free labor. He wouldn't have known what to do with himself all day.

"Let's just say I had a feeling I might find my way out to the pasture at some point."

"Get a move on then," she said, nudging him toward the door. "The guys are bound to be starving by now."

The sound of an ATV approaching caught Wyatt's attention. The Brangus and Hereford cattle were unbothered, already accustomed to the ATVs used on the ranch and surrounded on all sides by the vehicles gently driving them toward a new pasture.

This time of year, there was more grass than in winter, but it was important not to let the cattle overgraze, so they moved them more often.

Despite all four men working from ATVs, they took different points on the several hundred acres so they could urge any stragglers and wanderers toward the herd making its way gradually across the land. That meant none of them were close enough that Wyatt would hear them.

He turned in his seat, slowing to a stop, and watched the approaching vehicle. As it neared, he recognized Diego in the driver's seat, and a wide grin broke out across his face.

"You miss the cattle that much?" he called out.

"Hey, I'm just a delivery boy," Diego said as he rolled to a stop, lifting a small brown bag. "Rosie made sandwiches."

Wyatt rubbed his hands together. "Awesome, I'm starved."

Rosie was pretty good about sending food their way if seemed as if they wouldn't have time to make it back to the house. Some days, they packed their own lunches, but she'd told Wyatt not to worry about it this morning. Leave it to Rosie to find a way to get him and Diego together when he wasn't sure how to go about it.

"She send enough for the other guys?"

"Yup. I hit them first. Rosie and Papá both said you might be able to put me to use today."

Wyatt could think of a good many ways to put Diego to use, none of them for herding cattle. But they were in no place for that kind of blatant flirtation. Especially not after the mistake he'd made the day before, asking for too much too soon.

He wasn't sure that Diego wouldn't be gone before the end of the week—but damn, Wyatt wanted him. Even if all he got was a taste of what they'd had before, something he could savor during the long years ahead.

"Sure, I could use your company while I eat." Wyatt tested out a wink. "Make sure none of the cattle wander off."

As he opened the bag, reaching inside to withdraw a thick-cut ham sandwich with swiss cheese and mayo, he kept an eye on Diego's reaction. He didn't give Wyatt the flirty smile he wanted, but there was a faint glimmer of amusement in his eyes—unless that was just the glare of the sunlight. Whatever, Wyatt was taking it. He needed a morsel of hope, and Diego sitting on an

ATV, looking strong and handsome, just as at home as ever, was better than he'd expected after the way he'd stormed off the afternoon before.

Wyatt took a large bite, keeping an eye on the cattle as he ate, and Diego did the same. As long as they mostly stayed put, he could have lunch before he resumed urging them onward, but he didn't want to let any stray too far.

"So, was it your idea to get me out here for free labor, or my father's?" Diego asked. "I doubt Rosie came up with it on her own."

Wyatt grabbed his water bottle, taking a large gulp to wash down his too-large bite. "Hell no, is that what you think? I'm just happy to see your pretty face."

Okay, that might be too much too soon. Diego's expression froze for a moment, before he rolled his eyes and joked back, "My pretty face will be here for supper."

"It wasn't last night."

"And I got an earful from Papá and Rosie about that," he said with a less-forced smile. "Who am I to turn down free food, especially a home-cooked meal by Rosie? I'll be here."

"Oh, well, if you want to head back to the house—"

"Nah, I was just giving you a hard time. I don't mind helping out. Not like I've got much else to do."

Diego could visit his cousin and her little one, Wyatt knew. He had old friends in town. Wyatt was sure he could find ways to fill his time other than working on the ranch, but if Diego wanted to help out, he wasn't going to stop him.

"Okay then, I could use a hand."

"Wyatt, you're wound so tight, you could use a lot more than a hand," he said.

The statement could be taken a lot of ways, but there was an undercurrent to it that heated Wyatt's blood. He'd love nothing more than to let Diego use whatever body parts he deemed necessary to relieve the tension in his body.

"I, uh... I s'pose we oughta get back to work then," Wyatt said. "Before I take you up on that offer and abandon my men."

Diego's lips parted in surprise at being caught out in his sexual innuendo. Then he gave a clipped nod, the moment vanishing. Or perhaps the moment being decimated by Wyatt's lack of subtlety.

He could sense that, just like with the cattle, if he got too close, he would spook Diego. Just as he had yesterday. He'd have to apply gentle pressure, easing back when Diego tensed up, until he was ready to allow Wyatt in again. *If* he ever allowed Wyatt in again.

It would take time, and Wyatt wasn't sure they'd have enough. But he'd tried already to rush headlong for what he wanted. He was just going to have to be patient and hope Diego didn't leave before they had a chance to work out their differences.

"Should I head west?" Diego asked, turning Wyatt's mind to the more immediate task at hand.

"Nah, stay here. I want make a few rounds to see where we most need shoring up."

Diego nodded. "Colby seemed to be struggling a little. There's a ravine right along that eastern edge—"

"Got it. I'll check on him first," Wyatt said, marveling at how quickly they fell into sync when they focused on ranching.

Diego shifted to pull a red-and-white bandana out of his back pocket. Wyatt lingered long enough to watch him tie it over his head, his world clicking into place. Diego in jeans and a bandana, working the ranch. This is how things were supposed to be. He experienced a moment of disconnect from reality, suddenly feeling as if he was seeing a future that might have been if Diego had never left.

With a smile still tipping his lips, Wyatt turned on his ATV and circled around the cattle, heading east. Typically, they drove slow when moving the cattle; but since he was trying to make up some ground and keeping his distance from the herd, he picked up some speed, letting the breeze cool him for a minute or two before slowing to navigate uneven land.

ATV accidents could be deadly, and they were already short-handed enough without losing someone to injury. Wyatt proceeded with caution, checking on Colby—who was young but learning fast— before pulling away to head off a runner who seemed bound and determined to stray from the herd.

With the prospect of Diego working the ranch with him again, his mood was brighter than the sun hanging overhead.

4

Diego stepped onto the porch after dinner, taking a deep breath of country air redolent with the scents of grass and livestock. It was just dusk, the orange of the sun still tinging the sky. In front of the porch, dirt and gravel gave way to scrubby grass and an oak tree that cut an imposing figure against the expansive sky, branches stretching wide.

Diego had forgotten how wide open the world felt on the ranch. In Miami, there were tall buildings slicing through the skyline, but here? Just dusky blue highlighted with streaks of orange among the cottony clouds and land as far as the eye could see. In the distance, he could just make out the creek meandering through ranch property. Beyond it, he knew there was still more land covered in grasses and weeds, dotted with trees, and hiding all manner of critters: rattlesnakes, raccoons, foxes, coyotes.

"Heck of a view, isn't it?"

Wyatt's voice startled him. Diego had been drinking in the sight, absorbing the landscape and overlaying it onto his memories, sharpening soft images with the firmer edges of reality. He hadn't even noticed the cowboy sprawled in a wooden rocking chair, bottle of beer balanced on one thigh.

"It's beautiful," Diego admitted.

By the way Wyatt's smile spread, you'd think Diego had called him beautiful. Of course, he was. But Wyatt didn't need Diego to tell him that. He'd always been comfortable in his skin and well aware of the effect he had on people.

"Have a seat," Wyatt said. "Enjoy the breeze while it lasts."

Diego hesitated, not sure it was a good idea to get too cozy with Wyatt after yesterday's desperate proposal. *The marriage pact.* He hadn't thought of it in years. They'd been so naïve, too innocent to even understand what they were promising. Heck, at the time, they were too young to even understand sexuality. If they had turned out to be straight, that pact would have faded into the foggy edges of a happy childhood, not worth remembering. Hell, if they'd been straight, there would have been no ultimatum, Wyatt's decision wouldn't have broken his heart, and they might be sitting here, still the best of friends.

But they weren't straight, and Wyatt *did* break his heart.

They had a whole heap of baggage neither of them had attempted to unpack and only a few days until Diego would be gone again. But he wasn't ready to make the drive to town just yet, so he lowered himself into the chair beside Wyatt, groaning as his muscles protested the day's work. Diego was used to long hours on his feet, but he'd used whole different sets of muscles doing ranch chores.

Wyatt laughed, and Diego flailed out an arm, failing to make contact and too tired to care. "Shut up."

"All afternoon, I watched you. I kept thinking, damn, it's like he never left. Usually new guys can't keep up, you know?"

"Muscle memory," Diego said.

"Now your muscles are remembering they don't usually work so hard."

Diego grunted as he shifted, trying to get comfortable. "You're a real charmer. I thought you wanted to make nice with me."

Wyatt snorted. "By blowing sunshine up your ass? Unless

you've changed a helluva lot, I doubt that would work. But I will say this"—Wyatt leaned in close, lowering his voice—"your muscles are awful pretty even if they're not as tough as mine."

For a second, Diego forgot all their crappy history, forgot the awkward proposal of the day before, and just reacted as he would with any friend.

Using a hand, he shoved away Wyatt's face as he laughed. "You always were a cocky fucker."

Wyatt grinned, lifting his beer to take a long drink. "Don't be too hard on yourself, D. We can't all be in this good of shape."

Diego flipped him off before reaching out to steal his beer and take a long drink. "Asshole."

Wyatt smiled, letting Diego finish off his beer in companionable silence. When Diego handed it back, Wyatt set it on the floor by his feet.

Then, clearing his throat, he said, "About yesterday—"

"Let's not revisit that," Diego said.

"Fair enough." Wyatt seemed relieved to leave that topic alone. "But... while you're here, I can think of some ways for you to get in shape."

As if his words weren't come-on enough, his eyes fairly smoldered, the teasing smile of a moment ago replaced with parted lips that invited Diego to kiss him.

"Jesus, Wyatt."

Color rushed to Wyatt's face, and he looked down, mumbling, "It was just an idea." He peeked up at Wyatt from under thick eyelashes. "I can't seem to help myself when it comes to you."

Blood heating, Diego stood up fast, barely checking a pained sound as his muscles once again protested. If he didn't get out of there soon, he was going to give in to the urge to take two handfuls of Wyatt's shirt and pull that lean, hard body against him.

"I better get to town before I fall asleep out here."

Wyatt straightened in his chair, annoyance wiping away his sex-starved expression. Diego wondered idly just how long it had been for the poor guy. Probably not a lot of options around Cow Creek.

"Would you just check out of that damn hotel? You can have a room at Casa de Jones."

Diego smirked at the playful name Wyatt had given his house. "And where would this room be, down the hall from yours?"

"They're all down the hall from me, D. Ain't no gettin' around that. But I promise not to come in uninvited, if that's what you're worried about."

That wasn't at all Diego's concern, not that he'd admit it to Wyatt. He was more concerned about Wyatt coming in with an enthusiastic invitation. One Diego was tempted to extend to him right now, even though he should be remembering that he was angry at Wyatt. This was a man who'd made his choice a long time ago, and that choice hadn't been Diego.

"Ranch work starts pretty early in the morning," Wyatt added, looking up at Diego from beneath the brim of his cowboy hat. "Unless today was a one-time only offer?"

Ah, hell. The men had been so damn grateful for Diego's presence, especially Colby. His initial flash of jealousy had vanished when he saw how Colby and Wyatt interacted. The boy had a strong body and a good work ethic, but he really was like a colt, young and fumbling at times. He'd been happier than anyone to have Diego join in the work, rambling a steady stream about anything that popped into his mind.

"Nah, it's not a one-time offer. I'll be back."

Wyatt sounded relieved. "Good. I hope you know that the Triple J doors are always open to you. *My* doors are always open."

Irritation flared. Wyatt wanted Diego to treat the ranch like his home as if nothing had changed. But there was no undoing their past—or the pain Diego had felt when he realized he wasn't enough for Wyatt.

Leaning down, he braced his right hand on the arm of Wyatt's rocker. "Easy to say now, without Grandad here to pull your strings. But we both know that wasn't always the case."

"That's hardly fair," Wyatt said.

"Lot of shit isn't fair. I learned that six years ago."

"Yeah," Wyatt said, the light gone out of his eyes. "Me too."

As Diego walked away, he felt like the worst kind of asshole to snuff the first bit of real joy he'd seen in Wyatt since he'd arrived. Grief would take the light out of any man's eyes, but there seemed to be more to Wyatt's change in nature.

Maybe your resentment? You haven't given him much cause for cheer.

Diego turned on his heel, facing the porch, unable to leave on the sour note he'd put into the air between them. "I'll be here by six a.m. Will that work?"

Wyatt smiled faintly, causing Diego's heart to skip. "Yeah, that'll do."

Disconcerted by his heart's betrayal, Diego turned to flee before he did something truly stupid. Wyatt might be over six feet tall of sexy cowboy, but he was still the boy who'd let Diego down.

———

Wyatt was filled with restless energy once Diego left. That conversation had been a roller coaster, Diego seeming to respond to friendly banter only to lash out again seconds later, pushing Wyatt back to arm's length. And that was the rub, wasn't it? Diego didn't want to let his guard down.

It was a damn shame because Wyatt could feel the easy rhythm between them. They still clicked like the best friends they'd once been. He could also feel the spark of attraction. If he felt even a fraction of any of these things with any of his former hookups, he would have been elated and raring to go.

But it was Diego. It had always been Diego.

Diego was complicated. Even before everything went south,

he wasn't always the easiest guy to love. He was quick to anger. Wyatt could deal with that, though, because he was quick to forgive, their breakup notwithstanding. Even with the breakup, it wasn't really about anger. Diego was hurt, deeply hurt.

What Diego had yet to realize was that he hurt Wyatt too. When Diego left and cut Wyatt out of his life, it had devastated him. Wyatt wished Diego had had more faith in him, more patience, but he'd forgiven Diego and accepted his share of the blame long ago.

He'd told Diego time and again that he would come out, but he'd dragged his feet. And when Grandad's ultimatum had landed ... well, why *would* Diego believe Wyatt when he told him that his agreement to Grandad's terms was temporary. That with a little more time, they could have everything they wanted. The life they wanted, together, on the ranch.

Shaking off the melancholy that was fast descending, Wyatt walked down the porch steps and toward his pickup. As long as he was this antsy, he might as well get some work done on the plan to convert part of the ranch into an event venue. He'd done some research, and there were a few Texas ranches that offered wedding packages — some just for ceremonies and receptions, and others overnight stays — but none were too close by. The Triple J had some beautiful views, more than enough land now that the herd had been scaled back, and buildings to spare—even if they needed work.

It was the best option Wyatt had to infuse the ranch with new revenue. He'd considered other ideas. Agritourism wasn't as robust as it used to be and running a dude ranch would take even more work. Not to mention, it was a lot more popular at horse ranches, where folks could watch cowboys break stallions. Watching them feed and herd cattle? Not nearly so glamorous.

But they had the setting, more land and buildings than they needed, and horses for trail rides. Weddings and other events, they could do, he hoped.

"Where you off to?" Roberto called from the porch.

Wyatt turned. "Going to head down to the bunkhouse. See if I can do some work on it."

Roberto raised his eyebrows. "You sure? It's getting late."

"When else am I going to do it?" Wyatt said, some of his disappointment with Diego bleeding into frustration over the ranch. "Hell, an idea only gets us so far. We have to actually make it happen at some point."

Roberto held up a finger. "Hold that thought."

He opened the screen door, speaking to Rosie, then let it drop shut and jogged over to the truck. "I'll come with you."

"You don't have to spend your evening with me."

Roberto opened the passenger door. "Triple J is important to me too. We're in this together."

Wyatt blew out a breath, then climbed into the driver's side. "I figured I'd stop by the workshop to grab some tools. Maybe tear that awful carpet out of the bunkhouse."

The idea was to renovate the bunkhouse into guest housing. It was large enough for two rooms that could accommodate members of a wedding party. A small cabin on the ranch, where Roberto and Diego had lived for years, would serve as a honeymoon suite and bridal ready room.

At some point, the bunkhouse—which was originally built as a simple, one-room structure— had been updated. A bathroom had been added, which made good sense, but carpeting had also been laid over the wood flooring, and it hadn't held up well over the decades.

"With any luck, the wood will be in decent shape," Roberto said. "We can always refinish it, assuming it's not too bad."

Wyatt nodded. "I just hope this whole undertaking isn't a fool's errand."

Roberto drummed his fingers on the door as Wyatt pulled to a stop in front of the workshop. "I admit, I was skeptical when you first came to me. But the Triple J is bleeding, and you've got to try something to staunch the wound."

"If this fails, we may be worse off."

"Mm-hmm," Roberto agreed. "Maybe you should run it by Diego."

Wyatt was caught off-guard. "Really?" He paused. "Not that Diego's opinion doesn't matter to me, but... why would you suggest that?"

Roberto's expression told Wyatt that he knew exactly how much Diego's opinion meant to him on a great many things. "I don't know. Miami's a big city. It's probably got a lot of event venues. Besides that, he works at a hopping nightclub. He's more in touch with city folks than we are. It's just a gut feeling, but maybe he'll have some ideas." Roberto shrugged. "None of us are experts, but you did market research, Wy. Based on what you showed me, this is a solid plan."

Wyatt opened his door. "Thanks. I sure as hell hope you're right."

When Diego got back to the hotel, he hopped in the shower, hoping the hot water would soothe some of his aches and pains. He was pretty sure he would sleep like the dead tonight, so that was one benefit to hard labor.

When he got out, he discovered he'd missed a call from Josefina. It was the second one that day. She'd called once while he was working, and he'd forgotten to get back to her. He hit he return call button as he dried his hair. "Hello?" she answered.

"It's Diego. I saw you called?"

"Yes! I wasn't sure how long you were staying, but I'd love to see more of you before you go."

"Definitely. We should grab dinner or something," Diego said.

"I'm helping out at the ranch during the day. That's why I didn't get back to you sooner."

"Seriously?" She laughed. "You've been back two days and you're already slipping into ranch work like an old pair of boots?"

"I wouldn't go that far," he grumbled, but she had a point. Even if Rosie hadn't suggested he help out, he'd returned to the ranch in the morning, dressed in jeans and a T-shirt, itching to get a little dirty like old times. The labor was harder than he'd remembered, but it was satisfying too. Even in the heat, with sweat pouring, you were working toward a purpose larger than yourself.

"So tomorrow?" Josefina asked. "Dinner?"

"Sure, but let me take you out," Diego said. "I don't want you to cook for me."

She snorted. "Are you that scarred by my early culinary attempts? I promise not to serve you anything burned."

He chuckled. "No, no. You've got your hands full with Lakin, though. I bet you could use a night away from the stove."

"That's so considerate," she said, making his chest warm with the praise. "I'd love a night off."

"Great. I'll call you tomorrow when I get done at the ranch."

They exchanged their goodbyes, and Diego stripped down for bed and lowered the lights. He climbed into bed, muscles still aching, and set a phone alarm. No way he'd be waking on his own in time to arrive at six a.m. Damn, why *was* he working so hard for the ranch that he'd spent so much time hating?

But he already knew the answer to that. He wished he could say he was doing it all for his father, because the ranch was his livelihood and had been for Diego's entire life. But no. He was doing it for Wyatt, and there was no getting around it. *Why* he felt so compelled to help Wyatt was a mystery for another day.

His eyes were already getting heavy, so Diego texted Matias before he could forget.

I'm fixin' to hit the hay, he wrote. *How are things there?*

Diego had let Matias continue to stay at his apartment when he left for the funeral. It wasn't the first time Diego had served as emergency housing for one of his friends. The spring before, Julien had spent a few weeks on his couch. But usually he was there to keep an eye on the place.

Sleeping in hay already? You're getting into this cowboy thing!

Diego hadn't expected an immediate reply, but he must have timed it just right for Matias to be on his break.

My apartment? Diego prompted, not bothering to respond to Matias's tease.

Your building is still standing.

No parties, Diego replied. *In case that wasn't clear. Take care of my things.*

How's it going there? Matias texted. *Watch out for cows! Or better yet, watch cowboys.*

The statement was followed by a series of winky faces and lewd emoticons.

Diego rolled his eyes. People always had the notion that Texas was nothing but cowboys, tumbleweeds, and cattle wandering down the street.

No parties, Mati. I mean it.

Matias had been known to be flighty and irresponsible. His spontaneity could be fun, but he didn't always think through the consequences before he acted. Mati's daddy had kept him in check, but without Craig...

I'm not really in a party mood, Matias answered. He was taking this breakup harder than Diego expected. Diego didn't really get how the whole Daddy/boy dynamic worked, but he knew Matias and Craig had lived together, so their relationship must have been pretty damn serious.

Do you think you guys will make up? Diego asked. *Or...*

It's over.

Shit. Diego had nothing helpful to say. He wasn't your guy when it came to consoling broken hearts. His response was to either threaten harm to the other guy, or to tell you that you were better off without him. He didn't think Matias would appreciate either of those sentiments.

Sorry, he wrote.

Then, before he could rethink it, he added, *If it helps, you can stay at my place longer, but I'll need you to cover the rent.*

It does help! Are you staying in Texas?

Maybe, Diego wrote. *Not sure of how long.*

He'd planned to head out by Monday, but it felt too soon. Now that he'd seen how the ranch was struggling, he couldn't shake the feeling. Regardless of the history between him and Wyatt, or how much he'd once hated the ranch for being first in Wyatt's heart, he couldn't bring himself to walk away when Wyatt needed help.

I can cover the rent, Matias said.

It's due this week, Diego warned. *If that's too soon, let me know.*

Diego could cover it, but then he'd have to return to Miami ASAP because it would be tight. He'd spent more on gas and hotel then he could really afford.

I've been crashing here for weeks. It's fine. You'll be saving me from apartment hunting for a while. Just text me all the details.

Relieved, Diego agreed. Matias covering his rent would give him some flexibility on when he headed back to Miami. But before he committed to staying much longer, he wanted to find out more about why the ranch was struggling in the first place.

5

"Drink before you fall over."

Wyatt thrust a water bottle toward Diego, and he straightened from his crouched position on the ground in front of the wire fencing he'd been splicing. Double-checking the fencing was an ongoing job around the ranch— trimming away plant growth that would ultimately do harm to it, clearing away loose brush or limbs that had fallen on the fence or blown up against it, and mending any breaks they found in the wire.

Diego grabbed the bottle and upended it. He drank half of it down before pausing to breathe, using an arm to swipe at the sweat on his forehead. "Thanks. I got in the zone, but damn, it's hot."

"No need to do the work of two men," Wyatt said. "Considering I'm not paying you, you don't need to work so damn hard."

Diego squinted up at him. "Guess it's in my DNA. Don't know any other way to be, pay or no pay. Probably shouldn't be telling that to the slave driver, though."

He cracked a smile, and relief swept through Wyatt. For most of the day, the friendly banter they'd exchanged the evening before had been nowhere in sight. Once again, Wyatt had pushed too hard. He'd wanted to smack himself when Diego ran off to the hotel, looking as if Wyatt would bite him. He was trying too hard and he knew it. He'd hoped that if Diego didn't want to commit to forever, he might be open to a little bit of *right now*.

But Wyatt would have to be more patient. Diego clearly harbored resentment over their breakup, throwing it in Wyatt's face at every turn. Before anything could happen between them—friendship or romance—they'd have to unpack some of their baggage.

Diego had been all business today. As much as Wyatt appreciated Diego's help, it was starting to nag at him that it wasn't right, taking this much labor from a man with no compensation.

"Maybe we can work out a pay arrangement."

Diego shook his head. "The ranch has enough bills without adding me to the list."

Wyatt grimaced. He didn't like that it was so easy for Diego to see how much the ranch was hurting. He'd been so encouraged that Diego had agreed to continue helping. It had lit a spark of hope inside him. But now he realized that Diego was probably more worried about the ranch—his father's home and livelihood —than interested in reconnecting with Wyatt.

"I don't want to take advantage," Wyatt said. "Men work for me, I pay them."

"You're already feeding me," Diego said. He'd eaten lunch provided by Rosie that day, and he'd stayed for dinner the night before, but that hardly equated to hours of hard labor. "Except for tonight anyway. I promised to have dinner with Josefina."

"I'm glad you're catching up with your family," Wyatt said. "Tell Josefina she's welcome to visit the ranch anytime."

"I'll do that."

"As for the matter of pay, a few meals are hardly worth all this time and energy you're expending. We feed Hank and Colby, too, and they both get paychecks."

"They're ranch employees. I'm not," Diego said stubbornly.

"But I might take you up on the offer to stay at the house. Would that help? Free housing in addition to free food?"

Wyatt's heart leaped at the prospect. More face time with Diego? Hell yeah. Even if it was fraught with tension like the night before, he'd take it. If he was to have any chance of making peace with Diego, this was it.

"Absolutely. We're happy to have you."

"Good," Diego said. "Glad that's sorted, but I did want to ask you about the ranch."

"What about it?" Wyatt asked, instantly wary.

"Why is the ranch so short-handed?" Diego asked. "Used to be double the number of ranch hands working these lands. You've got a smaller herd now too. I know how tough this business can be, but it seems like something more is going on here."

Wyatt's first instinct was to deny it. It hurt his pride to admit that the Triple J wasn't everything it used to be. But Diego was devoting all his free time to working with them, and he deserved to know why they were working so damn hard.

"Things are tight," he admitted. "There's no single reason we're in this bind. We got hit hard by weather about two years ago. Lost more cattle than we'd prepared to lose. Grandad was ill for a long time, too. It took his focus away, made him unable to do everything he used to do, but he was too proud to admit that. Things got worse and worse. Then he died, and well, things haven't been the way they were before, the way you remember them, in a good long time. Guess I don't have the knack for running the ranch that Grandad did."

"Bullshit," Diego said, almost angrily. "You're every bit the rancher he was. Better, probably, because you're not so bullheaded."

Wyatt scoffed outwardly, though he was delighted by Diego's defense of him. "I remember you calling me stubborn a time or two."

Diego brushed off his attempt to reminisce. "No one's more stubborn than Grandad."

Hearing Diego call him that, so familiarly, did something squirrelly to Wyatt's insides. His heart squeezed tight, and he had to take a deep breath before he could speak. He didn't think he'd ever see Diego back on this land, much less talking about the family like old times.

"Maybe you're right," Wyatt allowed. "Doesn't change the fact the ranch is struggling."

"Guess not," Diego said. "I feel like there's something you're not telling me. Even with the operation scaled back, you should have at least a couple of more men."

Wyatt swallowed hard. Yes, there was more to it than Grandad's illness and death or some lean times. But he didn't want Diego's sympathy. Bad enough he was accepting practically free labor from him.

"We're just between hires," he lied. "We'll find some more men. In the meantime, your help means a lot."

After Diego took Josefina to dinner to catch up — turned out he was a bad cousin, who knew very little about her, including her growing Etsy business of knitted slippers, mittens, and hats — he stopped by the hotel to pack his one duffel bag of clothes so he could move into the ranch house.

He was still a little wary of staying so close to Wyatt, but it would do him good to conserve money.

When he pulled up in front of the house, his headlights cut across the porch, illuminating Wyatt in what seemed to be his favorite spot for drinking beer and gazing out at the horizon after dinner.

Diego got out of the car, closing his door. He waited for

Wyatt to react, say hello, or shoot a smile his way. When he didn't, Diego frowned. "Hey, you awake up there?" he asked.

Leaving his bag of clothes for the moment, he ascended the porch stairs.

Wyatt blinked slowly, as if waking from a dream. "Sorry. Just thinking."

"Anything you want to share?"

"Nah." Wyatt said. "Just got my mind on business. Tough to turn it off sometimes."

Diego sat down beside him. "It's a way of life, what you do. It's a lot different from bartending, that's for sure."

"What's that like?" Wyatt asked.

"It's still work," Diego said. "I'm on my feet all night, and I've got to be efficient. When we get slammed, it can be like a race. But... it's also a never-ending party." He glanced sidelong at Wyatt. "A great way to pick up men too."

"Must be nice," Wyatt muttered.

Diego felt a zip of pleasure at Wyatt's obvious jealousy, then a twist of guilt. Why did he want to make Wyatt jealous? He wasn't looking to get involved again. But... he supposed he didn't hate the idea of Wyatt feeling like he'd missed out on something great all these years. Wyatt had given him up without a fight, and Diego liked the idea he might regret that. But it felt juvenile, reacting this way, so he changed the subject.

"You wanted to talk to me about the ranch, didn't you?"

Wyatt stood. "Actually, I want to show you something."

Diego wasn't entirely sure this wasn't a ploy to get him alone, but he was curious. "What are you gonna show me? I've seen it all before."

Damn, that sounded like a sexual innuendo. He was talking about the ranch, not Wyatt, but they were one and the same, weren't they? Diego had thoroughly explored both in the past.

Don't think about it, Diego. Be cool.

Wyatt's lips curved, seeming to catch his slip but not calling him on it. "Don't be so sure you've seen everything worth seeing."

Diego still wasn't sure whether they were talking about the ranch or something else. He hesitated, and Wyatt saw right through him. "I'm talking about my plans for the ranch. I'm not about to drag you into the barn and have my way with you."

Diego huffed. "I know that."

He really hadn't been sure, and now he strangely felt a little let down. He didn't want to get involved with Wyatt, and yet ... he'd kind of enjoyed knowing Wyatt still cared. The proposal had shocked him, but the come-on... that had been flattering. It was stupid. Selfish, too, to want affection he never intended to reciprocate.

Wyatt held out a hand to him. "Come on, darlin'. Let's take a walk."

"Don't make me knock you on your ass, *darlin'*," he shot back.

Wyatt laughed, raising his hands. "My mistake. Come with me, *asshole*. I've got an idea for the ranch, and I could use a second set of eyes."

Wyatt led Diego across the yard and onto a meandering dirt path that led to the barn.

"You miss any of this at all?" Wyatt couldn't resist asking. It was a bit like poking the bear, but he couldn't help himself. He couldn't imagine just up and leaving the ranch and never looking back.

"Of course I did. No place quite like Texas."

Wyatt tucked his hands into his pockets so he wasn't tempted to grasp Diego's hand. "And us? You miss any of us?"

"I missed my father," he said, "and Rosie. Mama Jones, Josefina. Sure, I missed them a lot."

Wyatt smirked. Of course Diego wouldn't admit he'd missed

him. Pretty telling that he'd gone out of his way to list every other person around the place.

But maybe he really hadn't missed Wyatt. After all, he was the reason Diego had never returned, even for a visit. There was a wistful note to his voice that was enough to squeeze Wyatt's heart, always a tad soft when he was around Diego as it was.

"The barn again?" Diego asked as they approached its large doors. "I know I've seen every corner of this place."

"Dark corners were our specialty," Wyatt said. "Remember our first kiss?"

Diego nodded, eyes dark and fathomless. Wyatt wished he could read him better. He had a feeling Diego could always tell just what he was thinking. It was an unfair advantage.

Wyatt remembered that first kiss vividly. It'd been his sixteenth birthday, and Grandad had sprung a surprise party on him, complete with a barnyard dance with the daughters from the neighboring ranches. He'd danced with a nice girl named Virginia and then Charlotte, who Grandad would later push him to court properly, but his attention had been fully on Diego, who'd watched his every move intently. To this day, Wyatt wasn't sure how he'd known; only that he had. *Diego wanted to dance with him.*

Diego had watched Wyatt for damn near an hour as he mingled with party guests and danced with girls. When Diego slipped away, Wyatt followed him into the barn, knowing Diego would go there to hide out.

He found him sitting in a darkened corner of the barn half shielded by hay bales, and he'd lowered himself to the ground beside him.

"You okay?" he'd asked.

"Yeah."

"You didn't dance with anyone."

"You did."

Wyatt turned to face him, looking into Diego's eyes. He saw pain there, longing, jealousy. His heart had hammered, and he'd been more terrified than when he'd had to prove himself at his first kiddie rodeo event.

"What if I wanted to dance with you?"

"I'm not a girl."

"I know. I still wanted to dance with you."

Diego's eyes met his. "I wanted to dance with you, too," he admitted in a whisper.

Wyatt lifted a hand to Diego's cheek. "Maybe we can't dance out there, but we could kiss in here," he said hesitantly. "If you want."

Diego nodded, lips parting, and Wyatt leaned in brushing their lips together. He glanced up to check Diego's expression, and Diego curled a hand around his neck, pulling him into another kiss, one firmer and wetter.

That kiss had begun the summer of a thousand stolen kisses, followed by a year of glorious hand jobs and blow jobs and more happiness than Wyatt could have imagined, but it'd eventually turned into a tense time of hiding the truth and trying to dodge Grandad's attempts to get Wyatt to court one of the neighbor girls. By the time he was eighteen, Grandad was preaching the importance of a partner to share the burden of running the ranch, of starting a family before he was saddled with too much responsibility.

Wyatt was damn young, and he'd already found his partner anyway. He wanted to run the Triple J with Diego. But he couldn't exactly tell Grandad that, not when he was so adamant about traditional family values.

Then Grandad found them out. Made his threats. And Wyatt, in need of some time, agreed to break it off.

It was supposed to be *temporary*. Not six fucking years. But life had a way of taking its own course.

"So, are we here to stroll down memory lane?" Diego asked brusquely, bringing Wyatt's focus back to the present. "I thought you wanted to show me some idea?"

"Right." Wyatt pulled open the sliding door, walking inside. Diego followed him, taking in the large, mostly empty space. A few hay bales remained in the corners, arranged there for casual seating. The tractor had been removed, as had most of the animal feed supplements, antibiotics, and other supplies.

"What the hell ... ?"

"The ranch isn't what it used to be, as you've noticed," Wyatt admitted, as much as it pained him. "I'm looking to bring in new revenue. Did some research, and weddings seemed like the best bet." He waved an arm to the empty space around them. "This here will be a reception hall."

"But ... the animal stalls, the feed ..."

"Currently, it's all being stored in the small barn out closer to the northeast pasture. We built that a few years after you left. Makes wintering the cattle easier. And we've also got the workshop and storage shed, so we can make do."

"Weddings," Diego mused, looking around.

"There's not much to see yet. We plan to clean it, dress it up. Paint the outside. Barn weddings are trendy, so we are trying to take advantage of that."

He could hear the nerves in his own voice. He needed this to work, and he was hoping like hell it wasn't the stupidest idea he'd ever had.

Diego turned in a circle, taking in the wide, open space, then looked to Wyatt. "You need more than just this barn if you want to really make a go, don't you?"

Wyatt nodded. "The barn's the easy part. We're going to renovate the bunkhouse into guest quarters," he said, "and turn the cabin into a honeymoon suite."

"My father's cabin?" Diego said sharply.

"If we want to attract more than nearby townsfolk, we need a place for people to stay. At least the wedding part—"

"And what about my father?" Diego said. "That's his *home*."

"He moved up to the main house."

"By choice?" Diego asked, voice thick with suspicion. "Because if you're just pulling it out from under him after all the years he's given this ranch—"

"Of course, by choice," Wyatt snapped. "But that cabin belongs to the ranch—"

"So it's yours to take," Diego interrupted. "Because once again, you get everything you fucking want, the *king of the land*, and to hell with people like me and my father."

Wyatt took three big steps, bringing him chest to chest with Diego. He knew if they threw down, he'd probably come out worse for wear. Diego had brawn where Wyatt had lean, work-honed muscle. But he was too angry to care. Voice low, he said, "If I really got whatever I wanted, you'd be fucking me against a wall right now."

"Then pull down your pants, your majesty," Diego snarled. "I'd be happy to tear up your ass."

Their eyes locked, and Wyatt knew it was the wrong thing to do. He wanted Diego for the long haul, not just one angry fuck, but his veins were flooded with adrenaline with nowhere to go. He called Diego's bluff, yanking at his belt, and shoving his jeans down to his thighs. The denim had barely cleared his ass before Diego shoved him hard against the wall, pressing up behind him.

"Time to find out how rough you can take it," he growled in his ear.

6

Diego's pulse was roaring in his ears and his dick was hard enough to pound nails as he shoved Wyatt against the wall. It was best if he wasn't looking at that challenging, arrogant-as-fuck face right now. His brain was too chaotic to make sense of how they'd gotten here. All he could focus on now was the need to be inside him, the need to fuck some of that arrogance out of him. Fucking entitled asshole. Just because he was born a Jones, he thought he could run the world. Worst part? He wasn't wrong.

But right now, tonight, Diego was going to be the one to call the shots.

He'd left his wallet in the car, so he delved his hand into Wyatt's back pocket in the hopes he'd have something on him. Sliding out a condom and lube packet, he held them in front of Wyatt's face. "Planning to get lucky?"

"Pays to be prepared."

Diego grabbed Wyatt's right hand and pulled it away from the wall, squeezing a third of the lube onto his fingers. "Then prepare. You have ten seconds. Then I'm taking you hard."

Wyatt's breath sawed in and out of him even though they weren't fucking yet. Diego craned his head to look around Wyatt's left side, since he wasn't tall enough to get a good look over his shoulder. Wyatt's profile was something to behold: His face was already flushed red, his bottom lip caught in his teeth. He stifled a moan as he pushed his fingers into his ass. Then flinched, making a surprised sound, when Diego grasped his wrist and pushed, making his fingers go deeper. His pale dick quivered in front of him, tapping the barn wall. Diego sure hoped he didn't end up with a splinter in his dick. But not enough to stop and reposition him. Hell no.

With his free hand, Diego opened his own jeans enough to pull out his aching cock, then slid on the rubber and covered it with lube. Taking hold of Wyatt's hand again, he pulled back, drawing his fingers away from his glistening hole. "Time's up."

He pressed his left hand between Wyatt's shoulder blades, bending him over, and kicked his legs farther apart to lower his ass to the right height. Wyatt hadn't worn his cowboy hat for their evening stroll, what with the sun lower in the sky, and all his golden hair was on display. As Diego lined up and pushed his cock into the tight, hot grip of Wyatt's body, he slid his hand up his back to the hair at the nape of his neck. He grasped the strands, tugging on Wyatt's head, making his back arch, as he forced his way inside him.

And there was no other way to describe it.

Wyatt might have consented to this rough fuck, but his body was putting up some resistance. Diego paused, wondering if he ought to stop, but Wyatt urged him on. "I can take it," he gasped. "Just fuck me."

Taking him at his word, Diego drew back so only the tip of his dick spread Wyatt's rim, then rammed in so hard he saw stars.

Wyatt cried out so loudly, Diego was amazed Rosie didn't come running out to see who had just been murdered. He shifted to clap his hand over Wyatt's mouth, but Wyatt clearly had other plans. He parted his lips eagerly, laving Diego's fingers with his tongue. Diego knew what he wanted, and he shoved two fingers into Wyatt's mouth, feeling the velvet of his wet tongue as Wyatt closed his lips around them and sucked.

Diego's hips bucked out of sync with his rhythm as Wyatt's eagerness pushed all his buttons and damn near had him coming in seconds. Fuck, this man. Why'd he have to feel so fucking perfect around Diego's cock?

Diego fucked him harder, punishing his ass for tempting Diego when he didn't want to be drawn back into the love affair that had broken his heart. He fucked him so hard his own pelvic bones were throbbing from the impact of their flesh, and Wyatt was sure to be feeling him for a week.

Wyatt was far from quiet, even with Diego's fingers stuffed in his mouth. He was groaning around them, his voice muffled but still very much music to Diego's ears. He had both hands against the barn wall, needed them there to keep himself upright under the onslaught of Diego's hard trusts, and his dick had to be desperate for some relief.

"You gonna come like this?" Diego asked. "With me turning you out like some trick I picked up?"

Wyatt shuddered, and Diego pulled his fingers from his mouth so he could answer. "You could give me a hand."

Diego chuckled. "I don't think so."

He pulled out of Wyatt, ignoring his sound of complaint, and spun him around to face him. Wyatt's eyes were bright and glazed, as if he were high, his pupils blown wide. "Wha—"

Diego resisted the urge to kiss him. This was an angry fuck, not love, and he didn't trust himself to keep his distance in the heat of the moment. Instead, he shoved Wyatt to his knees as he stripped off his condom.

"Swallow me down," he ordered as he thrust his bare dick between Wyatt's pliant lips.

He grabbed Wyatt's head and thrust twice before unloading down his throat. His whole body lit up, electrified, as he shuddered through the hardest orgasm he'd ever experienced. Not in his whole life had he ever been so fucking turned on.

When he came back to himself, he jerked Wyatt to his feet. "Now, I'll give you a hand," he said, grabbing Wyatt's dick and roughly stroking it.

"Kiss me," Wyatt pleaded. "Please."

"So needy," he murmured, not sure he could resist his pretty begging. Tightening his hand around Wyatt's dick, he stroked harder. Wyatt went off, crying out harshly, and Diego slammed their mouths together.

Unlike the fucking, he was unable to keep his touch rough, and the kiss evolved into something gentler, just as he'd feared. Wet, sweeping tongues, messy lips, the taste of cum, but sweet nonetheless.

He jerked back, regret rushing in as he caught his breath and the lust fog lifted.

"I think we're done here."

Wyatt's eyes cleared, the blue turning ice cold in an instant. "We're not anywhere close to done, Diego, but you go ahead and fool yourself all you want."

Fuck! Diego jerked up his jeans. "This isn't happening again. I gotta go."

"Sure, you do. Run away like you always do—"

"Fuck you!" he shouted.

Wyatt still stood there with his pants around his knees, looking fully debauched and pissed off as hell. "Think you got that covered."

"Yeah," Diego spit. "Gotta admit, you take cock better than I thought you would. You liked it rough too. You get kinky while I was away?"

Wyatt flushed and lowered his eyes. *Score.*

When he looked up, face hard and cold, Diego regretted the petty words. He had no problem with people liking their kinks. It was the thought of Wyatt exploring his sexuality enough to discover his kinks that got under his skin. Well, that and he was lashing out because he was reeling over what just happened.

"I like to let go," he said evenly. "I work hard, and I have a lot on my mind. So, if that makes me a joke to you—"

"No," Diego said. "I didn't mean that. I just... This shouldn't have happened. That's all."

Wyatt flinched. "Well, there's the door. You know what to do if you don't want to be here."

"Yeah," Diego said. Scrubbing his hands through his hair, feeling like the worst kind of ass, he said, "Are you okay? I didn't hurt you, did I?"

"Just get the fuck out," Wyatt said, sounding enraged. "I'm not fucking fragile just because I like a pounding."

"I know, I—"

"Just go, Diego. It's pretty fucking clear you regret this. You still blame me for everything in our past. You don't want me. Hell, you don't even *respect* me. So, just go... and leave me a few shreds of dignity."

Diego hesitated, but Wyatt's eyes blazed, and he wasn't sure he'd ever seen him so angry. "Okay, fine, I'll go. I never should have come here."

"Then fuck off to Miami," Wyatt said. "It's what you do best."

Diego turned on his heel, stalking toward the door. "Real fucking nice," he shot over his shoulder. "I can just feel the afterglow."

"You killed it first, asshole!"

Diego slid the door shut behind him with excess force, grunting with satisfaction as it thudded. But once he was outside, reality swept in, causing him to clutch his hair and growl his frustration. "Fuckfuckfuck! Why did you *do* that?"

But he already knew the answer. Wyatt still had some kind of hold on him. Even after all this time, Diego was drawn to him like a firefly to a flame. And fuck if he wasn't going to get burned.

Roberto caught up with Diego by his car. "Hey, hold up, where's the fire?"

Diego laughed bitterly. "Right here. My whole fucking life is a trash fire."

His father instantly looked concerned. "What happened?"

Diego shook his head. "I fucked up. Maybe I should just go home."

"Already? I thought you two might be making up. Wyatt wanted to ask you about his plans to start up a wedding venue."

Fuck. Diego had nearly forgotten in the conflagration that had consumed him when they crashed together. "Yeah, he mentioned it." Diego almost didn't want to ask, knowing instinctively he'd overreacted. "Did you *really* want to give up the cabin?"

"Why wouldn't I? I eat up at the main house every night, and I'm just one guy. I don't need that much space. To be honest, it was kind of lonely out there without you."

Diego gripped the back of his neck, squeezing in frustration. "Damn," he said quietly.

In hindsight, it was so fucking clear. Of course Roberto would support Wyatt's decision. He needed the ranch to survive as much as Wyatt did. Diego had been looking for an excuse to be angry with Wyatt, to push him away, because he could feel his walls breaking down.

That had backfired.

Diego heard the barn door rattle open. "I should go. He won't want to see me."

"What did you do?"

"I'm sorry, Papá," he said, using the term he'd spoken frequently as a child. "I should probably go back to Miami and stop making messes I don't know how to clean up."

Roberto grabbed his arm as he reached for the car door. "Hold on now," he said. "You can't just hit the road. Not before we talk."

"I don't want to talk."

"And I don't care," he said in a hard voice. "I let you take off once; I even helped you. And I've spent six years wondering if that was a mistake. This time, you're not leaving until we have a good, long talk."

"Fine," Diego said shortly. "I won't leave town, but I *am* going back to the hotel. Wyatt won't want to see me right now."

Which meant he needed to hurry along this conversation before Wyatt reached them.

"Fine," his father said, sounding reluctant. "Just sleep on it— and come back in the morning," he said sternly. "I'm counting on you not to take off on me."

Damn it, why did everyone seem to think he was a coward who ran from his problems? Yes, he left once. He thought leaving was the right course. He didn't run out of fear or avoidance.

With a scowl, Diego opened the car door and got behind the wheel.

"I said I wouldn't leave, and I won't," he said shortly.

He'd return in the morning as promised, but he also wouldn't be surprised if Wyatt told him to turn around and leave again.

Wyatt reeked of sex and humiliation.

And his ass hurt.

The last thing he wanted to do was talk to Diego's father, but Roberto stood in his path to the house. Wyatt came to a stop a few feet away, hoping he wouldn't taint the air with the sharp tang of cum.

"I've got too much paperwork to do," he lied. "Going to skip doing reno on the bunkhouse tonight."

As usual, he lied badly. Roberto raised an eyebrow. "Diego seemed upset."

"When isn't he?"

"He was thinking about heading home to Miami."

Wyatt's insides curdled. He shouldn't have told Diego to fuck off. He was just so angry that Diego hadn't been out of his body two minutes before he backpedaled as fast as he could, regret clear in his eyes. Yes, it had been an angry fuck. Wyatt understood the concept. Tempers had run hot, and so had lust, and they'd made a mess.

But they'd done it together.

Wyatt had hoped they'd find something good in the wreckage of their lust. He'd felt it, the old connection between them snapping to life. He'd only found one sex partner, other than Diego, who'd ever been the right fit for his needs—strong, rough, a little controlling—and there'd been no emotional connection with him. With Diego, there were layers of emotion, their history embedded in his skin. Even while being brutally fucked against a wall, he'd felt everything click into place.

Him. Diego. Pleasure. Pain. It all melded into one.

But he'd been foolish. Diego had killed his hopes the second he opened his mouth, and then he'd called Wyatt kinky and acted like he was delicate just because he let Diego top him, and that pushed all kinds of buttons for him. He might not always be as strong in spirit as he'd like, but Wyatt was strong in body.

What a fucking catastrophe. Maybe they really weren't meant to be together. Maybe Wyatt had been wrong about everything.

"He was never going to stay forever," Wyatt said quietly.

Roberto looked at him steadily. "Would you want him to?"

"I don't know," Wyatt said. "I thought I did, but ... maybe too much has happened for us. Maybe we can't ever go back."

"Go back? No. I reckon not. Go forward? Maybe."

"He's leaving anyway, so..."

"I talked him into sticking around," Roberto added, "at least until we have a good, long talk."

"Oh. Well, that's..." He didn't know what that was. He was still too raw from what had happened in the barn to make sense of everything he felt. "Good," he said.

He was pretty sure he didn't want Diego to leave like this. If they parted ways, he'd hoped to at least do it as friends. If Diego didn't want to repeat tonight's actions, that might be for the best. Otherwise, they could end up with more pain and anger between them, and that's the last thing Wyatt wanted.

"I'll let you get to that paperwork," Roberto said.

Wyatt nodded and passed him. As he climbed the steps, exhaustion hitting him hard, Roberto added. "Don't give up on him yet."

He paused, glancing back. "What makes you think he hasn't already given up on me?"

"Just a father's intuition." He shrugged. "Diego is like a wounded barn cat. You got to earn his trust before you pet him. He might want that affection, but he's afraid of it too."

Wyatt smirked. "What do you think he'd say if he heard you comparing him to a barn cat?"

Roberto chuckled. "Reckon he'd hiss and show his claws."

Wyatt snorted a laugh, unable to believe he could laugh. Then turned and carried himself inside. Because he was a shit liar with a guilty conscience, he even went to the office and worked on paperwork like he'd said he would.

But he didn't get much done. His mind kept straying to Diego, trying to equate the passionate man who'd fucked him into the wall with the image Roberto had painted of a wounded animal full of fear.

7

Wyatt and Roberto walked down to the workshop the following morning. The crew often started their day there because the ATVs and other equipment were stored inside.

Hank and Colby stood out front, but Diego wasn't there. Wyatt didn't know whether to disappointed or relieved. Diego had yet to start work as early as anyone else—considering he was volunteering his time, that was fine—so he might show up any minute. Then again, he might not. Wyatt *had* told him to fuck off to Miami, after all. That didn't exactly scream, *Thank you for your help*.

Wyatt needed some distance from Diego, but not *that* much distance.

Hank held up a broken padlock as they neared. "We had a break-in."

"Goddamn it," Wyatt said, stomach sinking. "What's missing?"

He really didn't need this right now. Even if the insurance covered the theft, it meant a sheriff's report, an insurance report, headaches and delays. He had enough on his plate already.

"I don't know if anything is," Hank said. "It's a mess."

The door to the workshop stood open, and Colby leaned inside far enough to hit a button to raise the large garage doors on the building. As they rolled up, Wyatt saw for himself what Hank meant.

Tools and other supplies had been pulled off shelves, cluttering the floor in a jumbled mess. Chemicals darkened the concrete floor, dumped from containers that had been tossed aside like trash. In the center of the workshop sat their tractor and ATVs, seemingly untouched, but Wyatt couldn't be sure they weren't sabotaged too.

"Are these hazardous?" Colby asked, looking at the fluids leaking onto the floor.

"I wouldn't recommend drinking them," Roberto said dryly. "Grab that hose in the back. We'll have to clear out the shop and rinse the floor."

Wyatt swore under his breath. "This is not what I needed today!"

He kicked a spare coil of wire, sending it skittering across the floor with a screech.

Of course, that's the moment Diego jogged up to them. "Sorry I'm late."

Wyatt just stared. He couldn't seem to make words come out of his mouth. Diego hadn't left, but just looking at him, remembering what they'd done and said, made Wyatt's stomach twist up.

He turned back toward the mess in the warehouse. "Roberto, can you move the tractor out. Hank and I will work on clearing this mess—"

"Whoa, what happened?" Diego said, stepping forward to peer into the gloomy interior.

"Break-in," Colby volunteered.

Vandalism, more like. Someone had trashed the workshop. It was possible they'd stolen something they'd yet to notice in the mess, but that didn't seem like the primary motive.

"What the fuck?" Diego demanded. "Any idea who did this?"

Wyatt's jaw clenched. "Yup."

"You gonna tell me?"

Wyatt turned away. He wasn't ready to pretend the night before hadn't happened, and he couldn't turn to Diego for comfort either. He needed some space to process.

"Colby," he said, "take a quick inventory of the supplies we need to replace and take Diego into town with you to replace what we need."

"Sure," Colby said. "I'll grab a notebook."

"Just write notes on your phone," Diego said impatiently.

"Oh, yeah. Good idea," Colby said, pulling out his cell phone and walking into the workshop to note the supplies that had been dumped out or otherwise ruined.

Diego stepped in closer. "Seriously, who did this?"

Wyatt sighed. The day was only starting, and he already felt exhausted. "Same people who vandalized the barn, I reckon."

"Homophobic assholes," Colby volunteered. "You should have seen that graffiti. They wrote—"

"Let's not repeat those words," Hank interjected. "They wrote hateful nonsense. That's all Diego needs to know."

Diego's forehead creased. "You're shitting me."

Roberto paused in his climb onto the tractor. "It could be coincidence. I'm not convinced it's all the same person."

"I'm gay," Wyatt said. "This is what happens when you're a gay rancher and you're stupid enough to tell everyone. Now, the Triple J has a target on it, and it's my fault. That what you wanted to hear?"

"No," Diego said. "I'm sorry. That's shitty."

Wyatt huffed a laugh, eyes catching with Diego's. "A lot of things in my life are shitty right now."

Diego visibly recoiled, even though Wyatt hadn't meant it as an attack about the night before. He'd just lost Grandad; he was short-handed; the ranch was barely staying afloat. He had a lot of fucking problems, even without thinking about Diego Flores fucking him like a madman and treating him like shit afterwards.

The rumble of the tractor forced a halt to their conversation, for which Wyatt was relieved. They stepped aside, waiting as Roberto drove it out of the shop a short ways and parked it on the grass. They could bring it back in once they'd cleared up the mess.

Diego spoke again. "Let me stay and help with this—"

"Go with Colby," Wyatt said firmly.

"I think he can handle it on his own."

"I need you to go."

Wyatt didn't want to punish Diego, but he needed some time and perspective to decide how to move forward. If there was even a point to moving forward. Diego wouldn't be here much longer, either way.

"At least call the sheriff?"

"I've tried before," Wyatt said. "Without some kind of proof, authorities can't do much about it."

Roberto rejoined them. "Tell you one thing, if this is the work of bigots and I ever catch any of them on this land, I'll wring their fucking necks."

Wyatt gaped, and he noticed Diego doing the same. He'd never heard Roberto sound so furious. Usually, he was even-keeled and steady. But it was nice to know he had their backs. Being Diego's father, he probably took the homophobia nearly as personally as Wyatt did.

This wasn't just vandalism; it was a violation. Each time it happened, Wyatt felt the hate he'd feared before he came out. It reinforced the feeling that he was somehow wrong, and he knew that wasn't true—just as he knew it when Grandad was preaching to him in those earlier years—but it didn't stop the sick churning in his gut.

Colby returned, brandishing his phone. "I got the list. Let's go."

Diego hesitated, but Wyatt pointedly turned away, calling out to Hank, who was steadfastly working to clean up the shop while they all bitched and moaned. Wyatt felt a flicker of guilt and hurried into the workshop to join him.

"You get the ATVs," he told Hank. "I'll take over here."

Hank nodded. "Sure thing, boss."

When Wyatt glanced up, Diego and Colby were climbing into Wyatt's pickup. He always left the keys in it, and the ranch hands frequently used it when needed around the place.

Roberto cursed, and Wyatt turned. "What is it?"

"These ATVs won't start. I think the bastards did something to them."

Just great. Wyatt hoped like hell whatever sabotage had been done wasn't irreversible, because he couldn't possibly afford to replace the ATVs, and he'd let the insurance lapse on them months ago.

Fuck my life.

Diego climbed into the faded green pickup feeling like a chastened schoolboy, letting Colby take the wheel. Wyatt hadn't said anything about last night, but then he wouldn't. He'd done all his yelling in the heat of the moment, and Diego had to admit, he'd mostly deserved it.

He'd fucked him, enjoyed every second, then acted as if it was the worst thing that ever happened. There were worse things than falling into bed—or wall, in this case—with your ex. But Diego still didn't know how to feel about Wyatt. One minute he was angry about the past, and the next he felt the urge to help ease the burden he so clearly carried. He wanted to strangle those vandals every bit as much as his father did. But he also kind of wanted to kick his own ass for hurting Wyatt the night before, when he'd allowed Diego to take control of his body so thoroughly.

Diego knew that it was Wyatt's way to go quiet and distant when he was upset, but it still made him crazy. He'd rather have another screaming match than the cold shoulder. Probably not the healthiest approach either. They needed to have a conversation and talk through their feelings, but the very idea of it gave him hives.

"We lucked out, you and me," Colby said. "Buying supplies is gonna be way easier than cleaning up that mess."

"Yeah," Diego agreed without much enthusiasm.

Colby looked happy to escape the ranch for a while, though. He was mostly still a kid, somewhere around eighteen or nineteen. He had that glow that some people do, the one that says life hasn't really knocked them down yet. Being around him made Diego feel old, and it wasn't lost on him that twenty-five years old shouldn't feel so fucking ancient.

We sure thought it was old when we made that stupid marriage pact.

He hadn't thought much of the pact until Wyatt had brought it up again. His stomach tightened at the thought that Wyatt probably wasn't so eager to marry him now. If he ever really had been. Diego got the impression he'd blurted it out in a moment of desperation. He was grieving and overwhelmed by problems at the ranch. Last night, he'd set out to talk to Diego about his plans to generate new revenue, but what had Diego done? Made it about himself and turned it into a fucking mess, instead of offering support.

He really was a self-absorbed dick.

Annoyed at the direction of his thoughts, he turned to Colby as they drove. "So, how long you been with the ranch?"

"About a year," he answered, finger tapping idly on the steering wheel. "Uncle Hank's been with the ranch for a few years. Your Roberto's son, so I guess you grew up on the ranch?"

"Yep. I left for Miami six years ago."

Colby grinned. "Miami. Hoo boy, I bet there's some hot girls out there, huh? All those bikinis and tan lines, nngh. It's like famine around here. Ranch girls are nice and all, but there's not enough of them, and none of them look like those beach bunnies you must get around there."

Diego snorted, not quite sure how to handle the earnest yet chauvinistic ranch hand. He knew Wyatt was gay. Did he not realize Diego was too?

"Yes, Miami has some attractive people, women and men both."

Colby glanced at him, flushing. "Oh yeah. Are you..."

"I'm gay."

"Well, Miami guys are probably hot too, huh? There's not a lot for Wyatt around here. He takes off on the weekend sometimes. I figure he's driving to Dallas or Austin to meet guys. Like I said, it's famine around here, man."

The thought of Wyatt driving into one of the larger cities to hit gay bars and fuck around with men didn't sit well. It's not like he thought Wyatt was celibate out here, but... well, maybe he *had* thought that Wyatt was more focused on the ranch than on his sex drive.

Doesn't matter, he reminded himself. *He's not your boyfriend anymore.*

Diego cleared his throat, redirecting his thoughts back toward messing with Colby. "I work as a bartender at a gay club. One night, the prettiest thing you'd ever seen came up to me. Blond hair, blue eyes, lips made for sucking cock."

Colby looked uncomfortable but intrigued. "This is a guy?"

Diego smirked. "Yeah. He ordered drinks all night, just to spend time near me. He waited for me to get off shift, hanging around and flirting."

"Uh-huh?" Colby said, eyes locked on the windshield, body tense. Diego couldn't tell whether he was getting off on the story or really uncomfortable.

"He was so slim and petite, you'd never think he could handle the pounding I gave him, but *damn*—"

"Okay, we're here!" Colby blurted out as he braked too hard outside the small feedstore in downtown Cow Creek, making the pickup lurch. "Let's pick up the supplies and go."

"Don't you want to hear the rest of the story?"

Colby coughed, red in the face. "Nah, I mean, it's cool that you like dudes. But it's not my thing."

Diego thought the boy doth protest too much, but he didn't push him on it. "Okay."

"You and Wyatt ever...?" Colby asked.

Of course, two gay men in the same place—they *must* have had sex! Diego thought sarcastically. Although, it was actually true in this case.

"Does it matter?"

"No," Colby said. "I was just thinking you two could, y'know, get together while you're here."

"And then what, Colby? We live happily ever after? News flash: Life isn't a fairy tale."

"Yeah, well, I didn't say it had to be forever," Colby said. "Haven't you ever heard of a fling?"

Diego bit down on the urge to laugh. He and Wyatt were capable of some fiery passion, as evidenced by the night before, but a fling? It sounded so easy and uncomplicated. Just agree to have sex, no strings. That was tempting, if only because he wasn't sure he could resist having Wyatt again, regardless of what he'd said the night before. They were fucking explosive together.

Problem with explosions was that they rarely stayed contained. Wyatt and Diego already had enough collateral damage to last them six years. Diego didn't know if he could handle more fallout.

He trailed Colby as they picked up supplies and loaded the truck. They were still standing by the tailgate when Colby's phone rang. "Hello? Oh, yeah? Okay. Shoot me a text with a list? Thanks."

Turning to Diego, he said, "We're gonna pick up a few groceries for Rosie before we head back. Wyatt's planning a cookout for this Friday."

"A cookout, why?"

Colby shrugged. "Rosie said he wanted to have one before you left town. He's inviting his mama, Ella and the boys, your cousin. Pretty much everyone."

Diego's stomach clenched. Was this some sort of message to him? *Here's your goodbye party, now get out of town?* He hoped not. He knew he'd screwed up with Wyatt, but he wanted to leave on better terms than when he'd arrived. Maybe he should call Julien. If anyone had experience in confronting their past and finding closure, it was him. He could sure as shit use some advice because he was fucking this up.

No one had made him come home. That had been his call. He'd thought it might be time to move past old wounds. But all he'd done since he'd arrived was wallow and take it out on Wyatt. That wouldn't accomplish anything.

"Wyatt's been trying to make nice with Ella for a while," Colby said. "I think this cookout might be an excuse to get her over to the ranch again. Now that Grandad is gone..."

He didn't need to say the rest. Diego remembered the ugly arguments between Grandad and Ella when she'd told the family about dating Tucker Dalton. The Daltons and the Joneses had been at odds for generations, all over something that happened before any of them were born. Grandad had been adamant that Ella would have to choose between her family and her boyfriend.

When Tucker proposed, Ella accepted. She'd chosen love.

Wyatt, when given a similar ultimatum, had chosen to fall into line. For the first time, Diego was able to think of it a little more objectively. Wyatt knew his grandfather would make good on the threat, and the ranch was the only home he'd known...

Didn't mean it didn't hurt. Diego had been fully idealistic at nineteen. He'd thought he and Wyatt had an epic romance, one that couldn't be torn apart by anything. Now, he knew better. Life wasn't a fairy tale, like he'd told Colby. But it didn't have to be a tragedy either. He *could* forgive Wyatt.

No one should have to choose between the person they love and the future they want. Diego could see now that Wyatt had been trapped between two ultimatums. Grandad had wanted him to choose the ranch, and Diego had wanted Wyatt to choose him —but they'd both forced Wyatt's hand.

8

F riday night, it looked as if half of Cow Creek had converged on the Triple J Ranch. Wyatt had invited Mama, Ella and her family, Josefina and *her* family, and even a few high school friends to the cookout. He couldn't really afford to feed so many people—especially so soon after the memorial service luncheon—but he wasn't sure Diego would stay much longer, especially after Wyatt had lost his temper and asked him to fuck off.

He wanted to give him a proper send-off before he went, and maybe see if they could part as friends.

"How'd you get Ella out here?" Roberto asked as Wyatt placed beef patties and hot dogs onto the grill, the meat sizzling.

Ella hadn't set foot on the ranch since her falling-out with Grandad, except to attend his memorial service. Wyatt had been a little surprised to see her there, but even then, she hadn't stayed for the luncheon afterward.

"I ate crow," Wyatt admitted. "Told her I should have stood up for her when Grandad pulled his shit. That I was a coward back then, but I liked to think I've grown up."

"You were still a kid. Give yourself a break."

Wyatt shrugged. Ella had left when he was sixteen. He'd been

75

old enough to have a backbone. He should have definitely grown one by nineteen, when Diego left. He'd let fear cost him too much. Glancing across the yard toward where Diego stood with Josefina, he resolved not to be a coward ever again. If Diego left, fine. But he wouldn't do it because Wyatt hadn't apologized or tried to rebuild a friendship.

"Anyhow, I'm glad Ella is giving me a chance," Wyatt said. "I want to know her boys better. This will all be theirs one day."

Roberto raised an eyebrow at that. "You're young still. Don't put the cart before the horse."

"Kids aren't in the cards," Wyatt said. "I'm gay and single. These boys are the next generation. Doesn't matter to me that they're Daltons."

"Nor should it, but you never know. Your future may hold more family than you realize."

Wyatt turned his attention to the meat, unable to let himself believe there'd be a day he didn't feel alone. Even with his mama in town, his sister at a nearby farm, and Roberto steadfastly by his side, he often felt entirely alone in the world. None of them knew what it was like to be responsible for something so large—nine thousand acres, hundreds of head of cattle, farm outbuildings, a house, employees.

Wyatt thought he might only just now understand the message Grandad kept trying to send him: *It's not an easy life. You can't do it alone.*

If only Grandad had accepted him sooner, Wyatt could have had a partner to share the burden. He could have had Diego.

Wyatt left Roberto to join Ella at the picnic table. "Food's ready," he announced, watching as people rushed the grill. Thankfully, Colby had taken his place, helping slide burgers onto plates, while Rosie and Mama put out the side items and pointed people toward the coolers containing an assortment of beer, Dr Pepper, and bottles of water.

Ella looked to be in no rush to brave the lines, and Wyatt took a seat by her.

"I showed Ethan and Matthew the stables," he said.

Not the best ice breaker, but it was all he had for now. Ella had accepted his apology and attended the barbecue, but they still felt oddly formal. More like polite strangers than two people who grew up in the same house.

"Bet they enjoyed that. We don't keep any horses at the farm," she said.

"Ethan was especially taken with them. He asked about learning to ride."

"Oh, yeah?"

She didn't sound especially committed to the idea. But Wyatt had to start somewhere. "Yeah. I was thinking, Dolly is still your horse—"

"Oh, no," she said with a laugh. "I wouldn't know what to do with her. Besides, Diego rode her more than I did back in the day."

He glanced across the yard, his eyes involuntarily drawn to Diego. His anger had cooled, but left in its place was a disappointment that yawned so wide and deep Wyatt was afraid to fully confront it. He'd pinned so many hopes on Diego's arrival, he realized, and now reality was hitting hard. He and Diego might not be right for one another after all.

He'd loved Diego so much, for so long, that it seemed impossible. For now, it was easier to push the thought down and focus on Ella and the boys.

"Dolly could stay here, but maybe the boys could come over for some lessons? I'd love to have them see the place, learn more about the ranch that's been in their family so long."

"They're not Joneses," she said.

"Do you think that matters to me?" Wyatt asked. "Hell, Ella. A name is just a name. They're my sister's children. That makes them family. I'm not Grandad, you know?"

Matthew came walking up, precariously balancing a plate that was overflowing with a burger, a hot dog slathered in ketchup, baked beans, an ear of corn, and a mound of Jell-O. The plate was so crowded all the foods were running into one another, and it looked like an unappetizing glob.

Ella jumped up, helping him lower the plate safely to the table. "My word, did you get enough to eat?" she asked with a laugh.

"No," he said. "There's pie up there, but I couldn't fit any dessert!"

"Good thing there are more plates," Wyatt said with a wink. "Eat up, and we'll make sure they save you a piece."

Matthew looked at him skeptically. He'd been a little slower to warm up to Wyatt than Ethan, but then he shrugged and fell on his hot dog with enthusiasm, ketchup smearing halfway across his face.

Ella rolled her eyes. "You can see I'm doing a great job raising gentlemen," she said.

Mama paused on her way past them. "You should have seen Wyatt back then. You're doing just fine."

Wyatt rolled his eyes, grinning good-naturedly. "Who says I'm a gentleman now?"

"Everyone knows you're a sweetheart," Mama said, pinching his cheek until he batted her hand away.

Matthew giggled, and Wyatt felt the ice between them all begin to crack.

"Go on and get a plate," he told Ella. "I'll stay with this little cowboy."

"'M not a cowboy," Matthew protested. "I'm a farmer!"

Well, that was true enough. The Daltons raised goats and chickens, but they were smack dab in ranch country, and around here, everyone tended to get labeled cowboy.

"Okay, I'll watch over this farmer," he corrected.

"Thanks," Ella said as she stood up. Pausing, she said, "We can talk about the boys visiting more. I'm sure they'd love to learn to ride."

As she walked off, Wyatt exhaled in relief. Maybe if he could fix this relationship, there was hope for fixing his other ones. Once again, he glanced across the yard.

He didn't know yet if he and Diego could ever reconcile their differences, but he wanted to try.

———

Diego tried to give Wyatt some space at the cookout, which wasn't difficult to do because there were a crap-ton of people to greet, all of them fighting the flies for their chance to eat burgers, hot dogs, cucumber salad, potato salad, grilled ears of corn, and so much more. He didn't know how Wyatt was able to feed the hordes, but Rosie kept a garden, so hopefully they weren't demolishing his budget.

Josefina waddled up, her large belly leading the way, to give him an awkward hug. "You're still here, I see."

"Yep."

She looked at him thoughtfully. "Thinking about moving home?"

Diego startled. "No, I couldn't. I've got a life to get back to in Miami. For one thing, I've got a job there. Friends. You know how it is."

Josefina nodded. "Bartending, right? How much leave did you arrange?"

"Oh, I don't have benefits. I just asked him to leave me off the schedule until I called in."

Duke hadn't been happy, but there were two other bartenders on the roster—and Jake would love the extra hours—so it would be fine.

She smiled, looking pleased. "Ah, so you *could* stay as long as you wanted."

"I wouldn't go that far," Diego said.

It seemed as if everyone wanted him to stay. Well, everyone

except maybe Wyatt.

His father had come by the hotel for that heart-to-heart he was intent on having the night before. Diego had been afraid he'd pry into his feelings about Wyatt, but his father had surprised him by bypassing all that to ask him to stay in town for a while.

"I don't know the particulars of your breakup with Wyatt," he'd said. "And that's fine, it's your business. But I remember how close you once were, and seeing you two at odds feels wrong. I think you need to spend some time here, mijo. Reconnect with your home, and maybe... be a friend to Wyatt again, if nothing else. He's under a lot of pressure, and he won't talk to me the way he'll talk to you."

Diego had snorted. "He might never talk to me again."

His father's eyes had crinkled. "You know Wyatt isn't the type to hold a grudge. Give him a few days, and then apologize. *Sincerely*."

Diego had glowered. Of course he'd assume Diego was the one who needed to apologize. It was annoying, even if it was true. He clearly respected Wyatt, though, and Diego had seen for himself the stress that dimmed Wyatt's happiness.

"There's more to this than Grandad passing and the ranch struggling, isn't there?"

"Talk to Wyatt."

Roberto could be obstinate. Diego knew better than to try to persuade him to explain.

"Look, I want to help. I do. But I can only afford to stay so long. I've got responsibilities back in Miami. My apartment is covered, but I've got other bills."

Roberto nodded. "Maybe Wyatt could pay you—"

"No, he already offered," Diego said. "But I don't want him to be my boss."

He couldn't put words to it, but he couldn't work for Wyatt. Working *with* Wyatt was fine. Taking direction from Wyatt was fine. But being employed by him? He didn't want that.

But why? Because you don't want to fuck your boss? Wyatt might never let Diego that close again anyway, after the way he'd treated him.

"Okay, mijo. I understand." Roberto smiled knowingly. "Maybe that's for the best. Wyatt needs a friend, not an employee. I can cover you, if you agree to stay awhile. You don't have to worry about your bills."

"Why is this so important to you?"

"I want to get to know my son again." Damn, not the parental guilt. Shit. It wasn't even unfair. He'd stayed away so long. "I want you to make peace with Wyatt and your past. Maybe you go back to Miami in two weeks, maybe six. I just want you to promise me one thing: Don't leave until the time is right, until everything feels right in here." He touched Diego's chest, right over his heart, for emphasis.

"How will I know if it's right?"

"You'll know."

Diego had agreed, though the idea of taking his father's money made him uncomfortable. He'd been independent a long time. He didn't like the idea of taking a handout. But his father had been so sincere, he couldn't say no. He could float himself for a month, and he'd probably be out of here before then. If not, he could play catch up, work extra shifts and work harder for tips.

One way or another, he could take care of himself. But it was nice to know Papá was there, as a safety net, if nothing else.

Josefina excused herself to track down her husband, and for a while Diego watched the ebb and flow of people around the food and drinks, until he overheard Ella standing with a plate still in hand, joking with Mama Jones that Grandad would be turning in his grave to see the Daltons and Joneses breaking bread.

"Good to see you have a sense of humor about it now," Diego said to her as Mama Jones scurried off to help one of the neighbor kids get a piece of pie. "I remember some ugly yelling matches."

Ella huffed. "I'd give him a piece of my mind all over again if he was still in front of me," she said, and Diego sensed her sadness at his passing, even with all the anger between them. "He made me crazy, and all over a ridiculous feud that's probably a work of fiction."

Colby stepped into their little circle. "Feud? I don't think I've heard this story."

"Wyatt tells it best." Ella half-turned. "Wyatt! C'mere!"

The sun beat down on little Ethan's head of red hair when he ran over to report excitedly that they had seen a hawk overhead, and that Gramma—Wyatt and Ella's mother—said that sometimes hawks tried to eat the chickens for dinner, which was why they owned a black mouth cur, a species of herd dog who helped guard the coop.

Goldie, as she was called, had jumped up and herded the chickens under some nearby trees until the hawk had flown away. While Goldie mostly stuck close to her chickens, she came in at night, and enjoyed a good petting in her off hours, but the children had to be reminded not to try to play with her now. Goldie took her duties seriously.

"Wyatt!" Ella called from across the yard, grinning. "C'mere!"

Wyatt held up a finger, letting Ethan finish his story, before excusing himself. Ella stood in a small group with Colby and Diego. Wyatt was still smarting, and a little uncertain of where he stood with Diego, but he wasn't about to publicly snub him.

Wyatt's gaze briefly landed on Diego before shifting to Ella as he joined them. "You rang?"

"Yeah, tell these guys the old gossip about the Dalton-Jones feud. You tell it better than I do."

"I'm sure y'all have heard that by now..."

"Not me," Colby said eagerly. "I want to hear."

"I don't remember the details," Diego added. "In one ear and out the other, I guess."

"All right," Wyatt said, giving in easily. "The story goes that the Triple J Ranch, or at least a piece of it, wasn't purchased by the Joneses, but was won by our ancestor in a card game. The first owner was a Dalton man."

"Naturally," Ella said.

"The Dalton man bet money first, of course. Right down to his fancy shoes," he said, remembering to try to make the story fun. "When he lost all that, he bet his horse, hoping to win it back. Then he bet his few head of cattle. He kept trying and failing to win back what he'd lost. It's the gambler's curse," Wyatt said with a wink.

"Oh, I remember this now," Diego said. "The Dalton man bet his ranch."

"You're ruining the beauty of my storytelling," Wyatt joked.

"Keep going, Wyatt. Tell it right," Ella said, grinning.

Wyatt's eyes rolled up as he thought. "Well, let's see. Eventually the Dalton man had bet everything he could. There was nothing left but his very livelihood, his land, which was prime for ranching. This was before it'd been developed. It was just raw potential back then, and he'd already lost his cattle anyhow. So he tried one last time, and when he lost, he was so angry he swore to get even with the Joneses. One way or another, no matter how long it took. And that's how the feud began."

"Over a card game," Diego said skeptically.

"Yep," Wyatt said with a grin.

"That's awesome!" Colby crowed, laughing. "So, the families have hated each other ever since?"

"Close enough. Some family members take it more seriously than others," Wyatt said. "I'm hoping this old nonsense will be buried with Grandad."

"You and me both," Ella said. "Oh, don't forget the best part, about the name."

"Oh, right. The name of the Triple J is said to have come from the winning hand of cards. Three of a kind: Jacks."

Diego busted out laughing. "No way."

"Where *did* the three J's come from, then?" Colby asked, looking as if he really wanted to believe the feud story. To him, it was just entertainment though. To Wyatt and Ella, it had caused a real chasm in their family.

"Three Jones brothers started the ranch together," Wyatt said. "JJJ. But Triple J sounds better, so there you go. The very unexciting truth about the origin of the ranch."

"Oh. Well, still, it's so cool you've got something that's been in your family for generations. Your family created all this."

"It is amazing," Diego agreed.

———

While Wyatt was telling the feud story, which he and Ella clearly didn't believe for a minute, another sliver of truth had slid into place for Diego.

He'd always thought of the breakup with Wyatt as Wyatt's fault. He'd chosen an inheritance over Diego, and therefore didn't love him enough. But now, he was realizing it was much more than that. Had Wyatt walked away with him, he wouldn't have only been giving up the ranch, but a family legacy that was hundreds of years in the making.

That was bigger than the land they stood on, the herd of cattle or the buildings. It was history and heritage, two things Diego didn't have much of and hadn't really understood six years ago.

When the group broke up, with Colby seeking out seconds and Ella leaving to chase after one of her boys — her husband was kicked back with a beer, looking like the poster boy for the strong, silent type — Diego tilted his head toward the side.

"Walk with me for a minute, Wyatt?"

Wyatt fell into step with him. Now without the buffer of a

crowd, the tension between them swept in again. Diego cleared his throat, trying to fight past it.

"Thanks for having this cookout and all, but I'm gonna stick around, if that's okay by you."

Wyatt glanced at him sidelong. "'Course it is."

"Is it still all right if I move into a room in the house?" Diego asked sheepishly.

For the two days since their fantastic but disastrous collision in the barn, Diego had been too much of a coward to ask. Wyatt had been cool and distant, and Diego hadn't been ready to say the things that needed said.

"Yeah." Wyatt stopped, scratching at his jaw, a sure sign of his nerves. "Move in tonight, if you've got your things. I shouldn't have told you to fuck off to Miami. I didn't mean that." His eyes met Diego's. "Far from it."

"We both said some stupid things," Diego acknowledged. "I was a bastard."

One corner of Wyatt's mouth hooked up. No doubt he could go on at length about Diego's behavior, but he refrained.

"There's a lot between us, a lot we haven't resolved," Wyatt said. "We may never resolve it, but... I do want us to be friends."

"I want that too." Diego didn't want to step on Wyatt's toes, but he couldn't hold his silence. "And I wanted to talk to you, as your friend, about your situation here."

"What do you mean?"

"You can't let these vandals run roughshod over the ranch, especially if they're targeting you for being gay. It'll only escalate if hate is behind it."

"You think I don't know that?" Wyatt said. "The horse is out of the stables, though. I can't take it back. People know, and they feel how they feel. Most the ranchers have accepted me, thanks to Grandad backing me up. But the working men? Other folks in town? It's a mixed bag."

"So, let's focus on what we can change. You need more men. I know finances are tight, but even one or two part-time guys would be a huge help."

Wyatt grimaced. "Those guys aren't always the most reliable."

"Beggers and choosers, Wyatt. Something needs to change. If you want someone more reliable, and there's no one in Cow Creek, then go to Riggs or Little Mae. There's bound to be men who need to make a living."

"Yeah, but will they want to work for a gay man?"

Diego shrugged. "You won't know until you try. I think there's plenty of people who will put a paycheck ahead of their personal opinions, don't you?"

Wyatt took off his hat, ruffling his hair. "I reckon so, but that's not my biggest problem. I need more revenue. That's why I was working on the event venue."

"It's a good plan. I should have said so," Diego said. "And, uh, Papá told me he'd happily left the cabin. That was just me spouting off because... I'm a dick."

Wyatt huffed a laugh. "Not gonna argue."

"But you can't work all day with the cattle, keep up with the management of the ranch, and renovate all these buildings. Something's gotta give, Wy. You're just one man."

Wyatt looked off into the distance. The sound of voices drifted to them, even without a breeze. Car engines were starting. They'd have to get back to say their goodbyes shortly.

"I'm supposed to be able to handle this." He slapped his cowboy hat against one thigh in frustration. "I'm supposed to be strong."

Diego had felt their attraction since the moment he arrived, but now he felt something else unfurl inside him. He wanted to comfort Wyatt. But given the way Wyatt had reacted when Diego asked if he was okay that night in the barn—granted, it'd come on the heels of some truly insulting bullshit spewing from his mouth —Wyatt might take it the wrong way.

He seemed to have some issue with appearing weak. Probably

because Grandad had pounded into their heads that ranch life was tough, and ranchers needed to be tough, too. Wyatt was stressed, sure, but he wasn't weak. He was taking on a lot, and he'd barely had a moment to properly grieve.

"Hey, now, you are handling it," Diego said. "All good managers delegate."

"I s'pose."

"Okay, then, let's just take it a step at a time. You can show me these plans of yours for the wedding venue, and I'll put out a call to some friends of mine who run a resort up in Maine, see if they have any advice. If you can afford it, send Papá out to recruit one or two guys to free you up to spend time getting this event venue off the ground. We'll figure this shit out."

Wyatt snorted, returning his hat to his head. "I ought to be pissed, the way you're stepping up and trying to handle my business."

"Are you?"

"No. Feels right," he said. "You and me, running the ranch together."

"I'm not staying for good."

"I know."

"So no going down on one knee."

Wyatt rolled his eyes, looking a cross between annoyed and amused. "I jumped the gun with the proposal."

"More like built the gun and loaded it."

"Yeah, all right," Wyatt said, "but I meant what I said, even if it was too much too soon. That marriage pact, even though we made it as kids, is not something I've ever forgotten. I carried that promise inside me." His blue eyes implored Diego to understand. "I always thought we were forever."

Diego's heart squeezed painfully. He'd thought that too, before everything went sideways.

"Maybe we are," he said finally. "Just not in the way we imagined."

9

Wyatt was nervous when he finally took Diego on a tour of work he'd started at the bunkhouse and cabin. He needed this plan to work, but talking about it with others wasn't easy. And considering the way his last attempt had gone...

Maybe I should have brought a condom.

He almost laughed, but he checked the impulse as he opened the door and led Diego inside.

The old bunkhouse had once slept up to a dozen ranch hands when the Triple J required a larger work force. It was a long, narrow building that had originally been one room full of bunks — but had a bathroom added sometime later. Now, Wyatt was dividing it into two separate guest quarters, along with bathrooms for each.

They stepped into a small entryway, with a door on each side of them. Wyatt led Diego into the one on the left.

The renovation wasn't finished, but a wall had been added to separate the space into two rooms, and Wyatt and Roberto had ripped up the carpet to reveal a rustic, plank-style board. It was in better shape than he'd expected — and even with some scuffing, it fit well with the ranch theme — though it would need to be refinished. On one side of the room, there was another doorway that led to an attached bathroom. It would have to be gutted and updated, and a second bathroom still needed to be added for the other guest room.

"The idea is that these rooms could be used for the parents of the bride and groom, or the best man and maid of honor, if that works out better. Then your father's cottage will be the honeymoon quarters for just the bride and groom. We can't lodge an entire wedding party, and certainly not all the guests, but it's not far to other hotels."

"It's pretty gloomy in here," Diego said, glancing at the grimy, paneled walls. You're gonna do something about this décor, I hope?"

"Yeah, we'll hang drywall and paint. We still need a new shower surround, vanity, tile. The works, really, and that's just the first bathroom. I'll have to get a plumber out here to figure out the details, but that's the plan."

Diego nodded slowly. "If it takes off, this wedding venue idea, will you abandon ranching altogether?"

"I can't see doing that," Wyatt said. "Ranching is in my blood. It's my family's legacy. But running a smaller operation with weddings on the side? I could live with that. I'm still doing research, figuring out the bottom line and what services to provide. Deciding whether to exclusively offer weddings or other events too, and how to stand out from other Texas venues."

"It's a big investment," Diego mused.

"Tell me about it," Wyatt said with a stressed laugh. He gripped the back of his neck, squeezing the muscles that tensed whenever he thought too long on the ranch finances. He didn't have a lot of cash flow for this investment. He'd considered his options — everything from selling a piece of their land to taking out a line of credit against the ranch — but with the ranch technically still in probate, he wasn't sure he even *could* do that.

"What if it doesn't pay off?" Diego asked, echoing Wyatt's

own concerns. He knew that Diego wasn't trying to be an asshole; he cared about the ranch. Probably only because it was his father's livelihood, but hell, that was better than nothing.

Wyatt grimaced, gaze taking in the partially finished space around them. "It has to work, D. I don't know what else to do."

As they stepped out of the bunkhouse to visit the cottage where Diego grew up, worry over the ranch's debt weighed as heavily as ever. *This has to work, damn it.*

"If it has to work, you'll find a way to make it work," Diego said, surprising him. "I didn't mean to rain on your parade, Wy. It's not a bad idea."

Wyatt sighed. "I just hope I've made the right choice. Agritourism isn't as popular as it once was. There's a lot of competition, and in a way, it would take a lot more work to run a dude ranch or something similar. Require even more lodging. I imagine a lot of wedding parties will opt not to stay overnight."

"Hmm. Maybe. You should market yourself as a destination overnight event for the bride and groom, at least. Maybe add on to the package with horse-riding lessons, trail rides, home-cooked ranch breakfasts."

Wyatt felt some of his tension ease as Diego contributed to his ideas. Just having someone to share the burden was a relief. When he talked to Roberto, he was always aware that Roberto's opinions were colored by Wyatt's position as his boss. Mama would happily talk with him, but he didn't like to worry her.

"That's not a bad idea," Wyatt said.

"Remember how I mentioned Caleb and Julien, my friends with the wedding resort?" Diego asked. When Wyatt nodded, he added, "They suggested we send over any plans or photos you might have. They'll review them and offer any advice they might have, if you want?"

"That'd be great," Wyatt said. "I could use a second opinion. Or a third and fourth," he said with a little laugh.

Wyatt would take any insight he could get, but more than

that, he was just grateful for Diego's support. It looked like they really were going to try this friendship thing. After the mess in the barn, he wasn't so sure they could pull it off, but Diego wanted to help Wyatt—even with all the unresolved hurt between them—and that meant a hell of a lot.

It also gave him hope. Wyatt wasn't going to throw himself at Diego again. He'd learned his lesson; they weren't ready for a loving reunion and a happily-ever-after. Not yet. But now he knew Diego cared more than he wanted to let on.

When they reached the cabin, Wyatt paused outside. "Are you gonna be upset to see your house turned into guest lodging?"

Diego looked toward the cabin, an impassive expression on his face. Wyatt and Roberto had already repainted the outside, added some cute shutters. There was still a lot of work to be done before it'd be anywhere near ready, though.

"It's not my home anymore," Diego said.

"D, it'll always be your childhood home," Wyatt objected. "You grew up here."

"It looks good. Better than I remember it," he mused. "But I knew I'd never live here again. I gave that up." He shrugged, glancing Wyatt's direction. "When I talked to Papá about it, he said the place felt empty without me there." Diego grimaced. "Made me feel bad for leaving him behind. The ranch was his life, and I thought I made the right choice, that it would be better for him to stay where he'd invested so much time."

"He offered to leave?" Wyatt asked, not sure why that hurt his heart. He liked Roberto as an employee, and in a way, he felt like family, a good-natured uncle or something. But the pang in his heart wasn't for Roberto, it was for Diego. If Roberto had left, it would have removed the last tie between them. Diego might never have returned to the ranch, and Wyatt wouldn't have gotten even the few meager updates on Diego's life he'd managed through eavesdropping on Roberto's phone calls with his son.

"He offered to help me start over," Diego said. "Maybe I

should have taken him up on it. I know I was a shitty son, never visiting because I was avoiding this place. And neither of us with the funds to fly him out to Miami except the once."

"You weren't a shitty son," Wyatt said. "He talked to you every week."

"How do you know that?"

Wyatt smiled. "Because like clockwork, he made sure to be available for your call. Sometimes I watched him talk to you, and I wished..."

"What?" Diego asked as the sun beat down on him, setting off red highlights in his dark hair. "What did you wish?" he prompted when Wyatt didn't answer right away.

"That I could talk to you," Wyatt said. "Just to hear your voice."

Diego looked conflicted. "Well, I'm here now."

"You are."

"And when I leave, we'll stay in touch this time."

"You promise?"

"S'long as you don't fuck it up."

"Hey!" Wyatt protested as Diego laughed and strode forward to enter the cabin. Looked like he was ready to face at least one part of his past. Maybe before he left again, he'd be ready to confront their history too. For now, Wyatt would bide his time.

———

Diego wasn't sure what to expect when he stepped into the cabin that had been his home for so long. Wyatt was obviously nervous, probably prepared for Diego to lash out again. But he'd burned off most of his anger with that rageful fuck against the wall, and the rest had slipped away when Wyatt confided in him as a friend —even after Diego had hurt him with his distrust and accusations.

He still had mixed feelings about Wyatt. Their past and their present were all jumbled up. Sometimes, he looked at him and saw an entirely new man, one who was weighed down by responsibility, but also smart, strong, and dutiful. And sexy as hell. Other times, he looked at him and saw the boy who wouldn't step up to be what Diego needed. But he was no longer sure whether to blame Wyatt for that—or to blame himself for expecting Wyatt to be what Diego wanted him to be, rather than what was right for Wyatt.

It was damn confusing.

But one thing he knew: He wasn't full of that poisonous resentment anymore. And seeing his childhood home stripped of its furniture and without his father inside made him realize it was just a building. He didn't feel a great sense of loss. Sure, he had some nice memories of being there with his dad, but the ranch as a whole was his home as much as this single dwelling was. He'd had tons of sleepovers with Wyatt; he'd joined the Joneses for dinners at least once a week; he'd practically adopted Dolly as his own horse; and he'd had run of the Triple J — from its oak trees to its creeks to the barn.

Diego looked around the small living room, now just a dusty, scuffed-up floor and rough wooden walls. For all that it wasn't pretty, there was a certain charm that remained. The cabin had been the original structure on the ranch before the larger ranch house was built.

"This one's not as far along," Wyatt said. "I just haven't had as much time to get away."

"I still can't believe you've been doing this on your own. It's a hell of a lot to take on."

"Well, Roberto has helped here and there, but I need the guys to work the ranch. We cut back operations, but we cut back workforce even more. Things would be a lot more comfortable with six or seven men working the ranch, and we've got four."

"Which includes you," Diego pointed out.

Wyatt tipped his head. "I couldn't have gotten this far without

Roberto's assistance. He especially wanted to help with this place. Only natural that he has a sense of ownership in it. Hell, even I think of it as Flores Cabin."

"It's not, though," Diego said, remembering what Wyatt had told him at the barn when the topic first came up. As angry as it made him at the time, Wyatt was right. This cabin never belonged to them. "It's the Jones's Original Ranch House. It belongs to your family, always has. It's a historic place, and you should play that up for the wedding venue." He glanced at Wyatt. "I'm guessing. I'm no expert."

Wyatt lifted an eyebrow. "You seem to have good instincts."

Diego wandered into the kitchen, feeling oddly embarrassed by the compliment. He was talking out his ass. He didn't know anything about marketing. He needed to get Wyatt in touch with Caleb, not shoot off his mouth with bullshit ideas that might be wrong.

The kitchen was tiny as hell. He'd forgotten how damn small it was. They hadn't even had a stove, just a hot plate and a microwave. No wonder they'd eaten with the Joneses so often. No wonder Papá hadn't wanted to stay here when he could be well-fed every night by Rosie. Three cabinets on the wall, another three below the countertops. Not even as much storage as his apartment in Miami had managed.

"How the hell are you gonna bring this up to snuff?" he asked.

"I'm not." When Diego shot Wyatt a puzzled look, he added, "I'm tearing out the kitchen. This will be a honeymoon suite. They won't need to prepare meals."

"Is Rosie prepared to cook for extra guests all the time?"

Wyatt snorted. "All the time? I love that you think we'll do so well we're always booked up."

"You know what I mean."

"She's up for it, though I imagine we'll hire catering for receptions and rehearsal dinners. It'll be breakfasts and casual meals.

And I reckon it won't be every day, but if it does take off, we can explore other options. Maybe hire her an assistant."

Diego nodded. It seemed as if Wyatt had thought this through. "So, how do you plan to get these improvements done with no money and no workers?"

Wyatt looked pained. "Slowly but surely? There are some financing options I'm considering. I just haven't explored them yet."

Diego frowned. He didn't love the idea of Wyatt going into debt, but he knew launching a new business took investment. He decided not to overstep. Wyatt was well aware of the ranch's financial state without him butting in. Bad enough, he was butting in everywhere else.

"Well, I'm sure you'll figure something out," he said. "If you need any help brainstorming, I'm up for it."

"I appreciate that."

"I'm also up for helping with all this labor," he said. "Do the guys need us anymore today?"

They'd spent a portion of the day starting the process of putting up hay—mowing and scattering hay—but it needed time to dry out properly in the sun before it was raked into position to be rolled up by the baler.

"They'll call us if they need something," Wyatt said.

"Then tell me how I can help. Wanna grab a sledgehammer and go to town on that kitchen?"

Wyatt laughed. "That won't bother you, tearing up your old house?"

Diego shrugged it off. He'd accepted that Papá gave up his claim to the cabin and was at peace with Wyatt's plans.

"It's fine," he said. "I moved on a long time ago."

Wyatt didn't look pleased at that, but he nodded. "Okay, then. Yeah. Some help would be great. These projects have been weighing on me, stalled out like they are."

"So, let's grab some tools and get to work," Diego said.

They stepped outside and Diego turned in the direction of the storage building where they could grab gloves, sledgehammer, and other tools to tear down cabinets and demo counters in the kitchen.

Wyatt grasped his arm. "I wanna say one more thing."

Diego glanced back. "Yeah?"

"I know you think this is my kingdom, and that I do whatever I want. And I know what I said to you that night in the barn, about how this cabin is ranch property ..."

"I jumped to conclusions and overreacted," Diego said.

"Still, I want you to know, if Roberto hadn't been okay with this, I would have found another way," he said, his blue eyes locked on Diego's as if he could beam his sincerity straight into him, and hell, maybe he could because Diego felt the truth in his words. "I'm not just saying that. All those times I've said Roberto is like family, that you... are like family. I meant it."

Diego was more touched than he wanted to be. He'd grown up alongside Wyatt. Diego had lost so much more than a boyfriend when everything fell apart. He'd lost his best friend, a man who'd been as close as a brother as well as a lover.

"I believe you," he said, working to keep his emotion from his voice. He did not want to unpack all the things Wyatt's statement made him feel.

"I mean, obviously, you're not really family," Wyatt said with a grin, "because otherwise we committed a lot of incest, and I just don't know how I'd feel about that."

Diego cracked up, relieved that Wyatt had broken the serious moment.

"Amen, brother," he said with a playful wink.

Maybe they could do this. Maybe they could be friends, and he could help Wyatt set the ranch on a steady course again, and then he could leave, with fond memories of home instead of only pain and regret.

97

10

Wyatt was on his way back to the house to wash up for dinner when Diego fell into step beside him.

"Hey, Wy," Diego said casually. "What's the plan for tonight? Tell me we're done painting."

Wyatt laughed. "Yeah, we're done."

Wyatt was still adjusting to the new reality in which he and Diego were friends once again. There'd been no discussion of how long Diego would stay, but based on some of their conversations, Wyatt got the feeling he wanted to see the ranch in a healthier state before he went back to Miami. This gave Wyatt some mixed feelings. He wanted nothing more than to get the ranch through this rough patch, but if that meant seeing Diego go, he kind of wanted the ranch to struggle for the rest of his life.

With Diego at his side again, even if only as a friend, he no longer felt as if he were suffocating under the weight of responsibility. The ranch's tight budget, the work he needed to do to launch an event venue, even coping with the vandalism all felt more bearable. Not just bearable, but *possible* in a way he'd only dared to imagine before.

Roberto had agreed to start a search for new ranch hands.

Meanwhile, Diego continued to work with the crew by day and helped Wyatt with the renovation projects in the evenings—and whenever else they could sneak away for a couple of hours. They tore out the kitchen in the cabin, they hung drywall, and they painted walls. Within two weeks, Wyatt's vision for the event venue seemed more like reality than pipe dream, and he had Diego to thank for that.

He still wanted more. He'd always want more. But he couldn't force Diego to want the same things he did. He was just grateful Diego had stuck around as long as he had.

"You can take a night off," Wyatt said now. "I promised a few folks that I'd go to the rodeo at the fairgrounds tonight."

"Oh. The rodeo, yeah... I forgot." Sounding almost nervous, he asked, "Can I come along?"

Well, hell. Wyatt wanted to spend time with Diego, but... Brody would be at the rodeo, and he and Wyatt had history. Wyatt wasn't about to revisit that history — not when he had Diego Flores within his grasp, even if they weren't more than friends right now— but he wasn't sure he wanted Diego to know about him, either. It would be awkward. And it made Wyatt feel a little disloyal, even though he knew Diego had been with other men. Probably a lot more of them than Wyatt had.

But he wasn't going to turn Diego down. Not in this lifetime.

"Sure, you can ride with me," he said.

Diego nudged his shoulder. "Thanks. I'll buy you a beer."

"I'll hold you to that," Wyatt said.

It was a gorgeous Texas day, still light at eight o'clock, but a less intense sunlight that limned everything in gold. Wyatt's eyelashes fairly glittered as Diego watched him from the passenger seat of Wyatt's pickup. He could hardly keep his eyes to himself, but thankfully Wyatt didn't notice, his gaze trained on the road.

He found that now that Wyatt had stopped flirting with him, he missed it. Being friends with Wyatt was great—much better than being on his wrong side—but Diego couldn't forget that night in the barn, the heat that had flared between them. As the days went by, he began to think that Colby might have had the right idea. Maybe they *could* enjoy sex without all the emotional entanglements of a relationship.

He flipped on the radio, turned it off again. Shifted in his seat.

Wyatt glanced sidelong at him. "Something botherin' ya?"

"No," Diego said, heart hammering as if he was just a kid about to ask his crush on a date. To divert himself from his nerves, he changed the subject. "I heard back from Caleb and Julien. They suggested emails for now, but a video call when you have time to talk about your plans for the ranch. Does that work for you?"

Wyatt smiled, and it was such a free smile—free of worry, free of the wistfulness Diego had seen so many times since arriving—that it hit him square in the chest. He wanted to see that smile on Wyatt's face more often. He wanted to put it there.

Careful, now. All good things must end. Don't get attached.

"Yeah, I'll make time," Wyatt said, answering his question. "I appreciate them making the effort for me."

When they arrived, the fairgrounds were teeming with people and animals. Cars parked haphazardly in the dirt lot, while campers and horse trailers formed a little neighborhood behind the corrals where the bull riding, steer wrestling, and barrel racing events took place. Bleachers rose around the corral, gradually filling with folks from all around the region. Some rodeo fans were hard core, traveling to watch events. Others stopped by only when it was convenient to them. Diego had loved the rodeo when he was younger, had known all the competitors. He was out of touch now.

Cowboys in blue jeans, cowboy boots, and western-style shirts stood by one of the gates, talking animatedly. Numbers were pinned to the backs of their shirts, marking them rodeo competitors, but even without that, it wouldn't have been hard to guess. Even though there were cowboys in the audience, like Wyatt, there was just a different presence about these guys. There was an energy buzzing through them, like athletes about to go on the field. This was their sport.

Hank and Colby pulled up just after them, and they all walked toward the grandstands together. Diego's father had been cagey, saying he had other plans in town, which had seemed odd. Diego hadn't noticed him taking off any other evenings—though it was possible he'd come and gone while Diego worked with Wyatt out at the bunkhouse—and he couldn't think of any hobbies his father had. But Papá had been close-lipped about it, teasing him to mind his own business. Diego had been pretty amped up about getting off the ranch—even just to go to the rodeo—so he'd dropped it.

They weren't ten steps in before Hank excused himself to talk with some men who called out to him as they passed. In small communities like this, everyone knew everyone else. Plenty of faces looked familiar to Diego, but he'd been gone long enough that he only recognized a few definitively. Thankfully, they hadn't noticed him. He preferred not to get too drawn into talk, which would inevitably circle around to the price of beef, the amount of rain Texas had seen (or not seen) in the past few weeks, and the pesky illness or disease that had plagued their cattle/goats/crops.

"I'll grab you that beer," Diego told Wyatt before looking to Colby. "What about you? You old enough to drink yet?"

Colby laughed, looking down, cheeks turning pink. "Naw, not quite."

"Wow, you are green," Diego said just to see if he could make those cheeks go full red. Sure enough, Colby obliged him with a deeper blush and elbowed him.

"Shut up, I'll be twenty-one in a month."

"A Coke for Colby, then," Wyatt said, smirking as he caught Diego's eye, sharing his amusement.

"Wyatt!" a deep voice called.

Wyatt half turned toward the corral fencing, where a small grouping of men stood. One of them, with the number seven pinned to his back, waved an arm in Wyatt's direction.

"Uh, I better go say hi. I'll meet you back here," Wyatt said.

"All right," Diego said.

Wyatt walked a few steps backward, a big grin on his face. "Have that beer waiting for me. I'm feeling parched."

Diego flipped him off, and Wyatt laughed as he turned and jogged over toward Number Seven. Diego didn't realize he was staring after Wyatt with a wide smile like a besotted fool until Colby elbowed him again. "What now?"

"Thought you didn't like Wyatt." Colby jerked his chin in the direction Wyatt had gone. "Now you're staring at him like he's prime rib."

Diego scoffed. "Not true."

Wyatt leaned against the fence, clapping a hand to Number Seven's arm. They both laughed, talking, looking like two men who knew each other well.

"Well, if it's not true," Colby said, "then you won't care that this guy is one of Wyatt's regular hookups."

Diego tore his eyes from Wyatt. "Say what now?"

Colby shrugged. "Brody Carmichael, Number Seven down there? He's on the circuit. You'll see him in the bull-riding event."

Damn. A bull rider? How was Diego supposed to compete with *that?* Wyatt liked his lovers rough, and a bull rider had to have balls of steel. Each second on a bull's back was putting your life at risk.

When did this happen, he wondered? And, more importantly, just how did Wyatt feel about the guy?

Scowling, he tugged Colby's arm. "Come on, you can help carry the drinks. Should I get Hank a beer?"

"I'm not his keeper," Colby muttered, "but sure."

As they walked toward the concessions, Diego's mind still spinning, Colby added, "Keep that info on the downlow. I don't think the rodeo circuit is the safest place to be... you know... open about certain things."

Smart kid. Though if he were really smart, he wouldn't have blabbed about Wyatt and Brody's business.

"Which is why you shouldn't have told me," Diego said as they approached the concession stand. "Your big mouth could get Brody jumped. Besides that, you shouldn't be gossiping about Wyatt."

"But it's okay to lust after him?"

Diego turned a hard glare on him, and Colby held up his hands, backtracking fast. "Shouldn't have said that. Got it. Me and my big mouth ..."

Stepping into the line, Diego said, "Are they serious?"

Colby blinked. "You *just* said I shouldn't gossip."

Diego lifted a shoulder. "Cat's out of the bag. Just give me the facts. No rumors."

"I don't know," Colby said. "They see each other when he passes through with the rodeo. Not sure if it goes beyond that."

Once they'd ordered and gotten the drinks, Colby wisely veered off to deliver Hank a beer while Diego made his way over to Wyatt. Though he wanted to run up and insert himself between Wyatt and Brody, he forced himself to stroll casually toward them.

He took Brody's measure now that he had a closer view.

Nice enough face, friendly but boring. Typical lean cowboy build. Wyatt liked Diego's muscle mass too much for that to do it for him, surely?

Wyatt noticed him just before he reached them, half turning toward him. "Sorry, D. I got waylaid here."

"I noticed," Diego said, glancing dismissively toward Brody.

"Thought I'd bring your beer before it got warm," he said, handing it over.

"Thanks." Wyatt lifted it for a drink.

"Hiya," Brody said, sounding friendly. "How do y'all know one another?"

And wasn't that a loaded question they could hardly answer for themselves, much less someone else. Wyatt eloquently answered, "Uh," and Diego chimed in with, "Oh, we go way back."

He stood close to Wyatt. Not so close he'd draw any unwanted attention but close enough Brody could read it for what it was. His eyebrows shot up as he looked between them. "I see."

"This is Diego Flores," Wyatt said. "He and I grew up on the ranch together. Closer than brothers."

"But very much not brothers," Diego added with a wink.

Brody looked perplexed, but then seemed to shrug it off. "Well, I hope y'all enjoy the rodeo. Wanna grab a beer after?"

Diego tensed, holding his breath.

"Sure," Wyatt said, which had him grinding his teeth. He added, "But only if Diego is up for it. I gave him a ride here tonight."

Diego didn't want to go for a drink with Brody, but he also didn't want to be a jealous ass. The horses were probably out of the stable on that one — damn, now he was even starting to think like a rancher, instead of a bartender — but he did his best to smile and say, "Whatever you wanna do, Wyatt. I'm along for the ride."

"Y'all should come out then," Brody said, friendly as ever, as if Diego hadn't just cockblocked him. "I'm sure the Two Step will be jam-packed tonight. Gotta celebrate my victories while I can still win them. Won't be in the circuit forever."

Assuming Brody wasn't in the hospital with cracked bones by the night's end. Nah, Diego wouldn't get that lucky. Not that he wished injury on the man... well, nothing serious, anyhow. But he was asking for a bruising to be a bull rider.

Wyatt told Brody, "We'll look for you later, then."

"Sounds good."

As Brody meandered away, Diego murmured, "Isn't he worried about being seen with you?"

"I guess Colby told you," Wyatt said wryly. "There's folks around here who know, sure, but not the entire rodeo circuit. I'm not that famous."

Diego had kept an eye out for any sign of trouble when they arrived at the rodeo. After the vandalism at the ranch, and Wyatt's assertion it was the work of homophobes, Diego thought they might get some hostility thrown their way. But so far, folks seemed friendly enough. Wyatt hadn't been pulled into conversation yet by any of the old cowboys filling the stands, but that might be more because of his age. He was probably the youngest ranch owner in the county now that Grandad Jones had died. Then again, it could be they didn't want to associate with the gay rancher. It was hard to say.

Either way, it paid to be cautious.

"I hope it's worth the risk," he said.

Wyatt cast Diego a baleful look. "I like to think so. Remind me to thank Colby for sharing my personal business."

"Pretty sure I could have guessed by the way Brody was smiling at you," Diego grumbled.

Wyatt chuckled under his breath, shaking his head. "You're a piece of work, D. Acting like you don't want anything, then getting possessive. Do *you* even know what you want?"

"Not really."

Wyatt snorted. "Well, at least that's honest. Might be the first time you've been honest about your feelings since you've been back here."

"How about you?" Diego challenged. "You know what you want?"

Wyatt met his eyes, his expression serious. "I think so, but ... I admit, I've had some doubts since that night in the barn."

Diego stepped closer, wishing he could touch Wyatt. "I know I was an ass, and we've got a lot of shit to figure out, and I'll be leaving before long..."

"That's a helluva pitch, D."

"Let's stop holding back," Diego blurted, afraid he'd lose Wyatt before he could get his offer out. "We're crazy hot together, Wy, hotter than we ever were before. Why not enjoy the time we have together?"

Wyatt's lips quirked. "And then what? You just walk away?"

Diego's hand curled into a fist at his side. If Wyatt told him to take his proposition and shove it, it would suck balls, but ... "Yeah," he said. "I have to be completely honest. My life is in Miami, and I'll be going back."

"I see," Wyatt said quietly.

"But," Diego said hurriedly, taking a step closer, until the toes of their boots kissed. "When I leave, it'll be different this time. We'll be friends with some really good memories."

"Friends, huh?" Wyatt mused. "Will you unblock me on Facebook and let me call you, or am I immediately erased from your life again?"

Diego winced. "Yeah, of course. I'm sorry I cut you off, but—"

Wyatt held up a hand. "We can talk later. For now? I want to sit back and drink this beer. Watch some men get thrown around like ragdolls. But later ..."

Diego exhaled, already feeling the thrum of lust heat his veins. "Friends with benefits," he suggested, "for as long as I'm at the ranch?"

Wyatt turned toward the stands, and Diego fell into step with him.

"I should say no," Wyatt said, "especially because I think this was brought on by jealousy."

"I can't deny the idea of that guy bugs me...but that's not all it is. This is about you and me, and the sexual chemistry between us. Why waste it when we could make some really good memories?"

Wyatt laughed, shaking his head. "I must be out of my mind to even consider this ..."

"But you are considering it?" Diego asked hopefully.

Wyatt met his eyes. "I don't know if the reasons are right, but it's not within my power to say no to you."

Diego felt lighter than he had in days. "Yeah?" He grinned. "Do I get to turn you out against a barn wall again?"

Wyatt glanced over his shoulder, but Diego had lowered his voice and no one was close by. "Darlin', you can take me anywhere you like," Wyatt murmured. "So long as you treat me right."

"I will," Diego promised. "You've got my respect, Wyatt. I swear."

"I appreciate that," Wyatt said, his eyes twinkling. "Just don't respect me too much to give me what I want."

Diego snorted. "Too bad we have to have that beer with Brody. We'd be home so much sooner if you gave him a raincheck."

"Nice try," Wyatt said, looking mischievous. It was nice to see him without such a serious edge for a change. "It'll do you good to stew in your jealousy a bit longer, I think." He winked at him before dropping down next to Colby, where Diego couldn't openly protest.

But that was okay. Now that Wyatt had agreed to his terms, Diego could bide his time. Once they were alone, Diego would get his payback for all of Wyatt's teasing.

11

The Two Step was indeed packed. Wyatt followed Brody's broad shoulders through the crowd, the heat of Diego's body behind him. The bar was a little dive that usually didn't see much action, but when the rodeo came through, it was swamped with cowboys and their groupies. There were the cowgirls who also competed in the rodeo, dressed much like the men in jeans and button-down shirts. Then there were the women in short skirts and cowboy boots and fringe — fringed skirts or fringed halter tops or fringed jackets. Whatever they wore, at least one piece of item had some fringe going on.

Brody received backslaps and friendly greetings as he made his way up to the bar, ordering them a pitcher. He smiled at everyone, thanking them for their praise. He'd done well that night, despite getting tossed off the bull. There was really no other way for a bull-riding event to end. Once they'd gotten a pitcher of beer, they pushed their way to a corner, where they were able to claim an abandoned table littered with empty bottles. Wyatt pushed them aside, and Brody set down the pitcher and glasses.

Despite what Wyatt had told Diego, Brody usually took care not to be seen alone with him—or any other guy, he assumed.

They usually grabbed a beer somewhere a little more private before enjoying some post-rodeo calisthenics. He supposed Diego's presence had reassured Brody that this would be just a friendly beer with the guys, nothing that could be misconstrued.

Plenty of the crowd had taken to the dance floor for some two-stepping fun. Wyatt grimaced, remembering all the times he'd been forced to dance and pretend he wanted to twirl women around. He was glad those days were behind him. He glanced toward Diego, who lifted his eyes to meet Wyatt's gaze. He didn't have to speak out loud; Wyatt knew they were remembering the same thing, even if they had been in different positions. Wyatt forced to put on the act, and Diego forced to watch. Not that Diego had never taken a turn on the dance floor, but he tended to escape that duty far more often than Wyatt had managed. Roberto had never pressured Diego, as far as Wyatt knew, to be anything other than himself.

Wyatt leaned in close enough their shoulders pressed together. "They're not good memories for me either."

Diego's lips tipped up slightly. He nudged Wyatt, before putting more space between them. "Glad to hear it."

Brody cleared his throat. "So, how long are you gonna be in the Cow Creek area, Diego?"

The million-dollar question, Wyatt thought grimly. One Diego wouldn't answer, but Wyatt still felt himself tensing in anticipation.

"Not sure," Diego said, his expression suspicious. "I'll be around longer than you. How long is the rodeo in town?"

Brody smiled gamely. "Just through tomorrow night, but I'm staying on a few more days with my folks. They live near Riggs."

Diego's scowl said it all. He *was* jealous, even if he didn't admit it. Come to think of it, he'd looked happy when Brody got tossed off that bull, though Wyatt doubted he wanted any real harm to come to the man. Wyatt knew from experience that Brody would be sporting bruises over half his body. It had always amazed him that Brody had the energy to fuck after his body took such a beating, but he'd told Wyatt that he had adrenaline to burn after rodeo events. In fact, the rougher the ride, the rougher he wanted to ride Wyatt, which had suited them both just fine.

Brody had scratched an itch for Wyatt, but it'd never gone beyond the physical. Not like with Diego. Even when they were mad as hell and Diego was fucking him like it was a punishment, Wyatt had felt so much more between them. Some of it ugly, regretful history. Some of it beautiful, happy memories. All of it emotional and deeply rooted in him.

Now, they were agreeing to engage in a friends-with-benefits situation, Wyatt knew his heart was in for a rough ride of its own. He wanted so much more than a few hookups while Diego was there, but he was willing to take what he could get for now.

"That was a heck of a ride tonight," Wyatt said, changing the subject.

"Hoo boy, that bull was fired up," Brody said with a laugh. "He was a spirited one."

Brody grew tired of talking rodeo, and Diego was giving no more than cursory responses to his attempts at small talk, when their conversation veered into dangerous territory.

"Why *did* you leave Texas?" Brody asked, following up with, "I can't imagine anyone leaving Wyatt behind."

Diego failed to censor himself. He couldn't help it; this guy had had Wyatt, and Diego didn't like it. It reached inside and brought all sorts of buried feelings into the light. Feelings Diego didn't want to examine too closely. Feelings of possessiveness. Wyatt was supposed to be *his*, even if he didn't choose to be with him forever. Feelings of envy. Brody had gotten Wyatt, enjoyed him, while Diego was too far inside his resentment to know what he was missing.

"You don't know anything about me and Wyatt, and you never will," Diego growled.

Brody leaned back, as if Diego's anger was a physical force between them. "Easy, I didn't mean to touch a nerve. I just think Wyatt's great, is all."

"Yeah, but you'll never give him anything real. You're too busy hiding." He snorted. "Hell, maybe you'd have been just fine sticking around to watch him pretend with women for his grandad's sake, but I wasn't."

Brody glanced around wildly, but the bar was far too noisy for anyone to overhear. Didn't stop the panicked expression from crossing Brody's face. Diego jabbed a finger toward him. "There, see that? I didn't want to live like that."

"Diego, don't," Wyatt warned.

"Not like I have a choice," Brody said, eyes gleaming. "Not on the rodeo circuit."

"I'm sorry," Wyatt said to him. "You stepped on a landmine with that question. It was my fault Diego left. My grandfather gave me an ultimatum, and—"

Diego shot to his feet. "I need some air."

He didn't want to hear Wyatt rehash their breakup. Even if he was starting to see it wasn't all as black-and-white as it seemed, he wasn't ready to bring it out into the light and let someone like Brody weigh it on it.

Stalking away from the table, he tried not to listen to Wyatt and his ears strained for his voice anyhow, the traitors. To his relief, Wyatt abandoned his explanation of their breakup in favor of making his excuses and trailing Diego out to the parking lot.

Brody probably wished he'd never asked to meet up. *Good.* As soon as the thought surfaced, he winced. He didn't have any claim to Wyatt. They were friends who were going to hook up. With their history, it was easy to fall into old relationship patterns, but Diego couldn't let that happen. This was *temporary.* It had an expiration date, even if Diego wasn't sure exactly what day he'd leave.

A few more weeks, at most, he reminded himself. *Keep some perspective or bail now.*

He knew even before Wyatt caught up to him by the pickup that he wasn't going to bail. Couldn't. It'd been hell spending these past two weeks with Wyatt, working the ranch with him, joking around and laughing while they renovated the bunkhouse and cabin, and all the while, secretly burning for him. He wanted Wyatt again. He needed to know if the sex would be as good as it was the last time, or if their anger had infused it with something extra. He almost hoped it was a disappointment, and yet he was pretty damn sure it'd be phenomenal.

"Diego, I'm sorry about that," Wyatt said. "He didn't know."

"It's fine," Diego bit out. "I'm just not in the mood to share my personal life with your hookup."

Wyatt winced, moving in closer to him. "Yeah, I'm sorry. I know our past is messy, and—"

"Stop apologizing."

"Okay."

This was all wrong. They were supposed to be having great sex tonight, not worrying about Brody Carmichael. "Fuck, I'm the one who's sorry," Diego said. "I'm ruining the night."

Wyatt licked his lips, looking a little nervous. "If this changed your mind..."

Diego grabbed his shirt, pulling him in close. "Fuck no, I didn't change my mind," he murmured. "Drive me back to the ranch, where I can get at you, or I'm gonna take you right here against the pickup."

Wyatt's breath stuttered. "Fuck, okay, yeah. Let's go."

Rain spit from the sky as Wyatt and Diego headed back toward the ranch. Despite Brody's question pissing Diego off about the past all over again, he wasn't straying from their agreement to become fuck buddies while he was at the Triple J. Wyatt heard his whispered words again and again, heating up his blood and making him squirm in his seat as he drove.

Drive me back to the ranch, where I can get at you, or I'm gonna take you right here against the pickup.

He sure as hell knew how to push Wyatt's buttons.

The bar was closer to the ranch than the rodeo, but they still had a twenty-minute drive, and Wyatt was the one shifting in his seat this time. Diego had gotten him all worked up, and now he'd be suffering all the way home, where Diego probably intended to take out his frustrations on Wyatt's body. At least, he hoped he did. He squirmed again, mind fully in sexual fantasy mode, when Diego's voice broke in.

"Was I out of line about Brody?" Diego asked. Sounding reluctant, he added, "If you guys are serious, I don't want to step on any toes."

Wyatt blew out a breath. "It ain't like that. Brody's a friend. Being in the rodeo, he's closeted, and it's not like there's a lot of options in Texas. I'm just a sure thing, y'know?"

"Wyatt, you're not a last resort for anyone," Diego said.

Well, that was nice to hear. Wyatt was sure Diego was biased, but considering Wyatt wanted him to be, that was all to his advantage. Diego could think he was the most desirable man in the world and that would suit Wyatt just fine.

"We only see each other a few times a year," Wyatt said. "I wouldn't have asked you about the marriage pact if I was serious about anyone." Taking a risk, heart thumping, he added, "There's been no one important since you."

The rain transitioned from a trickle to a sheet of water pouring on them, and Wyatt flipped on the wipers. For a moment, the only sound in the cab of the truck was the swish-swish of the wipers and the pitter-patter of raindrops against the truck roof. He shouldn't have said that. He was going to scare Diego off again.

"Okay, good," Diego said at last. "I'd hate to ruin anything for you. Since this is just temporary."

Wyatt wondered who Diego was trying to convince, Wyatt or himself. He'd been awfully jealous for a guy who professed to want nothing but a good time. But Wyatt had poked the bear enough. He didn't want to push Diego too hard, too fast. He'd learned the hard way that it wouldn't get him anywhere.

He nodded. "Right. It's just sex. I know."

In the country, between towns, it was pitch black out, and Wyatt could only see as far as his headlights illuminated. He had to concentrate on the road because the last thing he wanted was to hit an animal. Armadillos and opossums were regularly roadkill, but occasionally cattle got loose, and that could be a deadly ending for the driver. But he could feel Diego staring at him.

Huffing a breath, he said, "Just ask what you want to ask."

"Did he know how you like it?" Diego asked.

Wyatt tried not to flush. He owned his desires, but sometimes it made him feel exposed to be so transparent in his wants. Diego seemed to enjoy being assertive, but for all Wyatt knew, that was just Diego's suppressed anger finding an enjoyable outlet. Could he dominate a man he loved and respected? It was unsettling that Wyatt didn't know for sure.

"He knew," Wyatt said shortly. "It suited him too."

Silence fell, and tension gathered between them. Wyatt had to know. Clearing his throat, he asked, "Does it, uh, suit you?"

"Topping you?" Diego asked. "Or do you mean making it rough?"

"Both. I don't know. I just wonder what you like. Or need—"

"Just you," Diego interrupted. "In whatever way I can have you."

Wyatt's breath caught. Fuck if he'd ever heard a more romantic line out of this new Diego's mouth.

Diego skimmed his hand over Wyatt's thigh, fingers tracing

the inseam on his jeans. Wyatt responded to the touch, his blood rushing south.

"I want you too," Wyatt said thickly. "However... whatever you want."

"Good, we're on the same page. Because tonight, I want you to suffer."

Wyatt glanced at him briefly, surprised. "What?"

"You tortured me all night, making me wait and socialize with your hookup, and now I'm gonna make you pay." He smiled evilly. "Don't worry. We're both going to *really* enjoy it."

Wyatt's heart skipped around erratically, but his cock throbbed with want. Whatever Diego had in mind, he had no doubt he'd enjoy being at his mercy, but it was still a little unnerving, the not knowing. Exciting, too.

He took the turn onto the drive into the ranch, navigating his way toward the carport attached to a storage shed behind the barn. The covered space where he would ordinarily park was filled with Diego's car, so this was the best he could do.

Shifting into park and cutting the engine, he looked to Diego. "I can drive you up to the house, if you don't want to get wet? This rain doesn't look to be letting up anytime soon."

Diego cast a look through the windshield. "The barn is close. Let's just make a break for it."

"You sure you won't melt in this water?" he joked.

Diego smacked his palm down on his thigh. "I'm sure I won't mind seeing you soaking wet and begging for my cock."

Wyatt leaned his head back, groaning at that image.

"Race ya," Diego said, opening his door and hopping out.

With a laugh, Wyatt followed.

12

They were drenched within two steps of the pickup, the sky dumping water without reserve. Wyatt caught up with him easily, and whooped with glee, spinning in a circle with his arms held up to the sky. He'd always been the type of guy who'd dance in the rain, the lunatic. Diego loved seeing him like this, more like the boy he remembered before stress or worry began to weigh him down.

Diego couldn't hold in his own laugh as he ran toward the barn. Just before he reached the door, Wyatt grabbed the back of his T-shirt and yanked him back.

"You cheater!" Diego accused, grinning. Wyatt had always pulled some stunt to win a race between them. But this time, instead of speeding ahead as Diego expected, Wyatt yanked him close. They kissed, the rain pouring down their faces like a waterfall.

When he pulled back, blinking, Wyatt's eyelashes were in sharp points, his hair was plastered to his head — he'd left his hat safely in the truck — and his eyes were fixed on Diego's face.

"You're so goddamned beautiful."

Diego rolled his eyes. "I was promised a dry barn, yet here we are, a couple of drowned rats—"

Wyatt chuckled. "You're a real romantic. Kissing in the rain is supposed to be one of those epic moments." His smile slipped. "Not that this is about romance, I know."

He turned away, but Diego grabbed his arm, pulling him back into his arms, and kissed him again, taking his time, letting the water plaster their clothes to their bodies. This might not be permanent, but that didn't mean it couldn't be passionate. He wanted to put smiles on Wyatt's face, not chase them away. He was done wallowing in pain; tonight was about pleasure.

Wyatt pulled back with a goofy smile on his face. *Better.*

"Okay, now we're drowned rats," he said with a laugh.

"Open the door," Diego suggested.

Turning, Wyatt pulled open the barn door, and Diego ducked under his arm, peeling off his T-shirt as he went.

Wyatt closed the door behind them, then set to unbuttoning his shirt. Diego let him remove it but stopped him before he could strip off his sleeveless undershirt.

"Hold it right there," he said, prowling up to Wyatt and enjoying the view of the white shirt plastered to his skin, molding to every muscle and the points of his nipples. Even though it had been beneath Wyatt's western-style button-down, he was drenched down to the skin, and the white shirt was practically transparent.

"I like this look on you."

Wyatt laughed. "Drowned rat is your thing?"

"More like wet T-shirt contest is my thing," Diego said with a grin.

Leaning forward, he sucked on Wyatt's nipple through his wet shirt. Wyatt hissed, his hands threading into Diego's hair as he sucked, then bit down, drinking down the moisture that came from Wyatt's shirt. Then he moved over to the other one, doing the same.

"Jesus," Wyatt muttered. "Gonna suck my cock through my jeans too?"

Diego straightened, smirking. "No, but maybe I'll have you give it a try." He gestured down to the growing bulge behind his wet pants.

Wyatt licked his lips. "I'm game if you are."

"Nah, I've got other plans," Diego said. He hadn't forgotten his promise to tease Wyatt in return for his evening of frustration.

Grasping the bottom of Wyatt's shirt, he drew it up and over his head. His skin was damp, but not dripping with water. Diego licked a line between his pecs, up to the hollow of his throat. He could feel Wyatt's moan vibrate against his tongue there. "You taste good," he murmured against his skin.

"I've wanted this for so long," Wyatt whispered, trembling faintly beneath his fingers and lips—or maybe those were shivers.

Diego stepped back. "Been wanting to strip you down ever since we fucked. Didn't get to see enough of you. Take off those pants. I don't want you getting too cold."

"What about you?" Wyatt asked as he undid his belt.

Diego was burning with so much lust he wouldn't be surprised if steam rose from him. But wet jeans weren't comfortable, especially when a hard dick kept chafing, so he yanked open his button and shoved them down. "Good idea. We'll both get out of our wet things."

They had to sit on a hay bale in the corner to get their boots off, the sharp hay prickling their skin. But finally they were naked, laughing a little at the complete lack of smoothness. But Diego was eager to get them back on track. He ordered Wyatt to the center of the barn. Unlike their teenage trysts where they had been so careful to hide everything they did, he now had Wyatt out in the open. Anyone entering the barn would see his naked body.

"Look at you," he said, his eyes roving over Wyatt's lean form.

His shoulders were broader than when they'd been kids, his pecs more built, his abs ... well, they weren't quite as defined as when he was nineteen, but Diego knew from experience Wyatt's body was still plenty hard. His cock stood out from his body, quivering and beading with a pearl of precum.

Fuck, he was gorgeous.

"Turn around," he said, twirling his finger in a circle.

Wyatt cocked an eyebrow. This was clearly not the kind of bossing around he had in mind. "Seriously?" he said, but he turned as ordered. "You're gonna make me blush."

Diego enjoyed the broad back tapering to a slimmer waist, the tight, round ass below it, the long legs. Wyatt was something to behold.

"Don't pretend you're shy," Diego said. "I know you."

Diego came up behind him, slipping a hand up into his hair on the back of his head. He grasped a handful and tugged Wyatt's head back, which pulled a gasp of surprise from him. "You don't need me to tell you how gorgeous you are. How sexy. You know already, don't you?"

Wyatt's lips parted, color seeping into his cheeks. Damn, he really was blushing. How sweet was that?

"Well?" Diego demanded. "Tell me."

"I'm okay," Wyatt said modestly.

"Nope, not good enough," Diego said. "Tell me how hot you are."

Wyatt chuckled, sounding embarrassed. "I've never had any complaints."

"Because..."

"Men find me... sexy," he said finally.

Diego kissed the nape of his neck, satisfied. Wyatt's implication that he'd been nothing but a matter of convenience to Brody had rubbed Diego the wrong way. Brody was *lucky* to get even a minute of Wyatt's time, much less his body.

So was Diego, for that matter. He was just beginning to

understand that. All those years he'd loved Wyatt when they were kids and young teens, he'd taken it for granted. Wyatt had always been there, and he'd believed Wyatt would always be there. But years apart had cured him of that notion. He'd been the architect of his own pain in a way, ripping them apart, but now he knew that he couldn't expect life to go the way he wanted.

He had to treasure the good moments, make them last, until it all fell apart again.

He wrapped his arms around Wyatt, sweeping his palms up his stomach to his chest. His cock pressed against Wyatt's upper thigh — damn height difference — and Wyatt leaned back into him.

"You are the sexiest man I've ever had," Diego confessed. "Do you believe that?"

"No," Wyatt said, a smile in his voice. "But it's nice to hear."

"It's true," Diego said. "All those gym rats and pretty boys in Miami, and not one of them could hold a candle to you."

Wyatt's breath hitched. "I feel the same about you. No one else could ever compare."

"Not even Brody?" he checked, even though he knew his insecurity was showing now.

"Not a chance," Wyatt said without missing a beat.

Diego kissed his neck again, this time nipping it. "Good boy."

He pulled away. "Now, lie down on the floor. I don't care if you get dirty. I'm gonna take my time with you."

Wyatt glanced down, hesitating only a moment before he lay down on the floor. The barn had been swept out when it'd been emptied of most its contents, but it was still dusty. He would definitely be dirty when they were done, but he could shower afterward. Diego straddled his waist, tipping down to kiss him, taking his time, tasting his lips and tongue, before moving down his body.

Wyatt slid his hands along Diego's flanks, and Diego grabbed them, pressing them to the floor beside Wyatt. "My turn to torture you, remember?"

Wyatt moaned. "Please, D. It's been forever. My dick is so hard."

Diego grinned. "Begging already? This should be fun."

He inched down Wyatt's body, using fingers, lips, tongue to seek out each sensitive spot. He tortured Wyatt's nipples again, twisting them, biting them, until Wyatt was arching off the floor, moaning enough that Diego thought he might come from that alone.

He moved on, and Wyatt's moans changed to ones of disappointment and frustration. "Fuck," he muttered.

His whole body trembled beneath Diego, and he knew this time that it wasn't because he was cold. When Diego took a look at his cock, it was weeping and flushed a much darker red than it had been at the start of their interlude. He kissed from one hip bone to the other, while Wyatt begged. "Please, please, touch me."

He skipped over his cock to kiss his inner thighs.

"I hate you," Wyatt said. "I hate you so much right now."

Diego laughed, his breath gusting, before he moved up, taking one of Wyatt's balls into his mouth. He laved it with his tongue, sucking gently, before moving to the other. Then ran his tongue along Wyatt's taint, down toward the puckered entrance to his ass. Gripping Wyatt's thighs, he pushed his legs back, draping them over his shoulders, and cricled his tongue around Wyatt's rim lightly, gently, not delving inside. This was all about the tease, and he doubted Wyatt had prepared for a thorough rimming, but the sound that jumped from Wyatt—a sort of tortured whimper —made Diego want to do this again, perhaps spread out on a bed where he could torment Wyatt into tears.

He nipped at the skin, using his fingers to spread Wyatt just enough to tease his entrance, and Wyatt bucked. "Jesus!"

Diego chuckled, letting his breath gust over him. "You like that?"

Wyatt let out a shaky breath. "I'm dyin' here."

At this point, they'd been in the barn for an hour, at least, as Diego played with Wyatt's body. He pressed a finger inside him, a little roughly without lube, and Wyatt cried out loudly and harshly. It was more pleasure than pain, Diego judged, by the way Wyatt ground down, taking him deeper. He groaned in frustration, clearing wanting more, and Diego loved that they didn't have to worry if someone heard.

Well, not entirely true. It would be *very* awkward if someone came to check out the noise.

He pulled out of Wyatt, sitting up on his knees. "Shhh," he said. "Wouldn't want someone coming in here to see what the fuss was about," he teased. "Imagine what they'd think when they saw Wyatt Jones, ranch owner, begging one of his ranch hands to let him come."

Wyatt's face screwed up. "I'll be quieter," he said.

It was kind of hot, though, thinking of someone witnessing how completely Wyatt put himself into Diego's hands. Diego would love to see it from their viewpoint, or maybe record it on camera so he could watch it again and again.

His hand strayed to his own cock, stroking, and Wyatt made a sound of protest.

"What?" Diego asked, smirking.

"Not fair. You've been tormenting me all this time, and you're touching *yourself!*"

He sounded so affronted, Diego laughed, stroking himself more intensely as he looked at the fine man beneath him. "I think I'll jerk off and come all over you."

Wyatt looked a mix of turned on and pissed off. "You don't want to come in my mouth?" he asked, sounding desperate. "We could come in each other's mouths."

Diego shook his head. "Nah, you're supposed to suffer. Remember?"

Wyatt huffed. "You know, when I said I liked being controlled in bed, this isn't exactly what I had in mind."

"I know," Diego said in amusement. "That's what makes it so satisfying for me. You do want me to be satisfied, don't you?"

"Yes," Wyatt said reluctantly.

"Good. Be patient, and you'll be satisfied too."

Wyatt appeared to be resigned to his fate, but his cock hadn't softened the slightest bit, so Diego wasn't too worried about his complaints. He liked it more than he was pretending. Diego had a feeling that while Wyatt enjoyed rough sex, it wasn't really about the pain for him, but about the loss of autonomy.

Diego moved up to straddle Wyatt's hips once more, continuing to stroke his cock over Wyatt, eyes roaming over smooth skin and hard muscle. "I'm thinking about how hard you let me fuck you against the wall," he said. "You loved every second of me inside you."

"Yeah," Wyatt agreed as Diego stroked faster and harder. "You could fuck me now."

"No condoms."

"I have—"

Diego groaned, shooting over his fingers. He pointed his cock toward Wyatt's chest and watched his cum spurt onto his pecs, spilling into golden hair and dripping down his body.

"Fuck," Wyatt said, sounding desperate. "Diego, I think I might—"

Diego reached behind him, running a finger down Wyatt's rigid dick, and he exploded. Jesus. Diego watched Wyatt's face twist in what looked more like pain than pleasure and wrapped his hand around his spasming cock, pumping him through the orgasm. He couldn't believe Wyatt had come from a single touch.

"That was so fucking hot, Wy," he said, leaning forward to kiss his panting lips. Wyatt's arms came up from the ground, encircling Diego, clinging to him. He let Wyatt clutch him close as he rode out his orgasm. Then, as the intensity faded, he gently kissed his cheek, and rolled off onto the dirt floor beside him. They were both going to need a thorough washing up.

———

Wyatt lay his head on Diego's broad chest, his fingers dancing up and down his lightly haired stomach. The hate fuck against the barn wall had been hot, but Wyatt liked the aftermath of tonight much better. A little cuddling, even on a dirt floor, made him feel a hell of a lot better about his prospects for a future with Diego. Not that he would be rushing into another proposal.

"It's funny how we keep ending up here, isn't it?" he said.

"In bed together?"

Wyatt chuckled. "Not in bed, I mean. Always the barn for us. When we were teens, we didn't have much choice, but it seems history keeps repeating itself."

He regretted the words as soon as they came out, worried their history would once more inject distance between them. But Diego only grinned.

"It's because you're such an animal," Diego said, leaning in to growl and bite his shoulder.

Wyatt flinched from the sting of teeth. "Me? You're the one that directed everything we did."

There was a lengthy pause, and Wyatt glanced up. "What? Did I say something wrong?"

The last thing he wanted after finally getting another piece of Diego was for there to be more conflict between them.

"No," Diego said. "I was just thinking. I've never really ... been with someone who likes it like this. So I don't exactly know where the lines are. I feel a little uneasy about how things went down the last time we messed around."

Wyatt sat up so he could better see Diego's face. "You mean

when you nailed me to the wall?" He pressed a thumb to the crease on Diego's brow, smoothing out the lines there. "Don't worry about that. I wanted it. I loved it. And yeah, we were both out of our heads with anger and lust, but..." Wyatt shrugged. "I sure as hell don't want you to feel guilty about giving me what I wanted."

"It wasn't really what you wanted, and we both know that."

Wyatt's chest constricted. Diego could still read him so well. He'd wanted Diego the way he'd had him tonight, dominating yes, but affectionate and controlled, not angry.

"Well, you just made up for it," Wyatt said. "And even though that night wasn't everything I wanted, it was still really fucking hot."

"Fuck, it really was. I've jerked off to memories of it ever since it happened."

Wyatt laughed, before lying back down in Diego's arms.

"You're different," Wyatt said. "Or maybe I should say, we're different together than we were before."

"I guess it was inevitable," Diego said. "We're both older. I traveled the country, moved to Miami, hooked up with hundreds of men—"

"Hundreds?"

"We've been apart six years."

"*Hundreds?*" Wyatt repeated.

Diego smirked. "Sorry? I had a lot of anger to work out of my system."

That dampened Wyatt's spirits. Would the past always be an obstacle between them, something to be worked around or avoided? Wyatt decided, dangerous as it might be, to stop dancing around the elephant in the room.

"About that day, when Grandad caught us together..." Diego groaned, but Wyatt persisted. "I wasn't giving up on you. I was trying to buy some time. I hate that you think I didn't care."

"Okay," Diego said mildly.

"Okay?" Wyatt thought Diego would take more convincing. Six years of radio silence, and now it was all fine? He didn't think so.

"I know you cared, and I know it's not all black-and-white, like I tried to make it all these years. It was just easier for me, hating you. Easier to cope with the end of us."

"Diego..."

He waved a hand as if batting away the words Wyatt might say. "There's no need to get into all this ancient history. Let's just enjoy this while we can. It's not going to last forever."

Ouch. That hurt, even though Wyatt had agreed to a no-strings affair. He'd agreed, because he knew it was all Diego would offer, and he knew better now than to tell Diego of how much more he wanted. He suspected Diego knew anyway, given the hasty proposal he'd made on his day of arrival. Just thinking of that moment made him cringe. Too much, too fast, too *desperate*.

But that was okay. Wyatt hadn't given up. He still planned to get more than sex, but it meant biding his time and waiting until Diego was ready. And if Diego wasn't ready by the time he had to leave for Miami? Well, they had the rest of their lives to figure it out.

In the meantime, Wyatt wasn't above indulging in the best sex of his life. And if he was wrong and Diego was never ready to love him again? Well, then, the only one he'd be hurting was himself. He could live with that. It wasn't ideal, but the reward was worth the risk.

13

Wyatt stood in the kitchen, pouring himself a mug of coffee, the next morning — which was almost jarring after the image that been imprinted on Diego's eyelids the night before, of Wyatt naked and begging for release. It made every one of his hookups at Caliente seem unimaginative and unsatisfying by comparison. How had he ever found it exciting to pick up some cute stranger and exchange blow jobs or a quick fuck? It all seemed so meaningless.

Not that Wyatt *meant* so much, he thought, his heart beating fast. This was just a convenient arrangement until he headed home. Great sex, but still just sex. He'd miss it when he left. He wasn't kidding himself there. But he'd move on, just like he'd moved on before. But maybe he'd be a little more selective about his future partners. Look for quality over quantity. Wyatt had already spoiled him for choice.

Rosie and Roberto sat at the kitchen table, talking over coffee. In the center of the table, a basket of biscuits sat, still steaming. Beside it, a boat of creamy sausage gravy, a dish of butter, and jars of honey and preservatives were ready for toppings.

But Diego couldn't take his eyes off Wyatt.

"Mornin', Diego," Wyatt said in that drawl that slid into Diego's ears like a sexual invitation.

Damn, he couldn't stop thinking about sex. He wanted more, pronto.

"Morning," he said, then forced himself to glance at Rosie and his father. "Everybody sleep well?"

"I slept like a baby," Wyatt said, smirking a little. Yeah, Diego had slept well too in his post-orgasm haze. It'd been the best sleep he'd had since arriving at the ranch and trying to adjust to new sounds at night. He and Wyatt had snuck back into the house late and showered together, sharing one more orgasm as they stroked and kissed in the water, before they went to their separate rooms.

It'd been fun, sneaking around. Not like when they were kids and they were so afraid of getting caught. Now, it was like a little special gift just for them.

Diego helped himself to a plate, letting Rosie and Roberto's small talk drift around him as he ate a pile of biscuits drowning in gravy, chased with a mugful of coffee that Wyatt delivered to him without being asked. Diego glanced up, and their eyes locked. From the heated look in Wyatt's eyes, he wasn't the only one thinking about the night before. He sucked his bottom lip into his mouth, letting his eyes roam over Wyatt's body, until the clatter of dishes in the sink startled him.

Rosie and Roberto had cleared away most of the breakfast plates. Diego finished his last couple of bites and added his dishes to the pile in the sink Rosie was filling with soapy water.

"Thanks, Rosie," he said, leaning in to kiss her cheek.

She beamed. "You're welcome, sweetie."

"What's on the agenda today?" Diego asked as he followed Wyatt and Roberto onto the front porch. Being a Sunday, Wyatt had given Hank and Colby the day off, but Diego was hoping they could still scrape out an hour or two to work on the renovation projects—and possibly work in a quick taste of what they'd had the night before.

Wyatt nodded toward Roberto. "Your dad recruited a new guy. He's supposed to start today. I'll let Roberto have the pleasure of training him."

Roberto laughed at that. "Thanks a lot."

"But I'll still make time to meet him, give him the official welcome to the place."

Diego nodded along. "What else? Any big projects for today?"

"Nah. Gonna take out some cow cakes to the herd today. The grass is dying in this heat," he said. "We'll save the rest of the baling work for next week, when we've got everyone here. Gotta leave something for the new guy to do, anyhow. I'm sure Roberto will want to get an idea of how much work he has cut out for him."

"How'd he seem?" Diego asked.

"He's got potential," his father said. "Young but strong as an ox. Big guy, but he seems a decent sort."

"He knows he'll be working for a gay man?" Wyatt asked. "I don't want any trouble."

"Yup, he knows," Roberto said. He hesitated. "We might have been mistaken about why we weren't getting much interest in the job bulletins we put in Cow Creek. In Riggs, the few men I talked to cared about reliable work, not anything else. I didn't come right out and ask, but I felt them out enough to get the impression that they just want to show up, do their work, and get paid."

"Which is how it should be," Diego said.

"Right," Roberto said. "But they had heard some things about the Triple J that concerned them..."

"What do you mean?" Wyatt asked.

"Seems folks don't think the ranch is doing so well. They're speculating about how long we'll last, or whether you might sell now that your grandfather is gone."

Wyatt swore under his breath.

"How would anyone know how the ranch is doing?" Diego asked.

Roberto shrugged a shoulder. "Couple of the ranch hands left after we started scaling back the operation. They probably ran their mouths some. There are other indicators, too, though. Bills with suppliers and the like."

"That isn't why those ranch hands left, though, and you know it," Wyatt said tersely. "They stayed for Grandad, but once he wasn't long for the world, they cut bait so they wouldn't have to work for a gay man."

Roberto didn't look convinced. "Your Grandad ran this ranch for a long time, and they stuck around out of loyalty, maybe, but change scares people."

"I was out there, working with them every day," Wyatt said. "I wasn't some new guy coming in out of nowhere."

"I know, but you weren't the guy holding the reins then. You didn't sign their paychecks or make the big decisions about running the whole operation. Not until your grandad became too ill, and that's around the same time we started scaling back."

"No," Wyatt said. "No way. I don't believe that."

"Your Grandad getting sick, that brought a lot of uncertainty..."

Wyatt jabbed his finger in the direction of the barn. "And what about that graffiti? It doesn't lie. I'm gay, and that's a problem for some folks."

"For some," Roberto said. "But maybe not as many as we thought. This is a good thing, Wyatt."

Wyatt shook his head. "They're just selling you a line so they don't look like bigots. Why else would everyone be so sure I'm gonna fail the ranch? I was born and raised to do this, same as most of them. Nah. They wouldn't be saying squat if I was straight."

"You don't know that," Roberto argued.

Wyatt waved a hand, cutting the argument short. "I've got

work to do," he said. "Come find me when your new guy shows up. *If* he turns up."

"I'll come with you," Diego said, stepping forward.

Wyatt glanced back, eyes distant, as he jogged down the steps. "I got this. You should take a day off too."

Like hell. Diego moved to follow, but his father stepped into his path. "Maybe you should give him a few minutes to cool off. I obviously caught him off-guard with all this."

Diego shook his head. "Not happening."

"Diego..."

Diego lifted an eyebrow. "You're the one who wanted me to stay and be his friend," he said. "So let me decide how to do that."

"Just a friend?" Roberto said. "I saw how you were looking at him at breakfast. You two got something going again."

Diego tore his gaze from Wyatt's retreating form. So much for their fun little secret. "So what if we do? That's between us."

Roberto opened and closed his mouth, looking unsure of what to say. Then he stepped out of the way. "Okay, mijo. I hope you know what you're doing."

Diego hoped so too.

He didn't have much time to think it through. Wyatt was already circling behind the barn, toward the storage shed and carport that had been added sometime after Diego left the ranch. He wanted to catch up to Wyatt before he got in the pickup and took off for the other side of the ranch.

He jogged across the yard, turning the corner to see Wyatt had moved the pickup, backing it up to a short trailer with a cake feeder on the back. This was the first time Diego had seen this set-up. The feed supplement was most often used in the winter, and last Diego had been here, the ranch hadn't had the same equipment, but a much clunkier process that involved more labor.

Wyatt was bent over the trailer hitch, cussing up a storm as he wrestled with it.

"What's wrong?" Diego called.

"Goddamn thing is stuck, I swear to— Fuck!" Wyatt flew back, falling on his ass.

Diego bit down on a laugh, sure Wyatt wasn't in the mood to see the humor. He said mildly, "Looks like you need to oil that sucker."

"Yeah, there's a lot of shit I need to do," Wyatt grumbled, "and not enough hours in the day to do them."

Diego took over hooking up the trailer to give Wyatt a minute to decompress. He was pretty sure Wyatt's frustration was more closely tied to his conversation with Roberto and not the hitch that was giving him trouble.

Wyatt stood and brushed dirt and grass from the seat of his pants. "Thanks, but I can take it from here. I told you to take some time off."

So, he was still determined to go off and brood alone. Diego turned a sharp smile on him. "Well, thing is, Wyatt, you're not my boss. You can't actually tell me what to do."

Wyatt's mouth dropped open in surprise.

While he was off-kilter, Diego stepped up close, placing his hands on Wyatt's shoulders. "And right now, I need *you* to do something for me."

Wyatt looked nonplussed. "Right now?"

"Right. Now."

Diego pressed Wyatt back against the barn, and his eyes widened as he realized what Diego had in mind. "The cattle—"

Diego kissed him.

Wyatt stilled, caught by surprise, but as Diego pressed him harder against the barn wall—which probably wasn't comfortable —he sighed and relaxed into the kiss, threading his fingers through the beltloops on Diego's jeans and pulling him closer. Diego's pulse quickened, as it always did when he had Wyatt in his arms. He could kiss him like this all day, but he had other plans for him.

Diego broke the kiss, pressing their foreheads together. "The cattle can wait a few minutes. Get on your knees."

"You're crazy," Wyatt said with a strangled laugh, but his eyes told Diego all he wanted to know. Wyatt was into it. And if it helped relieve some of the frustration that had Wyatt wrestling trailer hitches and cussing up a streak, Diego was more than happy to offer up an orgasm in the name of inner peace.

Wyatt wet his lips with the tip of his tongue, and Diego suddenly wanted this for himself, too. His cock throbbed behind his fly, demanding attention, as Diego remembered the hot velvet of Wyatt's tongue on his skin.

"I've got things to do, and we're out in the open," Wyatt said tentatively as he reached down to adjust the erection visible through his jeans.

"Then you better hurry before someone comes along," Diego said. "Unless you want the new guy to meet you with my cock in your mouth?" Diego said. "That'd be one way to make sure he's open-minded, huh?"

"The new guy. Shit, I hope Roberto knows what he's talking about. I can't believe—"

"Wyatt," Diego cut in, not angrily, but forcefully. "Stop thinking so much."

He pressed on Wyatt's shoulder, and he dropped to the ground without resistance. He glanced up at Diego incredulously, as if he couldn't believe he'd complied.

Diego brushed his thumb over Wyatt's bottom lip. "Good. Now, open my pants and take out my cock. This is for you. I want you to just let go. Your only worry right now is making me feel good."

Wyatt unbuttoned Diego's fly, and tugged at his boxer briefs, freeing his cock. "Can't believe I'm doing this," he muttered.

"Shut up and suck."

Despite his reservations of a moment ago, Wyatt fell on him like he was starving for it. He didn't waste time with kisses or kittenish licks, parting his lips and plunging down on Diego's cock as far as he could take him—which was most of the way.

Diego grunted in surprise, slapping a hand against the barn to keep himself upright. "Fuck, yes. Take it deep."

Wyatt back off a little, then sucked Diego even deeper.

"Damn, that feels... I'm taking over now," Diego warned, grabbing at Wyatt's head and knocking his cowboy hat flying in the process. His fingers sank into hair, and he gripped two handfuls as he thrust in and out of Wyatt's mouth. The rushing of his own pulse and his focus on the pleasure building in his cock and balls drowned out the birdsong and the rustling of the leaves in the trees, but Diego made sure to remain aware of their surroundings. For all his teasing, he didn't want anyone to see them.

He especially didn't want anyone to see Wyatt like this, so open and vulnerable. He gazed up at Diego with glazed, watering eyes, mouth stretched around his cock, and Diego could hardly stand how gorgeous he looked in that moment. *This is all for me,* he thought dazedly.

"Undo your belt," he ordered. "Take yourself out and show me how much you like this. You like me fucking your face, taking away your control, don't you?"

Wyatt groaned around his cock, while he fumbled with his belt and hurried to comply.

"Yeah, I decide when you breathe, when you touch yourself. When you come."

Wyatt shuddered, and Diego watched as he fisted his cock, whipping his hand over the rosy-colored head and shaft.

Diego picked up his pace, fucking Wyatt's mouth harder, letting the pressure build and build until he felt it crest. "Come with me," he gasped, pushing in hard as his cock pulsed and orgasm tightened all his muscles, then released them in a rush. He shot into the back of Wyatt's mouth.

Wyatt gave a garbled cry, muffled by Diego's cock, and came on the ground at their feet, swallowing convulsively as Diego flooded his throat at the same time. They shuddered through the climax together, Diego's cock slowly softening in Wyatt's mouth until he pulled free and tucked himself away.

Glancing around, certain they were still alone, he put a hand under Wyatt's elbow and tugged him up. His jeans were still undone, and Diego bent over, running his tongue over the end of Wyatt's cock.

Wyatt gasped. "Fuck, that's sensitive."

Diego chuckled, letting his breath wash over the twitching skin, then pulled back to carefully tuck Wyatt's dick back into his briefs and let him fasten his jeans and belt.

"How do you feel?"

"Uh, good?" Wyatt said with an incredulous laugh. "Fuck, you're crazy."

Diego grinned. "Bat-shit crazy, but only for you."

Wyatt picked up his hat, mashing it back on his head. "Well, hell. Not that I'm complaining, but why here and now?"

Diego shrugged. "You needed it."

Wyatt stared at him a long minute. Diego wondered if he'd misinterpreted what Wyatt had told him about using sex to let go. His explanation had been brief, and it'd come in the middle of an argument. It wasn't like Diego *knew* what Wyatt needed. He'd just seemed to need... something.

"I guess I did," Wyatt said, blowing out a breath. "I know I let these things get so big in my head. Sometimes I can't turn off the worry, but just now..."

"You forgot for a few minutes?"

"Yeah. Yeah, I did."

"Good," Diego said, relieved he'd gotten something right. "Let's go tend to the cattle now."

"You don't need to help—"

"I'm coming with you," Diego said. "It's poor ranch etiquette to put a guy on his knees and then make him do all the work on his own."

Wyatt grinned. "Is that right? I must have missed that ranching lesson."

"Good thing you have me here to teach you," Diego said with a wink.

———

Wyatt's body was still thrumming with pleasure as they got in the pickup, and he drove out toward the pasture. He could get used to this feeling—and he probably shouldn't. Diego kept saying he wouldn't be here forever. No matter how good it felt to let go and put himself in Diego's hands, not to mention, have someone who was willing to share the worry he let twist him up inside, he could lose it all tomorrow, or next week, or next month. But it wasn't in Wyatt to guard his heart. He'd thrown open the doors to Diego the moment he saw him again, and he'd do it all over again, even if it left him wrecked.

Wyatt braked, letting the truck idle, while Diego hopped out to open the gate into the pasture where the cattle were grazing. He drove through, then waited as Diego closed the gate again and returned to the truck. Behind them, Wyatt towed the trailer with the cake feeder, hooked up so he could operate the feeder from the cab of the truck.

As they drove through the pasture, the cattle came running from all directions, knowing they were about to get some extra treats. It was still early in the morning, the weather cooler. Once they were into the heat of the day, the cattle wouldn't have much appetite and would be more interested in drinking lots of cool water and finding shade.

Texas summers were no joke, and heat was a real danger for the cattle—especially when most of the herd were black. There were trees, but they were spread out in small clusters, so shade was limited. There was a pond on the far side of the pasture, and they had water tanks full of fresh, cool water pumped up through a well. But it still required vigilance. Wyatt would send someone out later, when the day was at its most hot, to check the cattle for any signs of heat stress, such as cattle lying down or excess drool around the mouth.

"Calves are looking good," Diego said. "That black baldy is a go-getter."

Wyatt looked out the passenger window, toward the Angus-Hereford calf Diego was pointing out. Like many of the mixed breed, he had a black body and white face. He was tagging after his mama, trying to drink from her as she ran toward cattle cakes. Around him, most of the cattle were midnight black—a surprisingly heat-tolerant Brangus breed, which was an Angus mix—and some were the brown-and-white of Hereford cattle.

"He's a feisty one," Wyatt agreed with a smile.

The cattle went nuts for the cakes, even though they were just pellets with protein and other supplementary nutrients. Besides supplementing their diet, Wyatt always thought the cakes were good for reminding the cattle where their bread was buttered. It kept them a little tamer when the ranchers needed to get in closer to check on them. Which they did on a regular basis. They had to keep an eye out for illness or injury, and they had to be able to check on the pregnant heifers' condition, especially closer to calving season.

To Wyatt's relief, the herd was strong this summer, and calving season had gone well this past spring. The ranch was already stabilizing, when he thought about it. Despite a ridiculously tight budget, they'd caught up on most of their debts when they sold off a portion of the herd. The loss of the three ranch hands who'd left after Grandad became bed-ridden had stretched them thin, but saving the cost of their paychecks had been a good thing. The ranch was on its way to better days, but Wyatt still wanted a long-term plan to add to and diversify ranch income so they were never in this situation again.

For the first time, he felt like he could think clearly about the ranch, instead of sinking into a fog of doubt. And he knew that was because of Diego, because he had a partner he could confide in—even a temporary one.

His phone rang, and he checked the display. "It's Roberto. New guy must be here."

He answered it. "Hey, I'm almost done out here with the cake feeder. I want to check the water levels, and then I'll be free to meet."

"Sounds good," Roberto said. "I've got TJ cleaning out the horse stalls and shoveling manure out in the corral. You got anything specific you want him to do?"

"Nah," Wyatt said with a chuckle. "Put him through his paces as you see fit."

"Will do," Roberto said. "Wyatt, I'm sorry if I overstepped earlier. I meant for it to be good news, not—"

"It's fine," Wyatt said, unable to bear listening to an apology from one of the most dedicated and hard-working men he'd ever known. "You had good intentions. You always do. And I'm a bit... Let's just say this particular topic is a bit of a trigger for me."

"I understand."

"Good. I'll come find y'all when I'm done here."

He disconnected and glanced over to find Diego staring at him hard.

"I'm fine," he repeated.

Diego nodded once. "You weren't wrong, you know. There's no reason you should accept what my father heard as the gospel truth."

"You don't think I'm paranoid?"

"I think someone vandalized the ranch. At least twice?"

"Three times since Grandad got ill enough that word spread."

Thankfully, the workshop vandalism had mostly been a cleanup job and the ATVs hadn't been seriously damaged.

Diego tipped his head. "Three times. And at least one of those times, the message was pretty damn obvious."

"It was," Wyatt said, gritting his teeth as the familiar feeling of anger and violation swept over him. He'd been relatively certain that Randall Bradshaw was behind it. He'd quit the ranch only the week before the vandalism, spouting some obnoxious shit about going to work for a real man, but when Wyatt had called the sheriff, he'd gotten nowhere quick. Without proof, Randall's homophobic comments weren't enough to arrest him in connection with the crime.

If this were a Western movie, Wyatt would have men staking out the ranch to catch the vandals red-handed and administer "frontier justice." But he needed his men working all day, not patrolling the ranch at night—which would probably be a waste of time anyway, seeing as the vandalism happened sporadically every few weeks. There was no way to predict when, and the ranch was large enough, he couldn't even predict exactly *where*.

"Not all bigots scream 'I hate fags,'" Diego said.

Wyatt winced at the word choice, the graffiti on the barn flashing before his eyes again. *This ain't FAG country. It's GUN country.*

"Sorry," Diego said, noticing his reaction. "I'm just saying that people can be subtle in their bigotry. Maybe they even convince themselves that the reason they don't want to work here is that you're bound to run the ranch differently, or that you're young, or that they heard the ranch is scaling back. But really, they're looking for an excuse."

"Yeah," Wyatt said. "I s'pose there's no way to know folks' true motives."

"Nope," Diego said. "I think it's fair to say it's probably a mix. Some people care too much; others don't care at all. But you've got enough problems on your plate without worrying about it."

"I don't want the Triple J to get a reputation as some sort of falling-down heap of trouble."

"It won't," Diego said. "Because it's going to get a reputation as a working ranch with a fantastic new wedding venue and an owner smart enough to make the ranch work for him, instead of killing himself to keep the ranch afloat."

Wyatt smirked. "Is that right?"

"Yep. Pretty soon people will see that the younger Jones is the smarter Jones. I have no doubt about that."

Wyatt's heart swelled, and he couldn't keep the sappy grin off his face if he'd tried.

He didn't try.

14

TJ was a quiet, intense guy. Roberto hadn't been kidding when he said he was strong. TJ's muscular build made Diego feel puny. TJ's muscles were shiny with sweat and fully on display in his dirty tank and jeans when they caught up with him and Roberto out by the stables. The guy was built like a tank, and young, so hopefully he'd take to guidance all right. Older, more experienced ranch hands required less training, but sometimes they were more bullheaded about the best way to get things done.

"Welcome to the Triple J Ranch," Wyatt said, stepping forward and extending a hand. "I'm Wyatt Jones."

TJ pumped his hand once. "Nice to meet ya. I appreciate the opportunity for some regular work."

"We've got plenty of it," Wyatt said.

TJ's gaze flicked around them, from the barn to the trees to the open land stretching out in all directions. "I'll do whatever needs doing. I'm not afraid of hard work."

"Good to hear."

"Mr. Flores told me that you recently took over after your grandfather died. You have my condolences."

"Thank you," Wyatt said. "I'll let you get back to work. You're welcome to stay for dinner. All the ranch hands are. Hank and Colby have been given the day off, but you'll meet them tomorrow." Wyatt gestured to Diego. He'd been hanging back, not wanting to insert himself into TJ's first meeting with the ranch boss. "This is Diego Flores. He's a family friend, and he's been nice enough to help out around the ranch while he's in town."

TJ nodded his head. "Flores? Any relation—"

"Diego's my son," Roberto volunteered. "He grew up here, so if ever you can't find Wyatt or me, and you have a question, Diego will probably know the answer."

"All right, thanks," TJ said. Hooking a thumb over his shoulder, he said, "I'm going to get back to it."

Once he was gone, Roberto said, "I'll take him out and do another check on the cattle later in the day. See what he knows and what he needs to learn. He's driving over from Riggs, so you might consider whether you want to give him housing, or at least an option to stay on our longest workdays. I know you need the bunkhouse for this event venue eventually, but maybe until we open it, that could work?"

"I'd rather not. It'll hinder work there, and we'll just have to find another solution at some point."

"He can take my room," Diego said.

Wyatt whipped his head to look at him. "You're not leaving yet."

He wasn't asking. It was a command, if a slightly fearful one.

"No, but I'll be gone soon enough, and until then I can sleep on the sofa or in the old office in the stables. It's short-term, so—"

"Hell no. If you leave your room, it's to sleep in mine."

Whoa, there. That went places Diego wasn't ready to consider yet. He glanced uneasily at his father, wondering what he'd make of it. "Probably not the best idea," he murmured.

Roberto cleared his throat. "I'll go check on TJ and get him going on his next task. Let me know what y'all work out. TJ is willing to commute, at least for now, so there's no hurry."

Once he was out of earshot, Wyatt winced. "I'm sorry. I shouldn't have spoken like that in front of him. If you didn't want him to know..."

"It's fine, he knows. Besides, I've never hidden," Diego said.

Hanging between them were the words he didn't say. *You're the one who wanted to hide.* There was a time when Diego wouldn't have held back the caustic accusation. He would have taken the opportunity to fling the truth in Wyatt's face. But he didn't want to be that guy anymore.

Wyatt's blue eyes filled with remorse even though Diego hadn't said the words. "I'm sorry I let fear get in the middle of us," he said. "What we had was something special, and I ruined it."

"No," Diego said, his chest tightening. "I expected too much of you back then. I see that now."

Wyatt moved in close and brushed a kiss over Diego's cheek. "No, darlin'. You expected exactly the right amount. I'm sorry I let you down."

Before he could form a reply, Wyatt added, "I'm going to catch up on paperwork. I'll see you later?"

Diego made himself nod, watching Wyatt walk away with a lump lodged in his throat and blocking his voice. He didn't know what he'd say if he could get words out.

I forgive you.

I was wrong too.

Or maybe even, *I'm the one who let you down.*

———

Monday morning, Wyatt gathered with his crew—finally feeling like he had enough bodies to work the ranch properly. He'd talked to Roberto the evening before, and they'd agreed that Wyatt should turn his focus toward his new vision for the ranch while Roberto supervised the crew. As it always should have been —*would* have been—if they hadn't been so short-handed.

"TJ is joining us from Riggs," Wyatt said, making a quick round of introductions. "You've met Diego, but this here's Hank and his nephew, Colby. Hank's been working with us for about five years now. Colby started this summer, but he's already got a pretty good handle on the job."

"Lotta family members here, huh?" TJ said.

Wyatt nodded. "Guess so. Hadn't thought about it. You'll be treated fairly. Hank and Colby are both employees, same as you. Roberto will treat y'all the same. And Diego isn't employed by the ranch, so while he does get special treatment, he doesn't get paid."

"Dude, you couldn't pay me enough to volunteer at a ranch," Colby said.

"That makes no sense," Hank said. "If you're getting paid, it's not volunteering."

"You know what I mean."

TJ looked impatient with all the jawing. Rubbing his hands together, he said, "So, where do y'all want me? I'm game for anything."

Wyatt and Roberto exchanged a look. Wyatt nodded, and Roberto stepped forward to take the lead.

"Now that we're better manned, it's time to play catch up on some of the maintenance that fell to the wayside. Colby and TJ, I want you to get a start on repainting the barn. Let's get her looking good as new."

Colby didn't look thrilled, but he nodded.

"Hank, I'll ride out with you to check on the cattle."

"I can go out, too," Diego volunteered. He glanced toward Wyatt. "Unless you need something else?"

Wyatt could think of a few things he needed from Diego, but they could wait. They'd been crashing together at every opportunity. That blow job behind the barn had been just the beginning; Diego had cornered him out at the workshop later, and they'd exchanged quick hand jobs, kissing like the fucking world was ending. But the night before had been a rude awakening when Wyatt had decided to slip into Diego's room, looking for a more leisurely love-making session. Maybe one that didn't involve a wall or a floor. Maybe one that *did* involve Diego's dick returning to his ass. They hadn't properly fucked since that first time, and he wanted Diego inside him again.

Diego, already stripped down and in bed, had shaken his head when Wyatt shut the door behind himself. "We're not doing this."

"We're not?"

Wyatt had sauntered closer, certain he could nudge Diego into agreeing. Bracing an arm on the headboard, he'd leaned down close to Diego's ear. "I cleaned up for you. Inside and out."

Diego's breath caught. Wyatt let his tongue flicker over the edge of Diego's ear, and he'd shuddered.

"Stop," Diego murmured.

"You sure? I could—"

Diego yanked Wyatt off his feet. He sprawled over Diego's lap, ass up, and Diego brought his palm down in a loud slap.

Wyatt jolted. "Jesus!"

He started to pull back, but Diego followed the slap with a caress that convinced him he wasn't in any real trouble. "You're a brat," Diego growled.

Wyatt chuckled, pushing up on his forearms to look at Diego. "You're just now figuring that out?"

"Nah, I just haven't seen this side of you in a while." Diego leaned forward, cupping Wyatt's face and kissing him.

The kiss was too brief.

"I'm glad you're feeling more like yourself," Diego said.

Wyatt could read between the lines. Diego's expression was too serious.

"You want me to leave."

He'd started to pull back, embarrassment heating his skin. He'd thought they were in a place where they both wanted each other all the time. But now that he thought about it, Diego had instigated all their hookups. Maybe—

Diego kissed his lips again. "Hey, stop thinking whatever you're thinking. I don't want you to stop being playful. I just think we need boundaries. This is temporary, and I'm not sure either of us can keep perspective if we start sharing a bed."

Wyatt withdrew, and this time Diego let him. "So if I'd done this anywhere but a bedroom..."

"I'd be all over you," Diego said.

Wyatt sighed, turning away to face the door. He didn't want Diego to see the disappointment on his face. He felt like a fool, getting shot down like this. No wonder Diego wasn't willing to consider sharing a room to make space for TJ in the house.

They'd connected so effortlessly once they stopped fighting their need for one another. He'd hoped they were on their way to a real, lasting relationship.

It was naïve, maybe. Diego still had a life back in Miami. It was probably too much to expect him to give it up for Wyatt.

"Sorry. I'm not trying to be a jerk."

"It's fine," Wyatt said. "You don't want to get attached. I get it."

He'd walked to the door, forcing himself to look back and smile for Diego. He wasn't doing anything wrong. Wyatt had agreed to a friends-with-benefits situation. That he wasn't honest with Diego, and wasn't really happy with that scenario, was all on him.

He had considered arguing that intimacy was intimacy, with or without a bed, but he feared he'd only talk Diego into calling a halt to everything, and Wyatt didn't think he could stand to have Diego within reach and not have him. Those first few days Diego had been back on the ranch had been difficult, but now that he'd had a taste of Diego—experienced the perfect match they were in bed—it would be torture to deny himself.

Bad enough that he might face exactly that kind of pain when Diego left. Wyatt hadn't given up on the idea of persuading Diego to give them another chance at something real—but he also knew that it wasn't realistic to expect Diego to uproot his life overnight. If this was going to work, they'd have to work for it. Make sacrifices. Diego would need time to decide if he wanted to live in Texas, and Wyatt would need time to decide if he was willing to walk away from the ranch, if that's what it took.

Either way, it wasn't a decision to be made lightly.

But before all that, Diego had to *want* him for more than sex. That meant getting past Diego's guard and sharing meaningful moments with him. If it couldn't happen with a bed in the room, so be it. Wyatt would find a way to reconnect with Diego, to redefine their relationship as two adults capable of love, trust, and commitment. He wasn't sure how, yet, but he would figure it out.

He'd left Diego's room disappointed, yes, but not defeated.

And now, standing with his crew outside the large workshop south of the stables, Wyatt forced his mind back to the present and the work at hand. He had to make some calls to the estate lawyer. With his grandfather gone only a few weeks, the ranch was technically still in probate. It was mostly a formality, since there wasn't expected to be anyone contesting the will, but it did complicate his ability to take out a loan using the ranch as collateral. He had to talk with the estate lawyer, figure out how to get around that hiccup so he could finance some of the final expenses in getting the bunkhouse and cabin fully operational as a venue, not to mention all the costs associated with actually launching the business.

"Go ahead and work with the crew," he told Diego.

"Okay, then," Roberto said. "Go with Hank. I'll catch up once I get Colby and TJ going on the barn."

The men parted, each headed for their respective equipment,

and Diego paused by Wyatt on his way by. "That ass should be illegal in those jeans," he murmured.

Wyatt laughed, his spirits lifting. Diego might not want him forever—not yet—but he did want him. Wyatt could work with that.

For now.

15

That afternoon, Diego and Wyatt met up at the barn to begin their video call with Caleb and Julien. They'd exchanged emails and snapshots up until now, but Diego wanted them to give them the perspective of a visitor to the ranch — and better illustrate some of the progress that had been made on the buildings while they talked about Wyatt's business plans.

"Ready?" Diego asked Wyatt as he pulled up Julien's number on his phone and prepared to video call him.

"As I'll ever be," Wyatt said with a nervous smile. Diego knew how important this call was to him. He was venturing into unknown territory, and Caleb and Julien were the only wedding/event experts he knew.

Diego tapped the call button, and soon his screen filled with Julien and Caleb. They sat close, heads together to both fit in the screen. Diego extended his arm, stepping in close to Wyatt, so they could see him. "Hi, guys. Meet Wyatt Jones, in the flesh. Or, in the screen, at least."

"Hi, y'all," Wyatt said.

Caleb chuckled. Julien beamed, smiling easy and free, while

brushing a lock of sandy-colored hair out of his eye. "Just listen to that Texas drawl! It's good to finally meet you, Wyatt."

"You too, Julien."

"You know which is which?" Diego asked, surprised because they'd only communicated via text and email. Julien had a very different personality from Caleb, but it wasn't as if he'd said much yet.

"Stalked them on the Internet," Wyatt said with a grin. Then added, "Just on the Bliss Island Resort website, nothing creepy."

"You should see their Instagram," Diego said in a low voice. "It's like lovers lane meets tourism."

"I heard that," Julien said. "Our Insta is totally professional." He pretended to glare.

"And that photo of you two kissing is just..."

"Good marketing," Julien filled in, then made a face. "Caleb made me take it down."

After they had a good laugh and teased Julien about his marketing tactics, they'd moved on to the business at hand. Diego panned the phone around, so they could see the view. It was a bright, sunny day in Texas with perfectly blue skies, cotton-puff clouds, and a bright ball of orange in the sky.

"Wow, look at all that space," Caleb said.

Diego had put them on speaker phone so they could talk while he showed them the views around the ranch.

"It looks better in spring and fall," Wyatt spoke up. "The grass is actually green. We get some beautiful colors in the foliage at the right time of year."

Diego turned toward the barn. "This is the reception space. It's about to get a paint job."

He moved in toward where Colby stood scraping old, flaking paint off the sides of the barn to prepare it for a new coat of paint. His face was red from exertion and heat, and his shirt stuck to him in places. TJ was working on a ladder a few feet back and above him.

"Colby, meet Caleb and Julien, a couple of friends of mine."

Colby half turned, smiling brightly despite his obvious misery. "Hi, y'all. Nice to meet you."

"Colby's been working with our newest ranch hand, TJ, to scrape and repaint the barn. How's it going with TJ?"

Colby grimaced. "Fine."

"That good, huh?"

Stepping in closer to them, Colby said, "He's too quiet. Never talks. I'd rather be working with you."

Julien snorted. "Never pegged Diego as much of a talker either."

Colby grinned. "Usually I can get anyone to talk. But this guy? He's a closed book." Lowering his voice, he said, "Doesn't seem normal, if you ask me."

"I only care about how much he works," Wyatt said. "Maybe you could learn a thing or two from a man who focuses on his task."

Colby pulled a face, while Julien and Caleb snickered, and resumed scraping with a sulky set to his mouth. Diego liked Colby, and he really was a hard worker. He was easy to tease, kind of gullible, but sweet and good-natured.

Diego patted Colby's shoulder as they passed into the barn. "You're a good worker, too, Colbs. Keep it up."

"Absolutely," Wyatt agreed. "And make sure you both stay hydrated. Don't let TJ work himself into a heat stroke. I'm countin' on you to be the smart one."

Colby puffed back up. "You got it, Wyatt."

Once inside the barn, Diego panned the phone around, doing his best to show Caleb the dusty wood flooring, the walls, the rafters over their head, anything he might find worth noting.

"This is a great space," Caleb said. "People are really loving rustic elegance right now. Are you planning to decorate the barn and keep it wedding-ready at all times, or have the couples come in with their own decorations?"

"I haven't gotten that far," Wyatt said. "Do you recommend one over the other?"

Caleb hummed thoughtfully. "I think you can charge more and save some trouble if you have at least a base package. For example, buy tables and chairs, with white tablecloths, and have a light fixture. Now, some venues might have two or three different design packages. One that's classic, one that's more rustic, and so on. But you could also just have a basic setup ready, which the bride can then add on to. There's no single way to do this, but with no decorations, you're asking couples to cart in their own tables and chairs. That's added expense and hassle for them."

"Gotcha," Wyatt said. "I reckon we can set something up that stays in place. We've already decided not to use the barn for anything but events, so that's no problem."

"Let's head over to the cabin," Diego said. "Then we can talk more while we make the hike to the bunkhouse since it's farther away."

Caleb and Julien were warm, friendly people—Julien especially. He smiled a lot, sometimes almost seemed to be flirting, but his husband didn't seem to mind. Caleb was nice enough, but he seemed more focused on business, while Julien was more social, making small talk and asking Wyatt questions about the ranch that had nothing to do with weddings.

"You grew up here?" Julien asked after they'd gotten a look at the "honeymoon suite," which at this point was an empty room with a bathroom that still needed a remodel. Wyatt needed money before he could finish that out—and he'd prefer to hire someone to do it right—but he'd yet to hear back from the estate lawyer about his options.

"Yup. Me and Diego have been friends since we could crawl," he said. "Two peas in a pod, my mama used to call us."

Julien gaped. "Wow. I knew Diego was from Texas, but..." He gasped. "Diego, are you a *cowboy*?"

Wyatt laughed as Diego grew red in the face. With his complexion, it wasn't often he blushed, at least not enough to be visible. Sputtering, Diego said, "I'm not— No, I... He's the one in a cowboy hat!"

Still snickering, Wyatt said, "Diego's been known to a ride a horse. And he knows how to wrangle cattle."

"Oh my God. It's like I don't even know you. The party boy bartender is a cowboy."

"Okay, okay," Diego grumbled. "I know my way around a cattle ranch. I'm not a cowboy. We use ATVs around here more than horses. It's not the Wild Fucking West."

Julien didn't seem put off by Diego's grumbling. Wyatt wasn't sure why the notion bothered Diego so much. He sincerely hoped it wasn't a sign that Diego never wanted to be associated with his way of life, or a future together would be mighty tough to build. Not that Diego had agreed to any such future, but one day at a time, and all that.

"We've got nine thousand acres," Wyatt said, "so there's a lot of options for outdoor weddings in pretty settings. I scaled back our herd size over the past year, so that helps too."

"Who will be managing the event venue?"

Wyatt fumbled. "Well, uh, me, I reckon? I've been focused on getting the buildings up to snuff. Ideally, I'd like someone else to do it, but right now..."

"Okay, well just be aware that it will take work. You'll have to market to couples, do consultations and bookings, and you should think about how involved you want to be in the planning before you start this. Do you want to coordinate with caterers, florists, and the like, or do you want to require the couple to plan their own wedding or hire a separate wedding planner."

"I think, to start, that it's best that Wyatt not take on too much," Diego said. "If you think the venue can be a success without it…"

"It can be, yes," Caleb said. "It really comes down to branding. You can market yourself as an upscale, all-inclusive wedding venue, like Bliss Island, or you can market yourself as a more affordable, down-home do-it-yourself sort of place, or something in between. What's the event venue going to be called? I'm not sure you ever said."

"I don't know," Wyatt mused as they approached the bunkhouse and opened the door. "The ranch is called the Triple J Ranch. Hadn't given much thought to naming the event venue separately."

"You don't have to give it a different name," Caleb said. "But it might be easier to market with its own name, and something that says weddings or events. Think about what a bride might want to put on her wedding invitations. That her wedding is at the Triple J Ranch, which is fine, or that it's at something a little more colorful."

"Too bad Bliss is taken," Diego said. "Bliss Ranch has a nice ring to it."

"Well, technically, I don't have the copyright on the word bliss. Besides, we're in completely different regions."

"It could be fun," Julien said. "We could do some cross-promotion. We'd be like sister wedding venues!"

"As long as it was clear, we weren't actually owned by the same entity."

"Of course," Julien said, batting away the concern. "Any opportunity to market is a good thing." He wiggled his eyebrows. "Photos of hot cowboys on our social media are a *very* good thing."

Wyatt chuckled. "I'll have to think about it. This place has been the Triple J for centuries."

"The working ranch can remain the Triple J. Or all of it can," Caleb said. "It's really your choice."

"Okay," Diego said, swinging the phone around once more so Caleb and Julien could see the view, "here's what we've got done in the bunkhouse. We haven't furnished it yet. We've been debating between a king-size bed with a sofa bed or doing something a little closer to its origins, fitting it out with bunks to accommodate more folks. Any thoughts?"

Diego panned the phone, showing them the hard wood flooring, a little rough but mostly stain-free, and the newly sheetrocked and painted walls.

"Maybe you could blend those two ideas," Caleb said. "With weddings, you want to hit the perfect balance of rustic elegance. You want that fun, rustic look combined with convenience and comfort. Maybe a king or queen bed, paired with bunks. That way, if you've got an older couple, parents of the bride, for example, they can sleep in more comfort, while other members of the wedding party take the bunks. If they prefer their privacy, they can book the whole room just for them, but it gives some added flexibility. It could also work well for family reunions, if you're open to other types of events."

"I like that idea," Wyatt said.

Diego walked over, showing them the one bathroom in place. "This needs an update. And a second bathroom needs to be added to the other side. There's another room, like this one, over there. So we essentially have the Bride side and the Groom side."

"I think this has a lot of potential," Caleb said. "You're not on an island like we are, so you don't have to provide tons of lodging. There are hotels nearby, I assume?"

"Sure, there's one about twenty minutes from here."

"I think having the space for the bride and groom, with the potential for lodging for some of the wedding party, is great. You might even see couples wanting to stay on for a few days on their own, a sort of mini honeymoon. I think you're in good shape. The biggest challenge, as I see it, is in managing the business once it launches. There's a lot of moving parts. You'll be familiar with keeping books for the ranch, but there's going to be a lot of organization needed for holding weddings, even if you don't plan them at the same level I do. I could go on and on about the challenges that crop up during events and the behind-the-scenes steps I take, but I can't really *show* you what's it like in a phone call."

Julien perked up. "Oh! You guys should come up here. Caleb could walk you through the behind-the-scenes process. Not just set-up and tear-down, which is a lot of work, but his project management software, his accounting process, and the event management we do while it's taking place. I think it could be really helpful."

"I don't know that Wyatt could get away from the ranch," Diego said. "That's a pretty big trip to make. Expensive, too."

"Oh, well... I guess." Julien said, frowning. "But if you could swing it, we have staff lodging so you could stay for free, and we could feed you. It'd just be the plane tickets and the time away."

"That does sound amazing," Wyatt said, feeling a flutter of excitement. To get away with Diego, travel to a beautiful setting, and get a hands-on training session before trying to launch an entirely new business venture? That was a very tempting proposition.

"We can have a few more phone calls, and I can send you a few links," Caleb said. "But obviously, it would be easier to show you some of the ins and outs in person. I understand that may not be possible. The ranch must take up a lot of time and energy— which is why it's essential you're properly staffed for this undertaking. Weddings won't stop and wait if you have a cattle emergency, and I imagine it's the same in reverse."

"You're right about that," Wyatt said. "I'd like to take you up on the offer. We've hired a new ranch hand, so we're not stretched as thin as we were, and I can't launch a new business without investing some money. I could probably only manage a couple of days."

Julien bounced on screen. "That would be amazing! Would it be you and Diego both, or—"

"Wyatt, are you sure you can afford that?" Diego interrupted. "The ranch..."

"I'm looking at my financing options. I need a loan to finish out the bathrooms and furnishings, and I'll need to do advertising."

"And you shouldn't expect a lot of bookings right away," Caleb added. "Brides plan far ahead. In fact, you should start marketing before you're ready to open. The sooner, the better. Set up the barn and take photos. Finish out one of these lodging spaces and get photos and a website going."

"Good advice," Wyatt murmured, feeling that old stress trying to creep in. He'd thought he was reaching the light at the end of the tunnel only to find there was another tunnel. And probably another after that. His whole life might very well be a series of tunnels he had to find his way through in the dark. He needed to accept that and find a way to move forward with confidence. "And to answer your question, yes, I'd like Diego to go."

"You sure about that?" Diego asked.

"I couldn't have made this much progress without you," Wyatt said. "I want you there as I see it through, if you're willing."

Diego looked hesitant. Wyatt's heart skipped, fear warring with hope. The more progress they made with the ranch, the more he worried that his time with Diego was running short. He'd have to make some kind of move soon, but he'd already learned he couldn't rush it. The timing had to be right. Which is why he really needed a reason for Diego to stay just a bit longer.

Things were coming together for the ranch. With Diego's help, they'd managed to get the ranch work done *and* make progress on renovating buildings for the event venue. And now that they had another ranch hand, Wyatt was freer to catch up on administrative work, too. Roberto was still keeping his eyes peeled for another hire, and if or when they managed that, it would be much smoother sailing. The only thing that they'd yet to make any headway with was the vandalism situation, but all had been quiet since the workshop incident. Maybe that would be the last of it. Maybe whoever had a beef with Wyatt had worked out their hostility or had more important priorities now.

That was all a relief, but it also meant that Diego would probably start thinking about returning to his life in Miami. Wyatt knew he'd only stayed because he'd been shocked at the state of the ranch, and probably the state of Wyatt's mind, too. He flushed every time he thought of that desperate plea he'd made to fulfill the marriage pact. Not because he'd wanted to marry Diego —he still did, always would—but because he'd gone about it all wrong. He'd made it sound like Diego was sort of safety net or last resort.

I'm tired of being alone. I'm tired of nothing but regrets.

If there was a prize for world's worst proposal, he surely deserved it.

"I guess I'll go to Bliss with you then," Diego finally said. "Might as well make the most of this vacation before I get sucked back into real life, huh?"

"Might as well," Wyatt agreed, throat tight with suppressed emotion.

He wanted Diego to think of him as part of his life, not just a vacation fling. And he didn't have much more time to make that happen. He wasn't sure if a week or two would make a difference in the scheme of things, but he had to try. The sex was fantastic, yes, but they'd also rebuilt a friendship, and proven they could work well together.

Now, it was time to show Diego that they could love one another, too. If only Diego would let him.

"Spill," Julien ordered later when Diego reluctantly answered the phone after three calls in quick succession told him Julien wasn't going to give up. That he was calling rather than texting said a lot.

"You already knew I was down here for Grandad Jones's funeral. I talk to Matias, and he talks to you."

"Blah blah bullshit," Julien said. "Tell me what I want to know."

Diego laughed under his breath because Julien could be so fucking direct sometimes. He'd always liked that about him.

"I missed this side of you," Diego teased. "I thought Caleb turned you soft."

He could hear the smirk in Julien's voice as he replied, "Believe me, Caleb makes me the opposite of soft."

There was a rumbling voice in the background as Julien laughed. "What?" he said to someone — probably Caleb — "He opened the door. I had to step through."

"Okay, enough about your love life. I see enough of it on Instagram."

Julien, continuing to snicker, said, "Yes, let's talk about your love life. You're hooking up with Wyatt."

"So?" Diego said, unable to mount a credible defense. Julien would never believe it if he denied it.

"So, this is huge! Isn't this the guy who broke your heart?"

Diego grimaced. "I may... have been too harsh in my judgment of what happened. Wyatt's a good guy."

"Oh my God," Julien said, sounding stunned.

"What?"

"You used to have so much anger. You wouldn't let anyone close. Not even..." Julien paused, and Diego felt a flicker of guilt. "Not even friends," Julien continued. "You'd never say exactly what happened, but I knew it must have hurt you deeply."

"Ugh, or I was a fragile little brat."

"Were you?"

"Maybe both?" Diego said. "My family didn't disown me like

yours. Wyatt's grandfather did insist we stop seeing other, though."

"He forced you to leave?"

"Not exactly," Diego said. Truth was, no one had made him leave. He'd made that decision all on his own. "No, he didn't say I had to leave. He told Wyatt he expected him to court and marry a nice country girl. Grandad was always going on about how much Wyatt was going to need family when he took over the ranch. A wife to share his burdens. Children to take over the ranch after him. He was a traditional kind of guy."

"You could have shared his burdens," Julien said, offended on his behalf. "And family—you could adopt! Or, get a surrogate. Whatever."

Diego chuckled, a little amused as Julien mounted a defense that was six years too late. "Grandad's dead and gone. No need to yell at him."

Julien huffed. "I'm just so mad for both of you." He paused. "But he didn't make you leave, you said. So, what did?"

Diego found himself oddly reluctant to tell Julien all the details. What if Julien blamed Wyatt? Diego wasn't sure he wanted that. But what if he didn't? What if he affirmed that Diego was a jackass who'd caused his own pain?

In the end, he kept it simple and vague.

"There was an ultimatum. Wyatt's inheritance was on the line," Diego said. "So... I left him to his ranch, and I ended up in Miami. End of story."

Julien sighed. "I have a feeling you left out a lot of the middle," he said. "But I won't pry."

Oddly, this freed some blockage in Diego, and the words began to pour out as they never had before.

"I'm not sure I made the right choice, leaving. It wasn't some selfless gesture to protect Wyatt's future. I was mad as hell. I demanded he choose, and well, I couldn't compete with a family legacy."

"Oh, Diego," Julien said softly, sympathetic but with just enough exasperation that he was pretty sure Julien agreed he'd been an idiot.

"I was young, just nineteen, and I had all these big ideals about love conquering all. I wanted Wyatt to fight for us. But I realize now, he was kind of between a rock and a hard place. He'd been worried about how his grandfather would react, hadn't come out when I wanted, and I was already growing impatient when Grandad caught us kissing and all hell broke loose. That was the end of us as a couple. I asked Wyatt to leave with me, and when he wouldn't, I left him. I swore I'd forget all about the ranch and have a fantastic life with someone who would love me right."

"And then you proceeded to hook up with half of Miami and never open yourself to a real relationship," Julien said dryly, but not unkindly.

"Yeah, I'm seeing that now."

"I bet you're seeing a lot of things," Julien said, a smile in his voice. "But it looks like you and Wyatt are mending fences nicely."

"Yeah, well, he's tried to apologize numerous times for how it all happened. He says he never intended for our breakup to last."

"That's something," Julien said. "How about you? Have you apologized?"

Diego winced. "Not yet."

"Mm-hmm."

"I should do that."

"If it feels right…"

Diego sighed. "I guess."

Julien laughed. "Don't sound so miserable. This is a major breakthrough. You've never opened up like this."

"Ugh, shut up."

He could hear the smile in Julien's voice. "No, this is good, Diego. You've always been so closed down. I think Wyatt might be a good influence on you."

"I don't know if I'd call it good. I'm a fucking mess of confused feelings. And it's all pointless because I have to go home soon, and the past won't ever change, so why obsess over it, right?"

"Then why get involved with him at all?"

"Because he's the best fuck I've ever had."

Julien laughed. "Same old Diego. My mistake. You haven't changed."

"Shut up, I'm serious," Diego said. "It's... unlike anything I've experienced with anyone ever."

"Huh, sex with a guy you once loved and still feel something for is better than random hookups? Shocking!"

"Aw, shut the hell up. I shouldn't have answered the phone."

"No, no, I'm sorry," he said, though he didn't sound sorry at all. "Let me impart some wisdom."

"Since when are you wise?"

"Fuck you very much," Julien snarked. "This is serious, so listen up. When I came back to Maine, I was really uneasy about it. Confronting my past was scary and uncomfortable, but it's the only thing that really gave me the freedom to move past it. While you're there, enjoy the sex, but don't pass up the chance for a little closure too. Talk things through with him."

"I'll keep that in mind," Diego said.

"You do that," Julien said. "I'd talk more, but Caleb needs me. Something about how not soft I am."

"TMI. Go be with your husband. I don't need a preview."

"Love you," Julien said, laughing as he disconnected.

Diego smile down at the phone. "Love you too."

16

Wyatt frowned at the flashing red light on the office phone he kept at the house. Who would be calling the land line? He gave out his cell phone number to anyone he could. It was more convenient since he spent most of his time away from this old room that still smelled of his grandfather's cigars.

Nostalgia swept over him every time he stepped inside, and this time was no different. He remembered sitting in the chair across from the desk, so young his feet barely reached the floor. Even in this memory, Diego was beside him in the next chair.

"You know why you're here?" Grandad had asked, his face stern.

"We're in trouble," Diego said.

"Be more specific," Grandad ordered. "Wyatt?"

Wyatt blinked hard, feeling shame Heat his cheeks. "We caught the old barn cat, Mrs. Fletcher, and we tried to put her in the chicken coop, so she could eat some eggs, but then the chickens and her fought, and um, she got pecked and was bleeding so we brought her inside to do first aid, but she got away and peed on the sofa."

Grandad nodded. "That about sums it up, though you know the real Mrs. Fletcher doesn't want a mangy cat named after her."

"Sorry," Wyatt muttered.

"So what did you do wrong in that series of events? We need to learn from this."

That was tougher to answer. Wyatt thought it was only right they try to fix Mrs. Fletcher because it was their fault she was hurt. But they wouldn't be in trouble if she hadn't peed on the sofa.

"We shouldn't have endangered the chickens?" Diego said.

"I'm not sure they were in as much danger as Mrs.—as the cat, but yes. You need to show respect for the animals here. They're not your playthings. They don't exist purely for your enter-tainment."

"I'm sorry, Grandad Jones," Diego said. He looked so miser-able, and it hadn't even been his idea. Wyatt thought Mrs. Fletcher looked bored, and that she might enjoy eating something other than field mice.

"I thought we were in trouble because the cat peed in the house?"

"Well, that surely didn't save you any trouble, did it? Rosie is having a fit, and your mama insists the smell will never come out."

"It ruined the sofa?" Wyatt asked in a small voice.

"It did, and now you boys will be earning the money to replace it. It's time I gave you two more work to do. Maybe you'll have less time to make trouble."

"We won't do it again," Wyatt said hurriedly.

"I know you won't," Grandad said firmly. "I'll tell you what I tell my ranch hands. Make a mistake once, and you'll learn a lesson. But make a mistake twice, and you're just wasting every-one's time. Understand?"

They'd both nodded, eyes wide. Grandad was full of little tidbits of wisdom, and they'd drank them down like Kool-Aid, awed by the big man who was in charge of their whole world.

Now, as Wyatt took a seat behind the desk, the memory made him a little sad. Not because it was a bad memory. Even though they'd been in hot water, Grandad had treated them like one of his ranch hands. He'd made them work, and his discipline had probably been more effective than a swat to the butt ever would have been. He didn't have sympathy for tears or softness, but he'd tried to raise Wyatt with a good moral compass and a work ethic that would serve him well.

Which made it all the more bittersweet that Grandad had taken so long to accept Wyatt—had threatened to withhold the ranch he'd raised Wyatt to operate—and had never really understood him.

He'd loved his grandfather, and he knew Grandad had loved him. But just like when the ultimatum drove him and Diego apart, Wyatt knew that love sometimes wasn't enough.

He wasn't sure he'd ever be able to think back on his memories of Grandad fondly, without the tarnish of a love that had come with strings.

Wyatt blew out a breath and let the memory go. Picking up the receiver, he dialed the code to access his voicemails.

"Mr. Jones, it's Mr. Montgomery here, returning your call. I'm open to discussing the process of obtaining financing, but I'll need to know more details. With the property in probate, there a few extra hoops to jump through."

Wyatt could have guessed as much. He'd probably left this a little late, especially if he wanted to purchase plane tickets to Maine in the near future.

"There are probate loans, which are essentially, advances against an inheritance. Generally, those require the full balance to be paid once you come out of probate. In your case, that'd require selling some of your holdings, as you don't have any cash equity—"

Well, that was out. Wyatt refused to sell off chunks of land. Grandad had drilled it into him over the years: That's the easy solution, but it's not the smart one. Your land is your most valuable asset. Give that up, and there's no getting it back. This property is our family's legacy and it's our job to maintain it for the next generation. Grandad was a man of many strong opinions, not all of them right, but Wyatt agreed with him there. He might not have children of his own, but there would be someone in the family—hopefully Ethan or Matthew—who'd carry the ranch forward one day.

Mr. Montgomery carried on explaining the various requirements of different forms of loans, along with possible hang-ups such as the ranch's shrinking revenue and Wyatt's lack of much credit history—living on the ranch, he'd never needed much personal credit. It seemed he could use the ranch as collateral, as long as the executor signed off on it, but they'd need to sit down and go over the numbers, Wyatt's business plans, and then there'd be a delay while the loan processed.

He jotted down a few notes, while a headache started up behind his eyes, then set down the receiver with a sigh.

"Everything okay?"

He looked up to see Roberto in the doorway. Wyatt waved him in, and he took a seat in front of the desk, resting his ankle over one knee.

"I was just listening to a message from the estate lawyer," Wyatt said. "He was explaining the ins and outs of how to get a loan against the property while it's in probate, and he's a bit of a rambler."

Roberto straightened. "You're pursuing a loan?"

"For the event venue," Wyatt clarified. "The ranch is in okay shape, but not so good I can dip into our accounts to finish off all the improvements and launch the venue properly."

"I see." Roberto swiped a hand over his lips, brow creased. Clearing his throat, he said, "I'd like to suggest something."

"Go ahead."

"Before I do, I should qualify it by saying that I already made this suggestion to your grandfather. He said no."

Wyatt nodded. His Grandad was always singular in his vision, but Wyatt appreciated the perspective of Roberto and Diego, as well as any of his men. The ranch might belong to him, but it was the livelihood of many people, and so it was bigger than him, regardless of who held the deed.

"I'd like to invest."

Wyatt's eyebrows shot up. He wasn't sure the ranch was a great investment, and he sure as hell hadn't seen Roberto offering to put his own money into the business. The ranch had been solely Jones property for generations, so the idea of taking on a partner of some kind never even entered his mind.

"Your grandfather didn't like the idea, and I could respect that," Roberto said. "It's been in the Jones family a long time. But I've spent damn near twenty-five years here, and it's home. I'd like to know that when the time comes for me to retire, I could stay, enjoy the land I've worked on for so long."

"I don't know what to say," Wyatt said.

"If you want to say no, too, I'll understand," Roberto said. "Just thought I'd offer before you pursue a loan against the ranch and have to pay interest. This might be a safer way to finance the changes you need to make here. And I don't need anything to change, really. I'd be a minority partner. I don't have the capital to be anything more than that. It would still be the Triple J Ranch."

Wyatt drummed his fingers on the desk. There were a few distinct advantages to taking on an investment partner, as opposed to a loan. But it would mean dividing the revenue the ranch did generate. "How much of an investment were you considering?"

"I have two hundred thousand dollars in stocks and bonds," Roberto said. "I could liquidate it in a matter of days and cut you a check. I'd be open to paying a portion of each paycheck as well, if you wanted a larger investment. It's a small fraction of what the ranch is worth. All I really want is a place to call home, as well as work, and maybe a space where I could build a little house of my own."

"I thought you wanted to live in the house? I wouldn't have usurped the cabin otherwise."

"I do. I did," he said. "But there's something else I have to be forthright about."

"Okay..."

"I'm seeing Sarah." He paused as Wyatt processed that. "Your mama and I are getting serious. I want to be able to offer her a home one day, here on the ranch, without living under her son's roof."

Wyatt couldn't say he was entirely surprised. Roberto and Mama had seemed friendlier of late, and Roberto had been slipping off to town in the evenings more often. In the back of his mind, he must have suspected something, because he was far from shocked. But it was still a lot to take in.

"Wow. Well, Roberto, I think you know how much I respect your knowledge and experience at the ranch. I've leaned on you during this transition, a heck of a lot."

"Not as much as you could have," Roberto replied.

"More than I felt comfortable with," Wyatt countered. "And I suspect you're at least part of the reason Diego is here now, and he's been... amazing. His belief in this fool plan I came up with, and his tireless effort in helping out around here, has been priceless."

Roberto's lips twitched, about the closest he came to an actual smile most days. "He made the decision to come back here on his own, but I admit to influencing him to stay a while longer than he planned. I'm relieved that gamble paid off. I wasn't so sure there for a while."

"That makes two of us," Wyatt said. "I think we're... friends again. Real friends, whatever else we might be."

"Good," Roberto said, "because if you take me up on this offer, there's one more thing you should know."

"What's that?"

"Whatever ownership I have in the ranch, I'd like to pass it on to Diego one day."

———

The kitchen smelled divine, like chicken-fried steak, mashed potatoes, and peppery cream gravy. Hank and Colby were already seated, and his father was setting the table, when Diego returned from the speedy shower he'd taken. He'd bumped into Wyatt outside the bathroom door, and they'd stumbled back into the bathroom for a frantic kiss that had heated his blood. He noticed Wyatt hadn't made his appearance at the table yet and smirked, imagining that he might have needed a few extra minutes to cool down.

I should have forbidden him to come. I wonder what he'd think of something like that?

Shifting in his seat, Diego decided to change the course of his mind before he had to excuse himself. "No TJ?"

"He didn't want to stay," Colby said. "Told you he was anti-social."

"Colby," Hank said, sounding exasperated. "Don't borrow trouble. The man probably has someone waiting for him at home."

"Well, I say he's crazy to miss out on Rosie's dinner," Colby said, earning a kiss on the cheek, as Rosie placed a platter on the table before taking a seat.

"That's sweet of you to say," she said.

"We all appreciate what you do, Miss Rosie," Hank said. He was always exceptionally polite with Rosie and Mama, when she visited, even though those two women were casual and considered everyone on the ranch family. His Southern manners were deeply ingrained.

The clicking of toenails on tile alerted Diego to Daisy, the black mouth cur who guarded the chickens by day and acted as Rosie's sweet pet by night. She was Mama Jones's dog first, but she'd left her with the ranch when she moved to town since Daisy was loyal to her duties. As a herd dog, her instincts came naturally, and they'd had to do very little in the way of training. She'd been a great asset in keeping the chickens safe from predators when they were out of the coop.

She sat on her haunches nearby, too well-trained to beg but licking her chops and sniffing the air. He didn't blame her. The food scents were making his mouth water, too. If she behaved—and she always did—she'd get a few choice scraps after the meal.

Wyatt entered the kitchen, taking his seat across from Diego at the square table. "Sorry for keeping y'all waiting. Smells great."

Rosie beamed. She couldn't get enough compliments about her cooking, despite hearing them every day. As they began serving—pausing to say grace, which Rosie had insisted upon their whole lives and was tradition as much as religion at this point—conversation turned to food, then cattle, then TJ's performance in his first couple of days.

"That man's a force of nature," Roberto said. "He learns quick, too."

Colby rolled his eyes as he shoved mashed potatoes into his mouth, and Diego bit down on a smile. There was something about TJ that got under Colby's skin, but he wasn't convinced it was only the fact he was quiet.

"Got a call from Ella, and she's going to bring the boys over on Friday," Wyatt said, when they'd exhausted the first few topics of conversation.

"That's great, honey," Rosie said. "Those boys should know you."

"I should know them," Wyatt countered, sounding serious as

hell. "I left it too long. Never should have let Grandad's beef with Ella create such a chasm between us."

"Well, you're on the right path now," she said, smiling. "When can we expect them?"

"Sometime Friday morning. I'm going to give them some riding lessons, teach them how to care for horses. Hopefully get them interested in the ranch. One day, maybe they'll be at this table after a hard day's work."

As the meal wrapped up and dishes were cleared, Wyatt and Roberto approached Diego, asking for a minute to talk. Diego followed them to Wyatt's office, curious as hell what this could be about. Perhaps Wyatt's tentative plans to go to Bliss?

"I take it this is business-related?" he asked as Roberto closed the door behind them.

Wyatt perched on the corner of his desk, his long legs braced against the floor, while Diego's father leaned a shoulder against the wall. Diego remained standing, too, suddenly aware of the serious vibe in the room.

"It is," Wyatt said, "but it's kind of personal too."

Diego raised an eyebrow. "I'm listening."

"I offered to invest in the ranch," Roberto spoke up. "I'd only have a stake in a small percentage of the ranch, but it'd give Wyatt some capital to work with, and it'd give me a retirement plan."

Diego wasn't sure how to feel about that. His father had given everything to this ranch, his sweat, his best years. But all his money too?

"Are you sure this is the best retirement plan for you?" Diego asked. He glanced at Wyatt. "No offense, but I know the ranch is running lean these days, and besides, it'll always be a Jones's operation."

"No offense taken," Wyatt said. "If we do this, I want everyone on board, and I don't want anyone feeling that I tried to take advantage."

"I don't think *that*," Diego protested.

"Good," Roberto said. "Because I'm damn well smart enough to look after my own interests. This ranch is home. I want it to be home, even when I'm no longer able to work the cattle. I hate watching the ranch struggle, when I have the ability to contribute. I'm not pouring good money after bad. Wyatt has a plan, and it's a good plan, but he needs some capital to pull it off."

"This is the financing you mentioned?" Diego said.

"No. I was pursuing a loan. Your father suggested I consider his investment offer instead."

It was reassuring to know that Roberto had approached Wyatt, not the other way around. Roberto had been loyal to the Triple J—though he'd almost left when Diego did, had offered to support him in any way he wanted—and he was dedicated as hell. If he wanted more than a job, if he wanted some ownership in it, then it wasn't Diego's place to argue.

"Well, sounds like you two are on the same page. I'm not sure why I should have any say."

"You tell him, Roberto."

Diego's father nodded, straightening his stance. "This is a business deal between me and Wyatt, but it'll affect you. Because I'll naturally be putting you in my will. You'll inherit my stake in the ranch when the time comes."

Diego scoffed. "That's decades away."

"Still... given how you left here before, I know there was a time you would have hated being connected to the ranch. If Wyatt and I do this, the Triple J will always be your home, not just symbolically, but legally at some point."

Diego shifted his gaze to Wyatt, wincing at the hurt that flickered in his eyes. His father wasn't wrong. He'd wanted nothing to do with the ranch. He'd cursed its name. He'd blamed it for being first in Wyatt's heart.

But things had changed. Or maybe *he* had changed.

"Do what's best for the ranch," he told them. "I've got no problem if it's what you both want."

"And what about what you want?" Wyatt asked quietly.

"I want the ranch to come through this rough patch stronger than ever. I want your plan to work, and for that, you need financing," he said. "I know my father loves this place, so... it only makes sense. I appreciate you taking my feelings into consideration, but it's not my place to argue. And I wouldn't even if it was. Y'all have my blessing, if that's what you're after."

Wyatt smiled faintly. "Your feelings will always matter to me, but thanks for giving this your blessing. It makes my decision easier."

Roberto cleared his throat. "Diego, this will tie up most my funds. I don't know how much longer you're planning to stay out here, but—"

Diego put up a hand to stop him. He didn't need to hear more to know his father was concerned about continuing to help Diego with his expenses. He'd already covered some of Diego's bills, and that was more than enough. Matias was still staying at his apartment, and that was by far his largest concern. He'd be fine. He certainly wouldn't get in the way of his father's future plans, even if he wasn't.

"It's fine. Don't worry about that."

Wyatt's gaze shifted between them. "Is this going to cause some sort of problem?"

"Nope," Diego said. "I appreciate the concern, really, but y'all should move forward with your plans."

Wyatt waited a beat, and when Diego didn't volunteer any more information, he nodded. "Roberto, I'll have some paperwork drawn up. We have a deal."

"I'll start the process of liquidating my funds, then." Stepping forward, Roberto held out his hand. "Thanks, boss."

"Hell, I haven't ever really been your boss," Wyatt said, pumping his hand. "Welcome to the business. You've always been a partner to me in spirit, and now you can be one on paper too."

17

TJ's old Honda broke down two weeks after he joined the crew, leaving him stranded halfway to the ranch. Roberto drove out toward Riggs to pick him up, but it cost them work-time during the cooler morning hours. Once again, Wyatt and Diego headed out to the pasture, side by side, on the ATVs. Hank rode ahead of them, while Colby resumed work at the barn.

Things had been going well on the ranch. So well, Diego was beginning to wonder what he was still doing there. His cell phone and car insurance bills were paid up, so there was no rush to leave, but was there a reason to stay?

You said you'd go to Bliss with Wyatt, he reminded himself. *And there's still the question of that vandalism.*

Thankfully, the ATVs ran like a charm despite the attempt at sabotage. The vandal had poured a mix of the chemicals they used around the ranch—like weed killer and de-wormer for the cattle —along with water into the gas tanks. The ATVs had to be completely drained and dried out, but they'd started right up once they'd been filled with gasoline again.

"Good thing you don't mind getting dirty with me," Wyatt called over the motor noise, a teasing grin on his face.

Well, there was another reason Diego continued to stay. Wyatt's smiles, Wyatt's flirting, Wyatt's goddamn sexy body. But he couldn't let his dick make his decisions, and he refused to believe any other organs would lead—other than his brain. He needed to think this through.

But not now. A chorus of low, echoing moos greeted them as they reached the herd. They'd ride among them, keeping an eye out for illness or injury, anything that might require an intervention. Pink eye was a problem off and on, and there were other, more serious health concerns.

As the hours slipped by, Diego's mind drifted to the evening before, when Wyatt and his father had become official business partners.

Diego still couldn't believe that one day, he could be a part owner of this land and everything on it. His father, yes—he'd poured years of his heart and soul into the place, and he deserved to enjoy it once he was too old to work it—but Diego? He'd tried so hard to let the ranch and everything it represented go.

Maybe now he didn't have to. He glanced ahead—Wyatt was yards away, working the other side of the herd—but he could see his cowboy hat and the straight set of his shoulders.

That was a man meant for this life. But was Diego? And even if he was, did he want to be? He'd been happy in Miami. Well, happy-ish. He'd enjoyed the vibe of Caliente, his flirty customers, and his friends. But he wouldn't say he felt a deep connection to any of them. With the exception of Matias and Julien, his relationships had been one of convenience and relatively shallow. It was hard to even imagine being surrounded by the club music, the strobing lights, the sweaty bodies. The smell of grass, livestock, and manure was in his nose—and that shouldn't be pleasing, and yet somehow... it was.

It smelled like home.

A couple of hours later, Wyatt's phone went off, and he lifted it to his ear. "Yep? Oh, they're here! Great. No, I'll come get them in a few."

Diego knew before Wyatt explained that his nephews had arrived at the ranch. Wyatt had been looking forward to this visit all week. All summer, probably.

"You mind finishing up here?" Wyatt asked. "Check on how Hank's doing for me?"

"Sure," Diego said, torn between pride that Wyatt was treating him, a temporary volunteer, like a trusted foreman, and disappointment that he didn't ask Diego to go along. But Wyatt didn't need him to play boyfriend. He needed him to work the ranch, so he turned back to his work as Wyatt drove his ATV back toward the house.

He made his way down the pasture to check with Hank as promised, and when Roberto arrived back from his drive to Riggs, Diego made his way toward the house, thinking he'd grab a bite of lunch and see how Wyatt was getting along with the boys.

He was happy Wyatt was getting this chance to bond with his family. From the sounds of things, they hadn't been close since Ella moved out when Wyatt was still a teenager. But when he got to the house, only to find that Wyatt had already taken the boys on a tour of the ranch property before starting their riding lesson at the stables, he couldn't help feeling a little disappointed. Almost... left out?

That was disturbing. He wasn't supposed to crave Wyatt's attention that much. And he wasn't jealous of the boys. They were just kids, so why would he be?

It took a while to put his finger on what exactly he was feeling, but as he scarfed down a sandwich and headed back out to the crew, he finally figured it out.

He wanted Wyatt to ask him to spend time with the boys and him. But why should he?

Diego had made it clear that this was a temporary arrangement, nothing but friends with benefits. He'd even shot down

Wyatt's attempt to hook up in his bedroom because he feared it'd become too comfortable, sleeping together. And here he was, wanting to be treated like a true partner who would be here to see those kids grow up.

Ridiculous. Get your head out of the clouds.

Wyatt was waiting when Diego stepped out of the shower after an afternoon in the hot sun. He pushed him back into the bathroom, shutting the door behind them, and kissed him. He'd shied from initiating anything with Diego since the bedroom fiasco, but they'd spent most of the day apart. While Wyatt enjoyed watching the boys' wide-eyed wonder—mixed with a little fear— as they worked with the horses, he'd felt Diego's absence at his side. If he hadn't felt that it would have been incredibly selfish, he would have invited Diego to spend the day with him and the kids.

"That's a hell of a greeting," Diego murmured.

It wasn't the first time they'd snatched a minute of privacy in the bathroom, but it was the first time Wyatt had started it.

He just smiled. He didn't think Diego wanted to hear how much he'd missed him. He wasn't ready for declarations like that, but tonight was all about moving that line an inch or two. Wyatt wanted to share his real feelings. Not the loneliness and regret and longing for what they used to have, which he'd felt when Diego first arrived at the ranch, but the warmth that filled him every time Diego walked into a room. The new, fragile thing they were building together, if only Diego would let it expand.

"Come with me to drop off the boys. I have a couple of errands to run in town. We can get off the ranch for a while?"

Diego's large hands gripped Wyatt's hips, then slid over his ass. Diego seemed infatuated with his ass. Any time they were alone, free to touch, it was one of the first places his hands strayed. Not that Wyatt was complaining. His ass was pretty infatuated with Diego. His biggest regret, in recent days anyway, was that they hadn't had a chance to fuck properly again. *But maybe tonight, if all goes to plan...*

Wyatt couldn't resist licking a dewy drop of moisture that clung to Diego's neck. His hair still dripped, dampening the top of his snug T-shirt that molded deliciously to his muscles.

"I guess I could be talked into running errands with you. With the proper incentive."

"Incentive, huh?" Wyatt said, pressing closer. "I'll do my best to try think of something you want."

Diego squeezed Wyatt's ass again, making it clear what he wanted, and they sank into another kiss before the doorknob rattled, startling them apart.

"Uncle Wy!" Matthew called. "I need to pee."

They collapsed in silent laughter, pulling apart so Wyatt could open the door. "Sorry, buddy."

If Matthew thought it strange that he and Diego were in the bathroom together, he didn't show it, rushing past them toward the toilet. They slipped out, shutting the door.

"Someone needs to teach him about nature's bathroom," Diego grumbled.

Wyatt slapped his chest. "C'mon, curmudgeon, get whatever you need and meet me and the boys outside in five."

Diego trapped his hand against his heart before Wyatt could pull it back. It was a surprisingly intimate move for a guy who kept insisting they maintain boundaries. Wyatt raised an eyebrow.

"We should look into some security cameras while we're there," Diego said, back to being all business. "In case those vandals come back."

So much for intimacy. Wyatt sighed. "The ranch is too big to surveil properly."

"You can still cover some key locations," Diego said. "Maybe you'll get lucky and catch something."

"Maybe," Wyatt allowed. He should probably thank Diego for

trying to help, but he really didn't want to think about his problems tonight. "We can take a look."

Diego released him. "Good, I'll meet you out at the truck."

The Dalton farmhouse was a much more modest size than the ranch house at the Triple J. It was square shaped, painted a white that had faded to nearly gray, and had red shutters. An old-model tractor could be seen in the field behind the house. It appeared to be empty and parked there despite there being an old barn on the far side of the field. The barn was leaning to the right and looked like one good shove would send it tumbling to the ground, but it still had four walls and roof.

Despite the weathered appearance of the buildings, the front yard was tidy, and Ella had planted some flowering shrubs close to the porch, giving it a welcoming appearance. Wyatt pulled in behind an old red pickup sporting almost as much rust as the old tractor.

Ella stepped onto the porch, waving, as they climbed out. The boys ran up to her, chattering at full speed.

"We rode a horse, Mama!"

"Just like Uncle Wyatt! We're cowboys now."

Ella's husband, Tucker, came around the corner of the house, wiping his hands on an old rag. It looked as if he'd been working on a vehicle, and grease streaks soon decorated the cloth in his hands. "You boys are farmers first. Don't forget that."

"Tucker..." Ella said, sounding exasperated.

"Daltons, too," he said. "You might have fun at the Jones's ranch, but you're not a Jones. Go on inside. Dinner will be ready soon."

The boys skittered off through the door. Ella turned to Tucker. "Was that really necessary?"

"Don't want them getting the wrong idea about their place," Tucker said.

Wyatt's jaw tightened. "They always have a place at the ranch."

"Ella didn't."

"That's different," Wyatt said. "I'm not our grandfather."

Ella sighed. "Tucker, please just give me a minute with my brother, all right?"

He nodded. "Daryl's joining us for dinner tonight. I just came over to tell you."

Once he was gone, she sighed and shook her head. "He's still a little distrustful of Jones men. I'm sorry. That old feud hasn't done any of us any good."

"I thought that was going to be buried with Grandad," Wyatt said, sounding disappointed.

"It is. Tucker just needs time to adjust. He'll come around."

Wyatt looked to be biting his tongue as he smiled tightly. "It was real nice having the boys over."

She smiled warmly. "I'm glad to hear that. I'll bring them by same time next week?"

"Sounds good. Thanks."

They returned to the pickup, and Diego's gaze was drawn to the two bumper stickers on the old red pickup in front of them: *Deport Illegals* and *Pro-Gun Texan.*

Great combination.

"Is that Tucker's pickup?" he asked.

"Nah, that belongs to Daryl. Remember him? He worked out at our place when we were teens. Looks like he works for Tucker now."

"Hmm. Wouldn't have thought Tucker needed any employees here."

Wyatt glanced in the rear-view mirror. "Yeah, you wouldn't know it from this view, but they've got a nice goat herd, along with some crops a few miles from here. Their land was sold off in bits and pieces, so it's not all connected to the house anymore."

"So, what errands do you have to run?" he asked as Wyatt swung his truck around in the drive and headed back toward the highway.

"About that..." Wyatt chuckled nervously. "There aren't any errands. I kinda thought you could use a night away from the ranch. I told Rosie we'd get a bite in town tonight."

"You did, huh?"

"We could grab a burger and a beer, if that'll do ya? Then we can catch a movie."

"Careful there, Wy. This is sounding almost like a date."

Wyatt glanced his direction. "Would that really be so bad?"

Diego remembered a time when he would have loved to go out with Wyatt like this, so even though this was blurring boundaries, he couldn't bring himself to say no. "I guess I could eat."

Wyatt's grin was worth saying to hell with the consequences of getting too close.

They parked in front of a row of brick buildings downtown, colorful awnings separating the different businesses. Directly in front of them, a plate-glass window was etched with a giant bull's eye.

"I hope you brought your appetite," Wyatt said. "In case you've forgotten, Bull's Eye serves burgers as big as my head."

"They must be massive then," Diego teased.

Laughing, they climbed out of the truck and headed toward the little diner. His mouth watered at the smell off cooking oil, and glancing over at Wyatt, at ease and smiling, he felt the warmth of nostalgia swamp him.

It would be really easy to get comfortable in this sort of life. Days working with Wyatt; weekends going out for a burger and beer. Easy conversation, plenty of laughter, sizzling hot sex.

He could see it all, laid out before him, an alternate life to the one in Miami. It was tempting to take that fork in the road, but was it real... or was it just a mirage? Being with Wyatt felt easy and right, but would it always? They'd fallen apart once before. Who was to say it couldn't happen again?

Abe, the proprietor of Bull's Eye, was a little grayer and a little rounder, but he was the same happy guy in an old-style white apron over jeans and a T-shirt. He swiped his hands on his apron front and came out from behind the front counter.

"Diego *Flores*," he said, recognizing Diego without even a moment of hesitation, "it's about time you got your ass home."

Diego laughed, accepting Abe's enthusiastic greeting and zealous handshake and arm pat combination. "Nice to see you too, Abe."

"How long you been back here?"

"A little while," he hedged. In truth, it'd been over a month. Wow. Time had certainly flown as he worked on the ranch with Wyatt. They'd made steady progress on the renovations, so he realistically knew time was passing, and yet, it didn't feel like more than a few days since he'd stepped back into his old life. It felt strangely comfortable to be here again, and at the same time, he was still off-balance, like a man straddling two worlds that couldn't possibly fit together. Miami, Florida. Cow Creek, Texas. The two did not have much in common, and yet... he fit into them both.

"You should have stopped by sooner," Abe scolded good-naturedly. "Now, let me see. I never forget a regular's favorite order." He cocked his head, thinking, then pointed at Diego. "The Black-and-Bleu Burger for you."

"That's right," Diego said, impressed. There was something magical about blue cheese melted over beef, and he was powerless to resist it. Always had been.

"And Wyatt's easy. A Cowboy Burger for a cowboy," Abe said with a wink.

"Thanks, Abe. Throw in a basket of fried okra, too?"

Diego groaned. "Damn, I forgot about the okra. I definitely

want some of that."

Wyatt held up two fingers. "Make it two baskets. Plus a basket of onion rings because I can't help myself."

They finished out their order with a couple of bottles of beer, then retreated to a table until the burgers arrived, each served on a plate of its own, taking every inch of the space, just like Diego remembered them. A steak knife stood from the center of each burger, because the only way to eat them was to cut them in half.

Goddamn, he'd missed Bull's Eye. His mouth watered at the sight of the familiar, artery-blocking meal. His burger was mostly contained within the bun, but Wyatt's Cowboy Burger was overflowing with jalapenos, pepper jack cheese, and onion straws.

"I still don't know how you eat that," Diego said with a shudder.

"With my mouth," Wyatt said with a wink. "Two lips and a tongue. You might be familiar with—"

"All right," he interrupted. "Tempt me with one vice at a time."

Wyatt laughed. "Didn't think I was any competition for your favorite burger."

"Right now? You're really not."

Diego pulled the knife from the bun with the satisfaction of a man pulling a sword from a stone and cut the burger into quarters. He sensed Wyatt watching him, glancing up as he lifted a wedge of the sandwich to take a bite.

Their eyes met just as delicious red meat and tangy blue cheese melted on his taste buds, the lettuce, tomato, and onion hardly gaining his notice. His eyes slid closed as nostalgia washed over him.

Wyatt's light laughter only contributed to the effect of reversing time by six years.

"Admit it. You like it better than me."

Diego opened his eyes. His best friend — his boyfriend — sat across from him, a crooked grin on his face. Sunlight streamed in the window, catching in his hair, making it shimmer. Wyatt Jones was so fucking gorgeous that he took Diego's breath away for a moment. But he couldn't leave him hanging.

Swallowing a huge bite, Diego washed it down with a gulp of Coke before answering. "Yup, nothing's better than this."

Wyatt kicked his foot. "Thanks, man."

"Hey, you said it first!"

They were still laughing when Charlotte and Emily approached the table.

"Hey, we're going over to the movie theater. Y'all want to come?" Emily asked.

Wyatt and Diego glanced at each other. "Nah, we're good."

"It could be fun," Charlotte said, batting her eyes in Wyatt's direction. She was always looking at him, and what's worse, Diego knew that Grandad had suggested Wyatt ask her out. What if he took the opportunity now? Stomach tied in knots, Diego knocked over his soda.

"Oh, shoot!" he exclaimed as it ran across the table, and the girls jumped back.

Wyatt laughed, grabbing some napkins to sop up the soda. "We're good here, and kind of a mess, so..."

"Yeah, okay. We'll see you at school then?" Charlotte said.

"Mm, yeah," Wyatt said, without looking up.

As they walked away, he said in a low voice, just for Diego, "You didn't have to do that."

"Do what?"

Wyatt's blue eyes met his. "I wasn't going to go to that movie."

Maybe not this time. Wyatt had gone on a date or two to appease Grandad, and while he assured Diego it meant nothing, he was afraid of losing Wyatt. Afraid Wyatt would eventually choose a life that didn't include him.

Diego forced a smile and said, "Okay."

. . .

187

"Diego?" Wyatt asked. "You okay?"

Diego blinked the memory away. "Yeah, fine. Just... a lot of memories here."

"Good ones, I hope." Wyatt tilted his head, studying Diego's face when he didn't answer. "Or not?"

Diego shook his head. "It wasn't a bad memory, it just made me wonder..."

"What?"

He hesitated, but Julien's advice to get closure as well as good sex came back to him. Taking a deep breath, he asked, "How long after I left did you... go along with Grandad Jones's wishes?"

Wyatt looked pained. "Too long," he said quietly. "He knew the truth, of course. He found out the day he caught you in my bedroom. But, um... he tried to tell me I was just confused. He pushed me to date."

"And did you?"

Wyatt met his gaze steadily. "No."

"Really?"

"Don't sound so surprised," Wyatt said. "I wasn't about to lead on some girl. Bad enough I'd gone on those few dates when Grandad didn't know the truth." He reached out, touching Diego's wrist. "I wish I hadn't done that. And I wish I had come out when you wanted."

"You weren't ready," Diego murmured.

"No, but I wish I was. It would have been better that way," he said. "I could have come out on my own terms. I was so side-swiped that day, when he—"

"Let's not rehash all that," Diego said quickly. "We're here to have a good time, right?"

"Right," Wyatt echoed, though he didn't look too sure.

Diego had had enough closure for one day. Leaning forward, he snagged one of Wyatt's onion rings, cramming the whole thing in his mouth obnoxiously.

"Hey!" Wyatt protested. "Not cool."

Diego grinned as he grabbed his beer and took a swig. "You snooze, you lose."

Wyatt retaliated by snagging a wedge of his burger, moaning obnoxiously as he chewed, but the burgers were so huge, it was no real loss. The last of the tension dissipated as they ate, stealing from each other's plates when it suited them, and Wyatt told Diego about what had changed in town and what hadn't.

"Mary Lou's is the same," Wyatt said. "Best bacon in Texas."

"Piles of whipped cream and pecans on the waffles?"

"You know it. And that Dutch apple pie you love," Wyatt said.

Diego sat back with a groan. "I'm stuffed, and you're making me hungry. I can't eat anymore, but that fucking pie was magical."

Wyatt snorted. "It really was. Maybe we can grab a slice some other time, 'cause I'm fixing to blow if I eat any more right now."

"Deal."

"How about we catch a movie?"

Diego grimaced. "I don't know. If that place hasn't changed either..."

"It has, actually. For the better."

"Yeah?"

"Yeah, got bought and remodeled. Decent movies there now, better seating."

"Tempting."

Wyatt threw a couple of twenties on the table and stood. "Come on. We can relax and digest, and then I have somewhere else I want to take you."

"Where?"

"It's a surprise."

Diego raised an eyebrow. "Way I remember it, Cow Creek has no surprises."

"Well, maybe just one. Trust me?"

Diego stood, gesturing toward the door. "Fine. Lead the way."

18

Wyatt held his breath as he led Diego to the truck after they'd watched an action flick with big explosions and little plot. He drove them out of town toward a tiny gay bar on the highway. By day, there wasn't much to see. It looked like a short, squat building that had seen better days. A sign stood in a parking lot riddled with potholes. By night, it came to life, marginally, with windows lit from within. A handful of cars could be seen in the lot as Wyatt approached, but this bar was no Miami gay club packed with pretty boys. This was Texas, and nowhere near a big city like Dallas or Austin. Being gay around here was a more cautious affair. It had to be.

"Woody's," Diego said with a snort when he read the sign. "Really?"

Wyatt felt a moment of hesitation. What was he thinking, bringing Diego to a dive gay bar when he worked at one of the most thriving nightclubs in Miami?

"I know it probably won't look like much compared to Miami's nightlife ... but it's the best gay scene we have without driving for hours," Wyatt said. "Do you want to check it out?"

"Yeah, of course," Diego said. "I had no idea a gay bar even existed this close to Cow Creek."

"It keeps a pretty low profile," Wyatt said. "Safer that way."

"Living in Miami, I sometimes forget how it can be in other parts of the country," Diego mused, shaking his head.

Wyatt almost regretted bringing him. It wasn't the best way to sell Diego on life in Texas. *Hey, you should totally move to Cow Creek, where we have to keep our gay bars on the downlow to avoid homophobes!*

Wyatt opened his door and hopped out. He'd been doing a good job pushing down his feelings so he could enjoy time with Diego and allow him time to deal with Texas, and Wyatt, and his memories. But tonight felt so much like a date, his emotions were floating close to the surface.

"You okay?" Diego asked.

"Yeah." Wyatt did his best to shake the lovesick swell threatening to drown him. "Come on, let's have some fun."

Wyatt pushed open the front door, putting his shoulder into it because the door wasn't quite even with the frame. Inside, three men sat at the bar, talking over beers, and six more sat at tables, watching big televisions broadcasting a mix of sports, news, and rodeo. A country song played in the background, loud enough to be heard but nowhere near the overwhelming volume of most dance clubs. There was a dance floor, but it was early still and remained empty.

Wyatt led Diego to the bar.

The bartender was an older bear with salt-and-pepper hair and a thick beard. "Well, if it ain't Wyatt Jones. You've been away too long, boy."

"Sorry, Roy. The ranch is keeping me busy."

Roy scoffed. "More like you've been raiding the city for better prospects. I know you." He glanced toward Diego, eyes appreciative. "Looks like you found one too. Hello there, gorgeous. What'll you have?"

"Shot of tequila," Diego answered without missing a beat.

"I like a man who doesn't mess around," Roy said with a chuckle. "Where did you find this guy? Surely not in Dallas."

"No, not Dallas," Wyatt said, feeling smug. Roy was eating up Diego with his eyes, and Wyatt was the lucky bastard who got to take him home that night. Forget jealousy; Wyatt was fucking happy to show him off, even if Diego wasn't really *his*. "He grew up around here."

"No kidding? Where you been hiding him?"

Diego laughed. "I live in Miami now."

"Aha." Roy slid the shot of tequila to Diego and began pulling a beer for Wyatt without asking what he wanted. He always ordered whatever was on tap so that wasn't surprising. "So you a city boy now? Or a Texas man?"

"Can't I be both?"

"You sure as hell can," Wyatt said, slinging an arm around Diego's waist.

Diego threw back his shot and asked for another. Then Wyatt motioned for him to follow him to a table.

"You troll for men often?" Diego asked, breath hot against his neck as he leaned close while they walked.

Wyatt shot him a look. "Not really."

They took a seat and Diego tossed back his drink, then stole Wyatt's beer for a long swallow. "You do look for hookups though. Brody wasn't your only one. Colby mentioned you take off some weekends?"

This was not how Wyatt had envisioned the night going. He was supposed to show Diego that there was a gay niche in rural Texas, even if it was small and somewhat hidden, not talk about his track record of sex with strangers.

He shrugged. "Sure, occasionally. I like sex."

Diego smirked. "I've noticed."

Wyatt rolled his eyes, but at least Diego didn't appear to be jealous. "I didn't bring you here to talk about that."

"Why did you bring me here?" Diego asked, grinning. "To show me off?"

"Nah, that's just an unexpected perk." Wyatt took back his beer, downing it in a few gulps, before wiping his mouth on his shirtsleeve. "Wanted us to have fun, relax over a few drinks, that's all. No reason to watch ourselves here."

He ran a finger over Diego's hand, glancing up to catch his eye. "We could even dance."

Diego's breath audibly caught. "Dance?"

"I've always wanted to," Wyatt said. "Ever since my first barn dance."

"Me too," Diego murmured.

Wyatt stood and held out a hand to Diego.

Diego glanced toward the empty dance floor. "No one else is dancing."

"Then we'll show them what they're missing."

Diego hesitated only a moment before placing his hand in Wyatt's and allowing himself to be led to the center of the room. Wyatt could feel eyes on them, but he wasn't bothered by it. He knew the picture they made together, and it was a sexy one. Let the other men watch, let them want.

Wyatt had wanted Diego far longer than any of them.

Despite never dancing before, they came together naturally, with no discussion of who should put his hands where. Diego placed his hands on Wyatt's shoulders, and Wyatt grasped Diego's waist, and they moved into a slow dance to a mellow country tune.

"This isn't the dance music I'm used to," Diego admitted. "Figures they play country even at the gay bar."

By the sparkle in his eyes, Wyatt didn't think he minded. "You prefer something faster?"

Diego pressed a little closer. "Well, there are some benefits to music that encourages a little bump and grind, but..." He leaned in close. "This isn't so bad."

He brushed his lips against Wyatt's as he finished talking, and Wyatt reflexively pulled him closer. They kissed, but just briefly, before continuing to dance. Another couple of men joined the dance floor, and then another.

"I can't believe we're finally dancing," Diego said with a laugh. Despite the smile, Wyatt could feel the weight of emotion behind the words.

"This is the real reason I brought you here," Wyatt admitted. Sure, he'd wanted to take Diego somewhere they could be themselves, be openly together, but he'd also wanted the dance they'd never gotten to share.

Diego looked up at him with gleaming eyes. "Really?"

Wyatt smiled. "Yeah. It's about time we got our dance. Don't you think?"

Diego nodded, looking serious but happy. "Yeah, I think you're right."

———

Diego struggled to process how it made him feel to be in Wyatt's arms on the dance floor. It seemed silly to get choked up about it. They'd been far more intimate. But this was something he'd wanted, pined for even, as he'd had to watch Wyatt at country dances when they were teens. Diego had danced once or twice himself, but he wasn't in demand the way Wyatt was. He wasn't going to inherit a ranch, or make the fine husband that Wyatt was supposed to be.

Wyatt had danced, had been courted—and Diego had been on the sidelines, yearning to be the one in his arms. That old ache inside him bloomed, and he held onto Wyatt a little tighter, more possessively. There was no one to stop him from having what he wanted now.

"This okay?" Wyatt murmured.

"Yeah," Diego whispered. "This is good."

He felt Wyatt's lips smile against his cheek. His warm breath fanned Diego's skin. It was a perfect moment. If he believed in fairy tales, he might even say it was fucking magical. But it wasn't. It was real. Just two guys holding onto each other as they circled a dance floor in a tiny gay bar in Texas.

They danced well together. Wyatt was graceful, with a natural rhythm. They drifted through twangy country-western songs, but Diego tuned out everything but the beat. His eyes kept slipping closed, but they snapped open when he sensed someone watching. Glancing around, he noticed a table with three men staring in their direction.

He nudged Wyatt. "Do you know those guys, or are they just getting off on watching?"

Wyatt looked over his shoulder, then chuckled. "Yeah, I know them."

"How do you know them?" Diego asked, then wished he hadn't. He didn't need to know if Wyatt hooked up with the men here. It wasn't important. Wyatt was his now, for however long they had together. He didn't have to ask to know that Wyatt wouldn't even consider being with another man right now, and he felt the same. While he was in Texas, they were a couple. Temporary or not.

"Met them here," Wyatt said. "Come on, I could use another drink. I'll introduce you."

They returned to the bar, and this time Diego got a water. His body was thrumming with the need to get Wyatt alone, and he didn't want to stay at the bar late, waiting for the effects of too much alcohol to wear off. Wyatt got a pitcher of beer and took it over to the table of men.

"Hey, guys," he said. "I come bearing gifts."

A guy with a dusky complexion and cheekbones sharp as a razor smirked. "Do you mean the beer or the gorgeous man? Because I could go for either."

The petite man beside him cackled and slapped his arm. "Oh, you're so bad!"

Wyatt set the pitcher and glasses on the table, then stepped back to slide an arm around Diego's waist. "I'm afraid he's not mine to give away. He belongs to no man." He winked playfully. "But he lets me borrow him from time to time."

That didn't sit right, though Diego wasn't entirely sure why. Wyatt had no claim to him, and vice versa. The dancing and romancing of the night had clearly gone to his head.

"Well, you two look gorgeous together," said the third guy at the table. He stood to peck a kiss to Wyatt's lips. "It's good to see you. It's been a while."

Wyatt and Diego took seats, Diego pulling up a chair from the next table and the guys squeezing together to make room for them all. Wyatt gave a brief round of introductions.

"Diego, this is Kyle, Mo, and Justin."

"Nice to meet y'all," Diego said.

"He sounds Texan," Kyle said. He was the oldest of the three men, somewhere in his late forties, with chestnut colored hair and eyes to match. He was handsome, in a cultured sort of way. This man definitely didn't work cattle. "Tell me, Diego, are you going to be joining our little club?"

"Club?"

Mo snorted. "He means the miniscule LGBT community around here."

"Hey, don't besmirch the club," Justin said. He was fair-haired with blue eyes and had a hyper sort of energy to him. "I love all the club members." He waggled his eyebrows. "And I do mean that literally."

He placed a hand on Diego's forearm, rubbing it. "Want to be initiated? All you gotta do—"

"Thanks for the offer," Diego cut in with a grin, "but I'm pretty sure Wyatt's already got my initiation covered."

Mo straightened in his seat. "Wait a minute. Your name is Diego?"

"Yes."

Mo's sharp eyes shifted to Wyatt. "This is the guy, right? The one who left you."

"What?!" exclaimed Justin. "Why would anyone leave Wyatt? He's the sweetest thing I've ever met!"

"Yes, why would anyone do such a thing?" Mo deadpanned.

"Stop it," Wyatt said. "He had reasons." Mo opened his mouth, and Wyatt said, "Reasons that are his personal business, not yours. You've got no business judging something you know nothing about."

Mo didn't look convinced, but he shut his mouth and took a long drink of beer. Kyle cleared his throat, and Justin drummed on the table, humming under his breath.

"Well, that got awkward," Diego said.

The guys laughed, while Wyatt grimaced. "I'm sorry," he said in a low voice. "I didn't ever tell them any details. I just—"

"It's fine," Diego interrupted, attempting to reassure him.

"—missed you," Wyatt finished. "I missed you, so I talked about you sometimes."

Damn it. Regret hit Diego with the force of a two-by-four. He couldn't put his feelings into words, so he leaned in and kissed Wyatt. There was a moment of silence, followed by a wolf whistle and laughter.

"Looks like he missed you too," Justin said.

"I did," Diego admitted.

He'd had fiery anger to help him cope with the loss of Wyatt, but there'd been a hole in his heart regardless. He'd never let anyone else in. He always thought that he had trust issues, but now he wasn't so sure it wasn't because he knew, deep down, that no one could ever replace Wyatt.

"Want to get out of here?" Wyatt asked in a low voice.

Diego nodded. "Take me home."

The drive back to the ranch was quiet and tense. Diego didn't know about Wyatt, but he was too ramped up to talk, and he knew if he so much as touched Wyatt before they got back, they'd end up fucking on the side of the road. Something had cracked open inside him when they'd finally danced, and he was burning for Wyatt. He was always burning for Wyatt, but this felt different, less want and more *need*.

Wyatt parked and turned off the ignition. They sat there, listening to the tick-tick-tick of the cooling engine. Then, at the same moment, they reached for one another. Diego locked a hand around the back of Wyatt's neck, holding him close, as he devoured his mouth. Hours' worth of restraint broke, and he couldn't get close enough. He deepened the kiss, bit at his lips, tongue-fucked his mouth. None of it was enough.

Wyatt pulled back, gasping for breath. "Want you inside me tonight."

Fuck, yes. Diego threw open his door, scrambling out. He took two steps toward the barn before realizing Wyatt wasn't following. He stopped and looked back. "What's wrong?

"I know you've got boundaries," Wyatt said hesitantly, "but I really want to do this in a bed. Just for tonight. You don't have to stay and sleep or anything."

Diego crossed the distance between them, grabbing Wyatt and kissing him hard.

"Anything you want."

"Really?"

His surprise sent a sharp pain twisting through Diego's heart. Was he really such a selfish bastard that Wyatt would be surprised? He'd only tried to maintain some perspective, but he knew that his so-called boundaries had been obliterated the second he stepped into Wyatt's arms on that dance floor. They weren't friends with benefits. They were friends, yes, but also lovers. They'd been young, naïve lovers once, and now they were older, more experienced, and in Diego's case, at least, more guarded. But still lovers, even if this time they knew it wouldn't last forever.

"Yes, really," he answered, kissing Wyatt again. He spoke to the rhythm of *Green Eggs and Ham* by Dr Seuss: "I'd take you on the breakfast table, I'd take you in a tree. I'd take you anywhere you'll have me."

Wyatt snickered with him. "Come on, poet. You can take me in a bed and give me really good head."

They hurried through the house, trying to keep quiet, but once Wyatt closed them into his bedroom, all bets were off. Diego shoved him roughly back onto the bed, where he bounced. Fuck, he looked good, the long length of his body stretched out for Diego. He climbed on top of him, both of them still fully dressed, and kissed him until his head was spinning.

"Want you to fuck me," Wyatt said. "Been too long since you were inside."

Diego flashed back to that ruthless fuck against the barn wall. His dick stirred at the memories, but part of him cringed at how he'd treated Wyatt. He loved the rough sex that Wyatt craved ... but he wanted to give Wyatt what he wanted in kindness, not anger. They'd get to the pounding, but first, he softened his kisses. The urgency was still there, but Diego fought it back so that he could revel in Wyatt. He deserved to be lavished with attention, not ravished in two minutes.

Between kisses, he unbuttoned Wyatt's shirt, pulling it apart and kissing each inch of skin he bared. He worked his way down toward Wyatt's navel, pausing to circle his tongue around Wyatt's belly button, making him squirm, before unbuckling his belt. They got tangled up briefly as Wyatt pushed up Diego's shirt, and he tried to push down Wyatt's pants, and they had to separate, laughing quietly, to remove their clothing.

Diego shed his T-shirt, then turned to pull off his boots and socks before doing the same for Wyatt. He grabbed the hems of

Wyatt's jeans and pulled, dragging the pants, which Wyatt had begun to push down, the rest of the way off him. He slid his hand up Wyatt's calf, feeling hair ruffle under his palm. Pushing Wyatt's legs part, he kissed his inner thigh, nuzzled at his balls, still encased in his briefs, and then tongued the top of his cock, which peeked out through the elastic waistband. Wyatt still wore his shirt, though it was spread open, exposing his torso, and Diego had a clear view of the full-body blush working its way up his chest.

"You're so fucking beautiful," he murmured.

Wyatt's eyes closed, but his lips tilted up. He was so modest it goaded Diego into spilling more compliments.

"Your body is so strong," he said, squeezing Wyatt's thigh and feeling the hard muscle under the skin. "And your dick"—he tugged Wyatt's briefs down, fully exposing him—"is mouth-wateringly perfect."

He dipped down, swirling his tongue over the head of Wyatt's cock, then sucking it into his mouth. Wyatt's breathing sped, and he lifted his hips from the mattress. Diego let his cock slide a few inches farther into his mouth while he pulled Wyatt's briefs down his thighs. He slid his tongue up and down Wyatt's shaft, thoroughly tasting him, before sitting back and stripping his underwear off completely.

Diego still sat in his jeans, and Wyatt surged forward, yanking at his button. "Take these off. I'm dying to have you."

Smirking, Diego slid off the bed to push down his jeans and boxer briefs. Wyatt watched, his eyes hooded and his skin glowing in the moonlight that poured through the window.

Once he was naked, Diego stood and let Wyatt look his fill. He wasn't modest. Gripping his dick, he squeezed it at the base, pointing it toward Wyatt. "You want my fat cock?"

"Yes."

"Where do you want it?"

"Inside."

"Inside your mouth?" he teased, stepping closer toward the head of the bed.

"If you want."

"I want to know what *you* want," he said.

Wyatt was growing frustrated, but Diego wanted to hear him ask for it. Wanted him to beg for it, just a little. It would make it better for both of them.

With a huff, Wyatt rolled over and pushed his ass up. "I want you to fuck me."

Diego calmly pulled open the bedside drawer, taking out supplies. "And?"

"Take me hard," he said. "Deep."

Fuck, yeah. They might be in a bed, but they were still the same guys who'd gone at it against a wall. He'd enjoyed slowing down, but now he was ready to own that ass.

He climbed onto the bed behind Wyatt, letting his cock slide through his crack and nudge at his hole while he reached for a condom and lube. "Do you want me to fuck you with my fingers?" he asked, half teasing. He was still working on getting some dirty talk out of Wyatt, but he also wanted to know if he needed some prep. Their first fuck wasn't exactly something he wanted to hold up as a shining example.

Wyatt was vibrating with want. He rocked his hips, pushing his hard cock into the bed. "Noo," he groaned. "I can take it. Just fuck me..." He paused, then blurted out, "Fuck me with that fat cock. Stuff me full."

Diego, now sheathed and lubed, leaned over Wyatt. "There we go. Now you're speaking my language."

Wyatt huffed a laugh. "You speak dirty talk?"

"You know it. Prepare to be stretched wide and pounded to within an inch of your life."

"You're all talk and no— ahh!"

Diego pushed in, catching Wyatt off-guard. His body didn't fight him, but it also wasn't prepared for the sudden entrance, and

Wyatt's ass clamped down around him, tight as fuck, once he was in. Diego kissed Wyatt's shoulder and stroked his flanks as he trembled beneath him.

"Too rough?" he asked.

"Don't baby me," Wyatt growled. "Take me like a man."

Well, okay then.

Diego pulled back and slammed in, setting a hard, steady rhythm. He focused on long, smooth strokes, putting as much force behind them as he could, shoving Wyatt up the mattress, until he braced one hand against the headboard to keep himself from slamming face-first into it.

"This ass is mine," Diego said. "I fucking own it."

"Yes," Wyatt gasped, pushing back to meet Diego's thrusts, taking every inch and begging for even more with his body. Diego adjusted his angle, nailing his prostate.

"Fuck!" Wyatt cried out, and Diego shifted to clap a hand over his mouth. There were other people sleeping close by, including Roberto. Bad enough his father knew they were hooking up; he didn't need to hear them do it.

Like that first night in the barn, Wyatt opened his mouth, licking at Diego's hand, and he gave him two fingers. Wyatt sucked them, moaning as Diego continued to fuck him. God, it was fucking scorching, the way Wyatt craved filling at both ends. He would probably enjoy a good spit roast, but Diego was too selfish to ever share him with another man.

Diego slowed his thrusts, rocking into Wyatt, trying to keep his orgasm at bay. "You feel too good. I don't know if I can last much longer."

Wyatt let Diego's fingers slip out of his mouth. "Don't come yet. Just a little longer. Please... I need more."

More, huh? Diego had already rammed him with every ounce of strength. Struck by inspiration, he slipped one of his spit-soaked fingers down to trace Wyatt's rim where it stretched around Diego's dick.

Wyatt whimpered at the sensation, shoving his face into the pillow to muffle the sound. Encouraged, Diego pulled his cock out to the tip, then thrust in, this time pushing his finger in alongside it.

Wyatt groaned deep in his chest, and his ass tightened up. Diego waited, not moving until Wyatt humped back against him, gasping, "Don't stop."

Diego fucked him with his cock, his finger moving with his thrusts, ready to blow from the sight and fantasies of DPing Wyatt with a dildo sometime. Goddamn, this man was hot as fuck, and so freaking needy. Diego loved it.

He slipped his finger free and leaned forward, draping himself over Wyatt's back.

"You're such a slut for me," he breathed in Wyatt's ear. "You love this, don't you?"

"Yes, yes, I love you," Wyatt gasped. "I love it so much."

Diego's heart missed a beat, but he was too caught up in the spiraling pressure of his impending orgasm to stop now. Wyatt didn't seem to realize what he said, and hell, he might not even have meant it. The man was clearly out of his head with pleasure, pleasure that Diego loved to provide.

Knowing he wouldn't last much longer, Diego wrapped an arm around Wyatt and leaned back onto his heels, bringing Wyatt up and onto his lap. He thrust up into Wyatt, while reaching around to fist his dick. "Come with me."

Wyatt wound his right arm around Diego's neck, fingers threading through his hair, as his entire body tensed. He made a hell of a view, his body pale, his muscles taut and defined under his skin, his dick wet with precum.

Diego felt wild and unmoored, his heart pounding as he raced toward climax.

Wyatt's cock pulsed in Diego's hand as he shot, muffled moans and groans escaping as he bit his own fist to keep quiet. Diego bit down on Wyatt's shoulder, grunting as he pulsed inside Wyatt's body, thrusting jerkily as pleasure washed over him in waves.

They fell forward into the pillows, breathing hard for several seconds, before Diego pulled out and discarded the condom. He flopped down next to Wyatt and glanced at him, noting he was awfully quiet.

"You good?"

"Yeah." Wyatt cleared his throat. "Uh, did I say what I think I said?"

Diego thought about lying. It would let them both off the hook. But in the end, he went for a simple truth. "Yeah, you did."

Wyatt covered his face with his hands and groaned. Dragging them down his face, he glanced sheepishly at Diego. "I'm sorry."

To Diego's surprise, he wasn't freaking out about it. He felt strangely calm.

"Don't be," he said. "If you didn't mean it, that's fine, and if you did..."

"I did," Wyatt whispered.

Diego pressed a kiss to his sweet lips. "That's okay too."

He felt the words on the tip of his tongue. He could say them, let Wyatt know he wasn't alone, but they wouldn't come out. He wasn't ready to open himself up that much.

He kissed Wyatt again instead, then pulled him closer, nuzzling his ear and kissing his neck. He couldn't say the words, but maybe he could show Wyatt that he cared. Maybe he didn't need words at all.

19

After their night out, something shifted between Wyatt and Diego. The distance between them closed another inch, or maybe even a few. Wyatt still couldn't believe he'd blurted out an "I love you" while getting rammed hard and fast. Hardly the sweet love-making that called for those kinds of proclamations. But the second the word "love" crossed his tongue, it hadn't mattered that he'd intended to reply to Diego's dirty talk. His innermost feelings had leapt from his mouth.

And amazingly enough, Diego had been okay with that.

He hadn't said it back. Wyatt hadn't expected him to, and certainly hadn't fished for it. He wanted Diego to say it when he was ready and not before. It wasn't easy to hand over his heart with nothing in return, but Diego already owned it anyway. In six years, Wyatt had never loved anyone else.

The next few days were a blur of work and sex. They returned to town and purchased surveillance cameras, installing them at the barn, stables, and workshop, as well as the small barn out closer to one of the pastures. Wyatt and Diego did a final walk-through of the bunkhouse and cabin, noting what furnishings and décor should go in each—sneaking in a quickie in the bunkhouse bathroom, Diego urging Wyatt to watch himself in the bathroom mirror while Diego fucked him hard and fast—and Wyatt called a local guy he knew to plumb and remodel the bathrooms in the buildings.

After placing some orders for furnishings and booking airline tickets to Bliss Island for two weeks later, it seemed everything was falling into place. As much as Wyatt wanted to enjoy that, each step forward was a step closer to saying goodbye to Diego unless he could convince him they belonged together for good. Diego had stopped fighting to maintain distance, visiting Wyatt's bed often, but he hadn't made any promises or so much as hinted that he might want to change the terms of their arrangement.

He knew Diego must feel something, too, even if he hadn't said the words. Wyatt had been his first love, after all. But he worried it wouldn't be *enough*. That there were too many obstacles for a little thing like love to overcome. And there were so damn many. The past was a big one, but it was hardly the only one. Diego lived a thousand miles away. Would he give up his new home for his old one? Diego wasn't a ranch hand anymore, despite picking up as if he'd never left this summer. He was a bartender at a popular nightclub. Would he give up his job, his friends, his freedom for Wyatt?

It was a tall order, and Wyatt was running out of time.

Their easy rhythm of sex and routine ground to a halt Wednesday, when he entered the kitchen to find Roberto and Diego in a discussion about TJ moving into the ranch house.

"He can take my room," Diego said. "I can't stay much longer."

The words were a knife to Wyatt's chest, and his voice came out gruff. "I thought TJ was getting his damn car fixed."

Rosie handed him a mug of coffee, kissing his cheek. "Morning, sweetie."

Ashamed of his bad manners, he wished her a good morning

and attempted a smile before sitting down with Roberto and Diego.

"TJ called me," Roberto said. "Turns out the engine head blew. He doesn't have the money to fix it, and it's an old car. Probably isn't worth pouring the money into. It's a long drive for him to make every day, anyway."

Wyatt nodded, sipping his coffee. He wanted to ask Diego to move into his room since he was sleeping there most nights, but that didn't seem wise. He didn't want Diego to leave the ranch to free up space, though.

"It's about time to move the cattle to another pasture," he said.

Roberto and Diego exchanged a puzzled look.

"It is," Roberto agreed.

"How about Diego and I ride ahead on the horses, check out the eastern fence lines." He glanced at Diego. "I thought we might take a couple of days, venture farther out, sleep out under the stars."

The ranch stretched for thousands of acres, but not all of it was put to use in their cattle operation. Grandad — and now Wyatt — still made a habit of surveying the property a couple of times a year.

"About TJ—" Roberto said.

"Give him my room," Diego repeated.

"I've already ordered furnishings for the cabin and bunkhouse," Wyatt added before Diego could offer to leave. "TJ's not on shift for two days. We'll get them set up and head out Friday. When we get back, you can stay wherever you're most comfortable."

With any luck, Diego would end up staying in his bed, but Wyatt wasn't going to press his luck by suggesting it.

"Just tell me I'm going to survive this trip without heat stroke," Diego joked.

"The creek runs along the fence line, and we'll stay hydrated and take to the shade in the afternoon. Trust me, darlin', and you'll be just fine."

Diego hedged. "Even if we do this, I can't stay forever. You know that, Wy."

"I know. I got our trip to Bliss booked for two weeks from now. You said you'd go with me."

He held Diego's eyes, willing him to agree. He wanted a lot more than two more weeks with Diego, but he could feel time running out. He was grasping at straws, anything to delay Diego's departure and give their relationship a little more time to flourish, and he wanted that damn trip to Bliss, even if it ended up being the last days they ever spent together.

Diego raked the fingers of both hands through his hair, ruffling it in aggravation. When he looked up, his eyes held a world of feeling that took Wyatt's breath away.

"Okay," he said. "I wanted to see this through, so... I'll stay and go with you to Bliss Island, but after that..."

Wyatt didn't care that Roberto sat at the table with them, or that Rosie watched from her spot by the stove. He stood and leaned over the table, smacking a kiss to Diego's lips. "That's what I wanted to hear."

Diego checked his phone for a response from Matias. There was nothing, and he was starting to get worried. He'd checked in frequently when he first arrived in Cow Creek, and Matias had assured him everything was fine and he was planning to stay at Diego's apartment until he returned. As time went by, he'd reached out less often. His schedule didn't often line up with Matias's, and Matias had seemed fine, if mopey, when they talked.

But lately it had been radio silence.

He tapped out a quick text: *Tell me you're okay. You've been quiet lately*.

Diego resisted the urge to ask about the state of his apartment. He'd know if Matias had managed to burn it down. He was a grown man who could water Diego's one sad plant and collect his mail. There was no need to worry. Yet, something felt off. Perhaps Matias was still depressed about his breakup.

Diego sent a quick text to Julien asking him to check on their friend, to see if he could get anything out of him, then pocketed his phone as Colby approached him. "The truck is here from the furniture place. Wyatt wants us over at the cabin."

Diego joined Colby on the trek toward the cabin, doing his best to push down his worry about Matias and the thoughts of his life in Miami that were beginning to tug at his conscience. He'd been gone well over a month now, and he was starting to feel the pull of responsibilities. It wouldn't be too long before he'd have another round of bills to pay, and this time he wouldn't have Papá to cover for him. After so long an absence, he wasn't entirely sure Duke would take him back at Caliente, either. He'd been ignoring his life, living in a fantasy with Wyatt, and it couldn't go on much longer.

Two weeks. You take the trip to Bliss, and then you go back to Miami. Rip off the Band-Aid, and just go.

He found Wyatt inside, wrangling the king-sized mattress onto a heavy, rough-hewn bed frame that fit the rustic surroundings perfectly. The moving truck sat out front, the delivery men carrying each piece inside and setting it near the door.

"What about the bunkbeds?" one of them asked.

"They're going in another building," Wyatt said. "Colby, can you take them over there?"

Colby looked surprised to be trusted with the responsibility. "Uh... yeah, sure. I don't know where you want everything, though."

Wyatt pulled out little notebook from his front pocket, and flipped it open to a room diagram he'd drawn. Tearing out the page, he handed it to Colby. "This is the general idea. I'll send over Hank to help you with it."

They resumed work after Colby left, directing the moving guys where to go next. They piled pillows and packaged bedding onto the bed and shifted the vanity over to the far wall. A small rocker sat in one corner, with a matching, rocking footstool. Paintings, mostly desert scenes, were stacked against one wall, waiting to be hung.

"You know, we don't have to take that weekend ride to check the fence line," he teased Wyatt. "I can start sleeping here tonight."

"Don't even think about it," Wyatt said. "I want that ride."

Diego's mind went straight to the gutter. Slipping his arms around Wyatt, he lowered his hands and squeezed his ass. "You can ride me right here."

He was only half-kidding. Diego had stopped fighting the pull between them, and he loved the idea of sleeping under the stars with Wyatt.

Loved the idea a little too much.

A weekend like that, spent alone with no interruptions, would only make it harder to leave when the time came. And now that he had a two-week deadline, reality was beginning to seep in. When he left the Triple J, he'd carry Wyatt with him. The new memories they'd made, the growing respect he had for the man Wyatt had become, the emotions that only Wyatt seemed able to stir. It was gonna hurt like hell.

"How about a compromise?" Wyatt suggested. "I'll ride you here *and* out on the range."

And... the time for rational thinking was over. Diego ground his hardening cock against Wyatt's thigh as he kissed the hell out of him. "You got yourself a deal."

20

The next morning, Wyatt woke Diego early, earning a few sleepy glares.

"Sun isn't even up yet," Diego muttered as he rolled out of bed and stumbled his way to the shower across the hall.

"That's kind of the point. Gotta get ahead of it, so we can find shade when it gets too hot," Wyatt said. "You'll thank me later."

Riding the fence line was something Wyatt tried to do once every few months, though sometimes life got in the way. While he could cover a lot of ground in his pickup, there were areas of the ranch that were too hilly or rocky for transportation, even on ATVs. He could send ranch hands to do it, but Wyatt liked to get out and see more of the vast Texas landscape. He never appreciated what an amazing treasure Grandad left him until he was looking out at the horizon, marveling at the natural wonder that had been the Jones's home for two hundred-plus years.

This weekend, it would be especially poignant. He had some thinking to do about this land, the feeling of connection he had to it, and the man who'd captured his heart and might very well walk away with it unless Wyatt had the courage to follow him. He didn't know how things would shake out with Diego, only that he couldn't let him disappear from his life ever again. He'd faced this choice once before, and right or wrong, he'd chosen his home. This time... whatever it took, he was choosing his heart.

The night before, Wyatt had packed up his saddle bags with tools for mending the fence where needed: a coil of wire that could be cut and spliced to mend the fence, fence staples, hammer, and pliers, along with work gloves. Stopping by the kitchen, he collected food, mostly things that didn't need refrigeration: beef jerky, along with some trail mix, peanut butter, and crackers. Rosie had also provided some sandwiches they could eat the first day.

He tossed in a few apples and oranges for some added moisture, then filled their canteens and packed a few extra bottles of water for good measure. They could refill the canteens from the creek; the water was mostly safe enough, but he preferred to avoid it when possible.

By the time, he was finished checking over their supplies, Diego appeared, hair still dripping.

"What can I do to help?"

Wyatt tossed him a sleeping bag. "Just grab your change of clothes and toiletries. We'll have access to the creek, so we can clean up and cool off as much as we like."

"Sounds good." Diego went back into his room to collect a few things, while Wyatt took his haul out to the stables and set to packing it into the remaining saddle bags that would ride on Dolly.

She was visibly excited as Wyatt saddled her up, clearly happy to get some time out of the stable. Wyatt needed to ride the horses more often, but it was tough finding the time. Maybe now that Ella's boys were coming to the ranch more often for lessons, the horses would get the attention and care they deserved.

It had been nice to see a couple of boys running around the place. Reminded Wyatt of some good memories from when he and Diego were that age. Wyatt had already decided that he wanted to have a chat with Ella about making her family's place at the ranch more official. Grandad had cut her out of the will, but that didn't mean Wyatt had to follow in his footsteps. He could give his sister what she'd always deserved and assure her the boys would get their share one day. And if he did make the choice to give up the ranch to have a life with Diego? Well, there were people here who could step up: Roberto could run operations. Mama and Ella could take a more active role. If there was a will, there was a way, though the thought of leaving pained him.

Diego came into the stable. "You're riding Dolly, right?"

Wyatt chuckled. "Nope. Silver's *my* horse."

This was a long-running joke from when they were kids. Diego used to moan up a storm about being stuck with a girl horse, since Dolly was both a mare and belonged to Ella, and Wyatt — sad to say — hadn't been inclined to share his horse. Boy, they'd had narrow views of things when they were ten. Heaven forbid one of them ride a *girl* horse.

Diego approached Dolly, and she whickered.

"Yeah, you're not so bad," Diego said. "Just try not to run off on me out there. I don't want to walk home, and Wyatt won't share Silver."

She snorted.

"I know," Diego said, shaking his head as he glanced at Wyatt, eyes smiling. "We'll have more fun together anyway, won't we?"

To Wyatt's surprise, and relief, Diego swung into the saddle easily, as if a day hadn't gone by since he'd ridden horseback. "You ride any horses in Miami?"

"I did plenty of riding," Diego said cheekily, "but horses weren't involved."

The joke fell flat. When Wyatt might once have groaned at the bad joke and laughed, all he could think now was that Diego would be returning to that life in two weeks. He'd go back to hooking up with men, and Wyatt would be left here nursing another broken heart.

Diego cleared his throat. "Bad joke. Sorry."

Wyatt turned and mounted Silver, urging him into the corral behind the stable so he wouldn't have to answer. When they reached the gate, he leaned down to unlatch it and the horses ambled through. Dolly wasn't the only one happy to be stretching her legs. Wyatt could feel the energy thrumming through Silver, but he was a well-behaved horse. He'd let Wyatt guide him. Dolly, on the other hand, jostled ahead, taking the lead once they cleared the corral.

"This girl wants to run," Diego said with a chuckle.

"Well, let's let them loose while it's still cool out," Wyatt said. "Soon enough she'll want to laze in the shade."

"We heading south?"

"Yup. Just follow the fence. It'll meander a bit, just like the creek does."

"I remember," Diego said, urging Dolly forward. "Race ya!" he called back, laughing, as the mare broke into a canter that soon transitioned into a smooth gallop.

Wyatt grinned, watching them go, man and beast, moving smoothly as one, their hair blowing back in the breeze.

What he wouldn't give for this view every day.

The creek wasn't deep, but the water was cool. After half a day on horseback, Diego was overheated and ready for a break. They'd kept their pace relaxed as they rode farther and farther from the house. So far, they'd stopped twice: once to splice the wire fencing where it had rusted through and another time to clear away some fallen tree limbs.

After watering and securing the horses, Diego waded into the creek eagerly, bare as the day he was born, his dick swinging in the breeze. Wyatt was ahead of him, his pale ass leading the way to the center of the creek, where the water slowly crept up to mid-thigh.

"Not the ideal swimming spot," Wyatt said, glancing back over his shoulder with a crooked grin.

Diego let his eyes trail down Wyatt's back to his ass. "Not a bad view, though."

Wyatt turned around, facing Diego and putting his dick on display. Just when Diego thought Wyatt might supply an innuendo that would bring them together, he dropped under the water. He came up a moment later. When he stood, the water came up to his chest. His hair was darkened by the water and dripping onto his face and shoulders. He used his hand to shove it back into spikes and swipe water from his eyes.

"That feels good," he said.

Diego's chest constricted. The knowledge he'd soon be gone hadn't left his mind all day. Each moment, no matter how small, took on added significance. Wyatt dripping wet in the creek and smiling like the devil? That was a vision Diego never wanted to forget.

He waded closer, until he was beside Wyatt, then dunked himself. As he came up, hands skimmed his torso.

Wyatt watched him surface with eyes too serious, and Diego knew that his impending departure weighed on him too. He wished he could say to hell with responsibility and just stay like this forever, in a cool Texas creek on a blazing hot day with an even hotter man. But Diego just wasn't built that way. Even now, thoughts of his apartment and his job nagged at him, like a pest trying to pull him from the moment.

Grasping Wyatt's arms, he tugged him close and kissed him, drinking the spare moisture that made it into his mouth along with Wyatt's tongue. Their bodies slid against one another, as slippery as fish, and Diego barely felt the twigs and pebbles jabbing his feet as he drew Wyatt to more shallow water. Being with Wyatt like this drove all other thoughts from his mind.

Wyatt broke from the kiss with a gasp, looking down between their bodies as Diego ran a finger along his now hard cock. It was wet and quivering above the surface of the water. In the heat of a Texas summer, the creek was cool, but far from cold enough to shrivel anyone's dick. Good thing too, because Diego had *plans*.

He glanced around. They were on a wide open range owned by the Joneses, nothing but nature all around them. There would be no other people out this way. But the idea of it was kind of sexy.

"Look at you," he murmured, "hard and dripping for the whole world to see."

Wyatt glanced around, as if checking their surroundings, then looked back to Diego. "How do you want me?"

"Just like that," Diego said. "You're perfect as you are."

Wyatt looked surprised for a moment, but Diego crushed their lips together again. He took Wyatt's nipples between his fingers, pinching them hard enough Wyatt jerked and cried out. Then he did it again, until they were pink and puffy.

"Do they ache?" he asked Wyatt.

"Yes," he said.

"Do they throb in time with your dick?"

Wyatt made a needy sound and thrust his hips forward, bumping his cock against Diego's hip.

Diego tugged his nipples again, but more gently now that they were hypersensitive. Wyatt shuddered.

"Please," he begged. "Touch my dick."

Diego grabbed Wyatt's waist, turning him around. Wyatt stumbled on the uneven bottom of the creek, and Diego steadied him. Then, he slowly sank to his knees in the water, and stared at the perfectly rounded ass in front of him. He gripped Wyatt's cheeks and slowly parted them. He let water slosh through Wyatt's crack, then pressed his tongue against the pink hole.

"Jesus! Diego," Wyatt gasped.

Diego took that for encouragement and stroked his tongue over him. He used his thumbs to spread Wyatt open and dip his tongue inside, which earned him a gasp. Then pushed it in deeper, which got him some whimpers. Wyatt's insides were boiling hot compared to the cool temperature of his skin, chilled by the creek water. He tasted earthy, and Diego curled his tongue, going as deep as he could with it before pulling back, then delving in again. Wyatt began to push back against his face.

"More," he gasped. "Please."

Wyatt reached for his cock, clearly desperate for release. Diego pulled back and swatted his hand away. "If you want to touch yourself, twist your nipples some more."

"Diego," Wyatt groaned in complaint.

"Do it," he ordered, then returned to Wyatt's ass, tugging at his rim, pushing his tongue inside, then adding his index finger. Wyatt trembled on his tongue; he could feel the vibration of his body. His asshole opened and closed, wanting more, and Diego inserted a second finger, spreading him wider, thrusting deeper.

"Fuck," Wyatt said. "I'm so close, but ..."

Diego leaned to the side, looked around Wyatt's body and up, saw him tugging restlessly at his red nipples. Yeah, that was hot. Making him torture his own nipples when he wanted nothing more than to jerk off.

Diego turned him back around, and Wyatt nearly fell over. They struggled, laughing for a second, as Wyatt flailed for balance. Diego looked up his body, his hair already mostly dried by the sun. "You're so fucking sexy," Diego said. "I could play with you all day."

"Please don't," Wyatt said so seriously that Diego had to laugh. The man was in a bad way. Diego loved making him come undone like that.

"Don't worry," he said. "I'll take good care of you."

With a wink, he leaned forward and sucked Wyatt's red cock into his mouth. Wyatt thrust hard, unable to control his need, and Diego gagged briefly. Neither them stopped. Diego relaxed his throat, reached around Wyatt to thrust his fingers back into his loosened hole, and sucked and finger fucked him until he came with a shout so loud some nearby birds took flight.

Diego wanted to laugh, but he was too busy swallowing around Wyatt's throbbing cock.

The second he stood up, Wyatt slumped against him, drained. But he grasped Diego, stroking him with a strong hand, and he didn't last long. He'd been suffering right along with Wyatt, after all.

After rinsing off once more, they made their way back to their spot under a tree, where they'd spread out a blanket, and lay down to air dry and eat lunch, before getting back to work.

———

They made it a little more than two hours before calling it a day. After another quick dip in the creek, this time without the sexual torment that Diego loved to dish out and Wyatt loved to take, they found a shady spot to eat an early dinner of chicken salad sandwiches. Rosie had packed a few into an insulated bag, and they wouldn't last much beyond a day, but at least they'd had some fresh food for the first leg of their trip.

"We didn't make it very far," Diego said, squinting into the still-bright sky. "Maybe we should have stuck it out longer."

"Nah," Wyatt said, unconcerned. "We're not going to make it all the way. That's all right. I'd usually make this kind of trip in cooler weather, but I wanted an excuse to get away."

Wyatt wanted to be alone with Diego. Really alone, just the two of them without interruptions. He loved Diego, and he suspected Diego felt the same, but the ranch was always such a big presence too. Out here, they could just be together, with no work and no worries hanging over them. He hoped Diego would realize how well they fit together, how right it felt to be together. More right than ever. They'd recaptured the friendship they lost six years ago, but they'd also discovered a new passion that surpassed anything Wyatt had felt before.

His memories of loving Diego were bittersweet. It had felt all-encompassing at the time, like his world would shatter without it, but it'd also been weighted with worry. He was afraid he'd disappoint Grandad. That he'd let Diego down. That he'd fail as he tried to be everything to everyone.

And he had.

He felt differently now. His love was less sweet, maybe. It was rooted more in reality. He knew Diego wasn't perfect, and neither was he. He knew the world would keep turning even after Diego left him. He knew it would hurt like hell, but that he would survive.

Trouble was, he didn't want to just survive. Now that he'd had Diego back in his life, he felt more complete, as if a part of him had been missing for a long time. The regular sex was nice, fulfilling in ways his random meetups with Brody or others had never been, but it was so much more than that. It was having someone to confide in, someone to share his burdens.

Someone to love.

Later that evening, as dark fell upon them, Diego broke the lengthening but companionable silence that had grown between them.

"What's the plan for tomorrow?" Diego asked. "More of the same?"

"Yep. More riding, more sex." He winked. "Maybe I'll take over and torture you for a change."

"If you think you're man enough."

Wyatt felt his hackles rise, even though Diego seemed to be joking. He liked to put himself in someone's capable hands and let go during sex. He wouldn't say he was submissive, but being told what to do was a turn-on. That didn't mean he was fragile. Far from it. He spent so much of his life being strong, capable, responsible. He needed an escape.

"I'm *not* weak."

Diego looked surprised. "I don't think you're weak."

"I let you take charge with sex most of the time because it's what I want," Wyatt said. "Doesn't mean I can't handle myself, or handle you, for that matter."

Diego arched an eyebrow. "You want to take charge of me? Prove yourself?"

"Maybe I do," Wyatt said.

Diego had been so guarded when they first came together that it had been easier to rely on Wyatt's kinks to give Diego a sense of security. He was in charge. He called the shots. But over the weeks, despite Diego often taking the lead, their love-making had become more organic. Wyatt still loved a good pounding, but there was more give and take between them.

Now, he wanted to take it a step further. He wanted Diego to give up a bit of himself.

Maybe it wasn't fair, asking that of Diego when they both knew he was leaving soon, but hell, it wasn't fair that Diego had come back to him only to take off again. It wasn't fair that Diego couldn't see what was right in front of him.

So Wyatt didn't give a rat's ass about being fair. He just wanted what he could get. Because life wasn't ever fair, especially when it came to the two of them.

Diego smiled invitingly. "Then take me, Wyatt, if you can."

Wyatt prowled toward him, a challenging look in his eye. Diego waited until he reached him, then grabbed Wyatt's arms and flipped him onto his back, pinning him down with his body.

"Well, that was easy," he said smugly as he looked into Wyatt's startled expression.

The world tipped, and Diego found himself on his back, Wyatt grinning. "Yes, it was."

They wrestled for a few minutes, each of them gaining the advantage. Arms were twisted. Ribs were jabbed. They grew sweaty again. But eventually Diego tired of the game. They were pretty evenly matched, but this had started because Wyatt wanted to prove he wasn't weak, and Diego had no desire to fight him on that.

When Wyatt pinned him again, he didn't fight back. He panted for breath, hands pinned to the ground. "You win."

Wyatt looked momentarily surprised. "Just like that?"

"Yeah," Diego said. "You think I don't know you're strong? You're the strongest man I know. Every time you let me take charge of you, it's heady as fuck because you don't have to do that. I get it, Wyatt."

Wyatt met his eyes, his expression serious. "You really do. A lot of men don't."

Diego nodded. He was sure that Wyatt's penchant for rough, controlling sex had been misconstrued a time or two.

"I get it," he repeated. "Now, fuck me. Or do whatever you want. Tonight, I want to give you everything you've given me."

Wyatt smiled slowly, his eyes simmering with lust. But when he spoke, Diego's heart lurched with fear. "Good. Because I want to make love to you."

"Wy—" he protested.

He was cut short by Wyatt's lips against his, firm and insistent. Diego had to resist the urge to take charge of the kiss. He parted his lips, letting Wyatt in, letting him lead them.

It's just sex, like every other time. Wyatt might call it making love, but that's just an expression.

Wyatt moved his lips to Diego's eyelids, pressing soft kisses on each one, then across his brow, then along his jawline. Fuck, what had Diego gotten himself into?

Wyatt tugged up Diego's T-shirt. Diego sat up enough for the fabric to clear his head, then lay back as Wyatt went to work on his jeans and boots. He helped as much as he could, but mostly let

Wyatt do as he pleased as he stripped Diego of every scrap of clothing.

Now the torture would start, the taunting and teasing for all the times he'd made Wyatt wait for his pleasure. Wyatt stood over him, his eyes roving over his body, prompting Diego's cock to thicken and stand, as if begging for attention.

Diego held his breath, waiting to see what would happen next. Wyatt didn't say a word, didn't touch him. Silently, he dragged his own T-shirt over his head. He unbuckled his belt, unfastened his jeans, and pushed them down. He didn't stop until he'd removed each piece of clothing, down to his socks.

Now, the teasing would start.

Only, it didn't. Wyatt lowered himself directly onto Diego, their moist skin pressing as chest met chest and cocks prodded one another and legs tangled together. Wyatt kissed him slowly, thoroughly. Not gently, exactly, but not roughly either. He lowered his lips next to Diego's ear, repeating his wish. "I want to make love to you."

Diego didn't answer verbally, though his heart skipped erratically in response. This wasn't how this was supposed to go. Wyatt was supposed to tease him a little, exert his dominance, and they'd both enjoy it.

"Tell me I can," Wyatt said.

Diego swallowed hard. "Wyatt…"

"You said I could have you however I wanted," he reminded Diego. "This is what I want."

Diego's eyes met Wyatt's, and he saw everything there. The longing, the love, the fear of losing him. He couldn't bear to look for long, so he closed his eyes and nodded. "Okay."

"Say it," Wyatt said, his voice holding the hint of demand.

"You can… make love to me," Diego said, aware that his voice was thready with uncertainty. This was uncharted territory. He'd had a lot of sex with Wyatt, and he'd always known, deep down, it was more than sex between them. But this was labeling it, deliberately announcing its purpose, and he didn't know how to feel about that.

"Good," Wyatt said, before kissing his way down Diego's chest to his cock. When his familiar velvety tongue licked over Diego's cock, he relaxed a fraction. Wyatt could call it whatever he liked, this was nothing they hadn't done before.

Wyatt sucked him, winding him up but keeping him far from the edge as he pressed fingers into Diego and prepped him efficiently. As he slowly coaxed Diego to relax and take his fingers, then pressed them expertly to his prostate inside, Diego realized that Wyatt must top more often than he'd expected. The man knew what he was doing.

The cool, wet sensation of lube touched his skin as Wyatt worked it inside. Diego had no idea when or where he'd gotten it, though he'd packed plenty for the trip. Soon, Wyatt's fingers glided in with ease, and Diego wanted more.

"Wyatt," he said, surprised to hear the strain in his own voice.

"I know," Wyatt said. "I've got you."

And he did. He read Diego's body perfectly as he withdrew his fingers and positioned his now-sheathed cock. Diego gripped his thighs, pulling back his legs as Wyatt pushed inside him.

He didn't even feel the burn, only the satisfying fullness of Wyatt inside him at last. Diego had always been versatile, though he didn't often offer to bottom for men. That required more trust than he usually had to give. But he had an excess of trust for Wyatt, he realized, even as he struggled with that notion.

Diego felt a frisson of fear mingle with the rising sexual tension priming his body. Wyatt thrust smoothly, confidently inside him, perfectly comfortable in this role even though it differed so much from their usual pattern. But it was his intense gaze, zeroed in on Diego's face each time he opened his eyes, that really undid him.

How can I give this up?

His heart thundered and his cock jerked as Wyatt hit his

prostate. He groaned with each thrust, unable to control his vocal cords and not liking how vulnerable he felt. He couldn't hide from Wyatt, not like this.

He and Wyatt were intrinsically connected. Even when they were apart, Wyatt had been a huge part of his life, if only through his resentment. And he'd come to realize, after spending time with Wyatt and so easily clicking with him once more that his grudge had only ever been a coping mechanism — a way to deal with the gaping wound left by Wyatt's absence from his life.

And for that he could only blame himself. He'd torn them apart. He had refused to listen to Wyatt's explanations or apologies.

"You with me?" Wyatt murmured, and Diego's eyes refocused on the perfectly imperfect man above him.

"Yes," he managed to say.

"You're gorgeous like this. Your face is so expressive."

"Fuck," Diego said, grimacing.

Wyatt laughed lightly, his voice reverberating through them both. "I like seeing you."

Diego knew he meant more than the arch of his eyebrows or the curve of his cheek. Wyatt liked seeing into him. To that knot of emotions that Diego kept a stranglehold on. He could feel the knot loosening, untangling, but he was afraid to let it unravel entirely. He didn't know if he could handle it. Didn't know if Wyatt could, though he seemed better equipped at dealing with his feelings.

He clutched at Wyatt's ass. "Make me come."

"As you wish," Wyatt teased, increasing his thrusts with incredible accuracy, his thick cock battering Diego's prostate. Diego's breath caught in his throat, his ass tightening around Wyatt's girth. This was better. He could hide inside the pleasure. Grasping his dick, he stroked it urgently.

His focus narrowed to the fullness inside him and the feel of his hand on his cock, tugging, squeezing, until the pleasure was too much and the coiled tension in his body suddenly released like the snap of a rubber band.

Diego came, back arching, harsh cry breaking from his lips for only Wyatt and nature to hear. The stars twinkled above in a dark blanket, or maybe he was just seeing stars from the intensity of the orgasm sweeping through him. He came harder than he had in a long time. He came with Wyatt inside him, on top of him, around him. Holding him close, filling him up.

It felt like home, being held like that, and it scared the shit out of him. He wasn't supposed to feel this way. Hell, Diego couldn't even remember the last time he'd felt something even close to it. He hadn't been sure he even *could* feel the way he had when he was seventeen.

But just now, his emotions ran so deep, he realized the terrifying truth: He wasn't feeling something new. He was feeling something very old. Something that had always been there.

He was still in love with Wyatt Jones.

21

The next day was much of the same. They rode during the cool morning hours, keeping a close eye on the fence line and making repairs as needed. They discovered a downed section of fence at least six feet long, and Wyatt shook his head. "What on earth..."

"Looks like someone drove through here," Diego said. "Maybe some off-roaders got carried away?"

"Maybe." Wyatt glanced in both directions. They were damn close to the section of land that would be rough riding for any vehicle. The ground was rocky and uneven. But occasionally, someone took out his pickup or Jeep and set out to prove his dick was big enough to drive over any terrain. "Probably."

As they got to work on repairs, Diego mulled it over. "You don't think this is vandalism? This far out?"

"We used to drive the cattle out here every summer," Wyatt said. "Now that the herd is smaller, we don't have to venture so far to avoid overgrazing." He smiled wryly. "I mostly brought you out here for my own selfish reasons. There was no real need to ride this far, but I can't leave this fence now that I've seen it."

Diego chuckled. He understood the feeling. Leaving that

section of fence down would feel wrong to a rancher who spent his days trying to keep his cattle safely contained. Even if he logically knew they wouldn't be up this way, it would nag at him.

Wyatt's words did make him wonder, though. If the cattle used to graze out here, and this vandal happened to know that, maybe he'd knocked down the fence in hopes of causing a little havoc. He might not realize his actions were harmless due to changes at the ranch. Hell, he might have even done it weeks ago. If they weren't here, Wyatt still wouldn't know.

After repacking their things into the saddlebags, they led the horses to the creek and let them drink their fill before resuming their ride. Diego's ass was still a little sore from the night before —even though Wyatt had gone easy on him comparatively—and he was eager to finish the morning's work so he could soak in the creek.

Later that afternoon, they tied the horses up under the shade of some trees and rinsed in the creek. Afterward, still naked and air-drying, Diego stood beside Wyatt, staring out at the land spreading in all directions. He felt as if they were the only two men in the world. It made him feel incredibly small, and at the same time, it made the importance of Wyatt seem that much larger. He knew instinctively that if he ever had to choose just one person to have by his side, it would be this man.

"Look at all this land," Diego murmured. "Is this all yours?"

"As far as the eye can see," Wyatt replied.

"Wow. Sometimes I forget."

"Forget what?"

Diego waved an arm around them. "All this. Earth. Life. You own a piece of the world itself."

"Yeah," Wyatt mused. "There are more important things, though."

"Like what?"

Wyatt looked him in the eye. "Love. Family."

"You've got all that here."

Wyatt smiled sadly. "Not all of it."

Diego's heart constricted, but before he could say anything, Wyatt cupped his face and kissed him.

They stood there, two men naked and natural in the middle of a vast Texas landscape, kissing like it really was the end of the world. Maybe that'd be easier, Diego thought, as they stumbled back to the blankets they'd laid out earlier, lowering themselves to the ground in a tangle of limbs.

If it was really the end of the world, Diego wouldn't be tearing himself apart over his decision to leave. If it was really the end of the world, he and Wyatt would go out in a blaze of passion instead of parting with memories of a bittersweet love affair.

They rode back north on Sunday, making it most of the way home before spending one last night under the stars. They were too exhausted for sex, worn out from hours of horseback riding and baking in the sun, even with breaks for food, water, and dips in the creek. They could have made it home that evening if they'd pushed hard, but Wyatt wasn't sorry to prolong their time alone without the distractions of ranch hands and cattle and a new problem every day—though the problems had certainly grown more manageable of late. Now that he was coming out from under the dark cloud that had hovered over him, Wyatt realized that nothing had been as bleak as it'd seemed in those early days after Grandad's death.

Grief and stress had combined to overwhelm him, but he was seeing more clearly. He was stronger now, more optimistic, and he knew that was partly because of Diego's unwavering support. In these past weeks, he'd become the partner Wyatt had always wanted, the partner Grandad had always told him he'd needed. An irony Wyatt now realized, considering Grandad had spent most of his years alone after his first wife died and his second marriage failed. But maybe that's why he was so determined that Wyatt should start a family.

They rolled out their sleeping bags, just lying on top of them because it was so hot and draping a sheet over them to keep away some of the bugs. They both smelled like bug spray, but it was a necessary evil.

For once, Diego crashed before he did. Within two blinks, he was out, but not before he'd wrapped his arms around Wyatt and tugged him close like a teddy bear. No doubt they'd push apart in the night, too hot to sleep entwined, but for now Wyatt was content to hold Diego and be held in return.

He tried to memorize the feel of it as he closed his eyes. He didn't know how long this would last, or what the future would hold, but he knew that come what may, he would put Diego first this time. The biggest mistake of his life, the day Grandad burst into his room while they were stupidly kissing in the house, surfaced in his mind.

"What in damnation is going on in here?" Grandad blustered, face red, as Wyatt shoved Diego away so quickly he fell from the bed.

"Nothing!" Wyatt exclaimed. "We were just—"

"Nothing is right," Grandad interrupted. "You'll do nothing of the sort under my roof. I won't have that kind of perversion. I raised you to be a good man, a God-fearing man."

Diego spoke up. "It's not a sin! It can't be. We love each other, Grandad Jones."

"This isn't love," Grandad spat.

"It is!" Diego insisted. "I love him like you loved your first wife."

Grandad advanced on him, grabbing his arm and pulling him hard toward the door. "Don't you talk about my wife! How dare you compare this sickness to the sanctity of marriage. Go home to your father and tell him what you've done, and that if he wants to work here, you'll stay away from my grandson!"

"But—"

"Please, don't," Wyatt said. "Don't threaten him. It's my fault."

Grandad turned on him, and Wyatt had never seen such fury in his expression, not even when he had vicious fights with Ella over her decision to date and then marry Tucker Dalton. He'd exiled her from the ranch, but he looked ready to kill just now.

"I'll threaten anyone I damn well please. Don't think I'm through with you. If you continue this"—he sounded utterly revolted as he said the word, and Wyatt's stomach twisted up into knots—"I'll disinherit you, you hear? No more ranch. You can pack a bag and get the hell out."

"You can't do that!" Diego protested from the doorway.

"I can, and I will. I want your promise, Wyatt. It's this boy or the ranch. What's it going to be?"

Wyatt looked at Diego, imploring him with his eyes to understand. Grandad wasn't rational right now. With a little time, maybe he could talk him around, but not right now, and Grandad was worked up enough he might just send Wyatt packing this second if he didn't hear what he wanted.

"Okay," he said quietly. "It's over with him. I promise."

Diego sucked in a sharp breath, betrayed eyes cutting into Wyatt like knives. "Fuck you both then! Fuck your precious ranch."

He spun on his heel, darting from the room. Wyatt moved to follow, but Grandad blocked his way.

"Let him cool off. You made the right call." He squeezed Wyatt's shoulder, looked at him like he was the chosen one once again. The future of the Triple J Ranch. But Wyatt was left feeling cold and alone.

Wyatt pushed the ugly, shameful memories from his mind. He'd found Diego later, tried to explain that he just needed some time to figure out a solution, but the damage had been done. Diego had insisted he was leaving, and that Wyatt had one more chance to choose him. But he hadn't. The ranch was all he'd ever known, and he'd begged Diego to just give it more time. But after so long waiting for Wyatt to come out of the closet, Diego was all out of patience. He'd left the following day without saying goodbye. For some reason, that had cut the most deeply, but why say goodbye to someone who'd thrown you away?

God, he wanted to reverse time and change something, anything about that day. But he couldn't.

It was a miracle Diego had come back into his life at all, much less as a lover.

He wished he could tie him down and refuse to let him leave. If only you could wrangle a man the way you wrangled cattle, he thought wryly. He'd have married Diego years ago. He'd marry him tomorrow if he could. But his desperate proposal had failed him. Wyatt had to rely on something much scarier—whatever lay in Diego's wounded heart.

Wyatt pulled Diego against him more tightly, even though it was plenty warm, and whispered into his hair. "I love you, and deep down, you love me. I know it."

Diego didn't stir, but that was to be expected. He was sleeping peacefully, while all Wyatt could do was think.

Think about what they used to have, what they'd lost, what they'd found once more.

You didn't get a second chance very often in life. But he couldn't make Diego take it. Couldn't make him want the life Wyatt wanted.

All he could do was hold him close for a little while longer, and when the time came, accept Diego's choices were his own. In the meantime, he'd remember the fragile, almost frightened honesty on Diego's face as he thrust inside him. The emotion blazing from his every pore. Wyatt wasn't alone. Whether Diego accepted it or not, they loved each other.

Wyatt reckoned they always would.

22

They broke camp early Monday morning and made good time as the horses galloped on the more even, flat land closer to the ranch house and stables. Diego's phone started chiming with incoming texts and social media notifications. They'd been without service while out on the range. He thought about checking it, but Wyatt's colorful cursing drew his attention.

He pulled Dolly from a gallop to a canter, falling back to ride beside Wyatt. "What is it?"

Wyatt glared down at his phone. "Cattle are loose," he said. "Section of fence went down sometime overnight, and far too close to the road for my liking." He reached down to flip open a saddle bag and shoved his phone inside. "We gotta go."

Wyatt took off again, turning west, and Diego urged Dolly to follow at a gallop. It didn't take much work; the horse loved to run. Diego felt like he was flying, the wind whipping past as they covered the ground between them and the pasture where the cattle had recently been moved to graze. This pastureland was farther from the house, with its western edge closest to the road, though there were a few acres between the fence and border of ranch property.

They arrived to find chaos. Colby and TJ were shoving each other, yelling. Roberto and Hank were nowhere to be seen.

Wyatt rode up, looking like a gunslinger out of a Western, face hard and eyes narrowed. "What the hell is going on here? You should be rounding up the goddamn cattle!"

Colby jabbed a finger toward TJ as Diego rode up too. "He says he saw someone suspicious on the ranch last night. Didn't mention it until *after* we discovered the cattle were out."

Diego circled around, scanning the horizon, but it was hard to say how many cattle were missing. This pasture stretched out for several hundred acres, and the cattle had plenty of room to roam without a section of downed fencing. One thing was certain though: A break in the fence didn't necessarily mean the cattle would run from the pasture. It was more likely something had spooked them into a stampede in that direction.

Or someone.

"I don't know all the vehicles around the ranch," TJ protested. "Nobody ever told me about any vandalism. How should I know to tell anyone?"

"Maybe we didn't tell you because we don't know you," Colby said. "You're not trustworthy—"

"That's enough," Wyatt barked. Seeing him go all authoritarian was really doing it for Diego. He liked taking charge of Wyatt in bed, but seeing how strong and confident he could be? It only made it that much hotter that he made himself vulnerable to Diego. "We'll worry about who did this later. Right now, we've got cattle to wrangle. Where's Roberto and Hank?"

"We came across an injured heifer," Colby said. "They were working together to get her to the small barn and call the vet."

TJ added, "We've fixed the fence and been rounding up cattle, but it's taken all morning. There are still some missing strays."

Diego checked the time. It was nearly ten a.m., which meant the guys had been working for about five hours by now. He felt guilty for persuading Wyatt into more sex when they woke,

75

followed by a wash in the creek and breakfast before they headed home. They'd taken their time, neither of them eager to return to the grind of the ranch, and yet Wyatt was needed here. Of course he was. It might have been Wyatt's idea to take off for the weekend, but Diego had selfishly kept him to himself as long as possible.

"All right," Wyatt said. "Diego and I are gonna ride through the herd and get an accurate count, so we can figure out what we're up against. I want to find every last head of cattle. You two, head out and resume rounding up any strays you find. But cover the ground closest to the road first. We don't want any car accidents."

Wyatt grabbed the reins. "Looks like we get to do ranch work like real cowboys today."

"You've got the hat for it."

Wyatt shot him a grin before wheeling his horse around and charging across the pasture.

For hours, everyone — including a couple of neighboring ranchers that Roberto had called for an assist — did what they could to hunt down and round up the last of the cattle. By the time they'd accounted for every last stray, and that last one was a doozy, having gotten stuck in some fencing along the opposite side of the pasture, where they weren't looking, they were exhausted.

The vet had been out to treat the cattle after their ordeal. The first heifer injured had made it onto the road and been clipped by a truck. The trucker had kept going, probably not even realizing he'd hit her, but she'd been thrown into the ditch and suffered a leg break and some abrasions. The one tangled in the fencing had some deep gouges, and several more had become dehydrated and overheated after wandering too far from a water source. They had been taken to the small barn, where they could receive medical attention and fluids.

But their work wasn't done yet. There was still the matter of how this had happened.

"Is it possible this fencing came down on its own?" Rosie asked as she filled glasses of ice water for the worn-out, dirty men collapsing into chairs around the kitchen table when they straggled in. "Maybe it's just an unfortunate accident. I can't imagine anyone wanting to cause this kind of trouble for you."

"I don't see how," Roberto said with a sigh. "We just checked those fence lines when we moved the cattle a couple of days ago."

Diego and Wyatt had ridden out ahead of the crew checking the eastern fence line. It would have been up to the crew to survey the western border. Wyatt trusted Roberto to have done that.

"I wasn't the one checking that far south," Colby said. "TJ was supposed to do it."

"Here we go again," TJ said. "If y'all wanna blame me, go ahead. I'm the new guy, and I sure as hell can't force you to trust me."

"Didn't I hear mention of a truck on the ranch last night?" Diego asked.

"Yeah, an old red pickup," TJ said. "It wasn't nowhere near the house, but it wasn't at that pasture either. It was cutting across the fields down past the bunkhouse. Seemed strange, but I don't know everyone who comes and goes around here."

"What were you doing out there anyway?" Colby asked.

Wyatt waited for TJ to answer. Colby's hostility wasn't doing much good, but TJ *was* newer to the ranch, and Wyatt couldn't discount the possibility he'd only hired on for better opportunities to fuck with him. It seemed unlikely, but ... Wyatt was grasping at straws. This harassment had to end, or it was going to end up causing them more than a big headache. Had more of the cattle gone for the road, it could have been a nightmare scenario, and considering where the fence was downed, he reckoned that's exactly what the asshole who did this wanted to happen.

"I was going for a walk."

Colby made a scoffing sound, and TJ shoved back his chair, rocking to his feet. "You wanna take this outside?"

"Sit down," Wyatt ordered as Colby blustered.

"I'm not afraid of you," Colby said, though Wyatt thought he was an idiot if he wasn't. TJ could break him in half with one arm tied behind his back.

TJ thumped back into his chair, crossing his muscled arms over his chest.

"You were going for a walk," Diego prompted.

TJ looked unhappy. "Y'all don't have any reason to believe me. I couldn't sleep. New place, new bed, and all."

"I know that feeling," Diego said.

"I was just wandering. Thought I might check out the bunkhouse, see what y'all had done, whether I could crash there instead." He shrugged. "I wouldn't have even noticed the truck, but he almost ran me down in the dark before cutting across the field."

Wyatt exchanged a look with Diego. They'd installed cameras at the bunkhouse and other outbuildings, just in case a vandal decided to target them. The camera would mostly capture only the area right in front of the building, but it was worth a try.

"Just red? Notice anything else?"

"It was too dark," TJ said. "Reckon I wouldn't have even known it was red if I hadn't nearly become a hood ornament."

"You said it was old. How'd you know that?"

"Just gut instinct. It was shaped like an older model farm pickup. No extended cab or monster tires."

Diego drained the last of his water, swiping at his mouth, and glanced at Wyatt. "I think we better check those camera feeds."

Wyatt nodded. "Let's do it. The rest of you get some rest." He paused as he stood, looking hard at Colby. "No more accusations.

The truth will come out, but fighting amongst ourselves won't help."

Colby flushed, casting his eyes down. "I'm sorry."

Wyatt squeezed his shoulder as he rounded the table. "You love this ranch, and you're a good man. But I need you to give TJ a chance."

Colby nodded, mumbling another apology, and Wyatt let him be. He was embarrassed for getting called out, but he was a good guy, and Wyatt knew he'd come around and do the right thing.

Diego and Wyatt went out to the bunkhouse, pulling the small USB drives from the cameras and returning to his office to watch the footage on his computer. They could operate on Wi-Fi, but living out in the country didn't yield itself to such modern convenience. The USB held up to a few days' worth of footage before the camera recorded over it, but if the vandalism happened the night before, it *should* still be there. Assuming the truck passed within the camera's range.

Wyatt took a seat in front of his computer, and Diego leaned over his shoulder to watch the screen. Roberto came in at some point, back from working with the vet and looking ready to fall over. "Anything?" he asked.

"Still checking," Diego murmured, his eyes going back to the screen.

A flicker of movement at the edge of the screen caught his eye. "There!" He jabbed the screen, but it was already gone. "Go back. I saw something."

Wyatt hit rewind on the video player, backing up the file until Diego saw it again. "Stop!"

Roberto came closer, leaning in. "Looks like a bumper and a tire."

"The back of a pickup," Wyatt said, nodding. "This is our

guy. He passed by the bunkhouse at 3 a.m. Plenty of time for him to use his truck to ram down that fencing and spook the cattle into a run. Pasture was far enough away, no one at the house would hear it even if he'd honked the horn or fired a gunshot."

"But why was he by the bunkhouse at all?" Roberto asked. "If I was doing it, I'd drive right back out that downed fence."

"Maybe the cattle blocked his way," Diego guessed. "The bunkhouse has been abandoned for years, right? He probably didn't expect anyone out that way."

"There's a clear access to the road over there too," Wyatt said. "Back when ranch hands did stay there, they came in that way all the time. He may have been coming and going on that back road all along. It's rutted to hell and overgrown, but it's passable."

"Still, a bumper and tire don't tell us much."

Diego squinted, leaning in so close to the screen his nose nearly touched it. "There's bumper stickers. Hard to read, but... yeah, I can just make it out. Holy shit, I know who this is."

"What?" Wyatt asked, leaning closer. He could just make out the words *Deport* and *Pro-Gun*.

"This is fucking Daryl's truck," Diego said. "The one that was parked at your sister's place."

"How can you be sure?"

"I read the bumper stickers. There was one about deporting immigrants, and another about guns. I remember thinking it was a real nice combination."

"Bumper stickers are hardly evidence," Roberto said.

"TJ said it was an old truck, and it was red. Daryl's got a rusty, old-model red pickup."

Wyatt pressed his lips together. It wasn't much to go on, but it was more than they'd had yet. He checked the time on his computer monitor. It was just now going on four-thirty. With any luck, they could get out there before Daryl left for the day. "Okay, let's head over to Ella's place and have us a chat."

"Maybe you should call the sheriff," Roberto said. "Sometimes these things can get out of hand."

"Nah, you were right. We don't have solid evidence," Diego said. "Our best bet is to bluff Daryl into admitting what he's done, then scare him into never doing it again."

"Frontier justice?" Wyatt said, amused. "I think you've been watching too many Western movies."

Diego snorted. "You got a better idea?"

"Nope. Reckon we'll ask some pointed questions, make like we've got him on camera, and watch him squirm. If we can get him to admit it, maybe we can call in the sheriff." He sighed, rubbing his eyes. "I just really hope Tucker Dalton isn't behind all this."

Diego dropped a kiss on his head, casual as you please, before stepping back to give him room to stand. "Seems likely, doesn't it? The Daltons and the Joneses and that ancient feud."

Wyatt rolled his eyes. "Thought we were finally done with all that."

"Maybe after tonight you will be."

"Let's hope," Wyatt said, smiling grimly. At least they had a lead, and a real suspect. But if Tucker Dalton was behind this, it also meant Wyatt would be eating some crow with Roberto, because it wouldn't have anything to do with Wyatt being gay and everything to do with him being a Jones.

Either way, he couldn't fucking win.

23

Wyatt pulled into the Dalton farm, and sure enough, Daryl's pickup was parked out front. It sat gleaming in the sun—well, the parts of it that weren't rusted to hell, anyway. The truck had seen better days, sporting a smattering of small hail dents, in addition to metal that looked ready to disintegrate over each wheel well and one nasty scratch along the driver's side door. Nothing that proved he'd driven through fencing, though.

Diego sat beside him, their thighs and shoulders touching, and Roberto was pressed up against the passenger door. He'd come along to keep them in check, Wyatt suspected, but he didn't mind having the backup. Besides, Roberto was a partner in the ranch now. This was his concern, too.

"Let's check it out," Wyatt said, cutting the engine.

They spilled out onto the drive, circling the pickup. Diego pointed out the bumper stickers.

Deport Illegals, read one.

The other proclaimed the driver a *Pro-Gun Texan.*

Wyatt had saved a screenshot from the surveillance video and sent it to his email, and he pulled it up now to compare the shots.

It was pixelated, but now that he knew what he was looking at, it was easier to match up.

"I think this is it," he murmured.

"Won't hold up in a court of law," Diego confirmed, "but it should be enough to confront this bastard and get some answers."

"Let's just all keep our heads," Roberto said. "I don't want any violence."

Voices came from around the house, and Tucker and Daryl emerged, talking about the price of gasoline. "Highway robbery," Tucker said, scowling.

"You aren't kidding," Daryl said. "I just had to fill up again this morning."

"Been using a lot of gas driving around pastures?" Wyatt called out.

Daryl and Tucker's heads snapped up at the same time.

"Wyatt, what brings you out this way?" Tucker asked. "The boys aren't due at your place for another few days."

"It's not a social call, unfortunately."

"Hey," Daryl called, "what are you doin' to my truck?"

Wyatt glanced over his shoulder. Roberto stood a foot behind him, but Diego had circled to the front and was bent over examining the grill, still searching for evidence of the truck driving through their fencing. Wyatt figured Daryl would probably be smart enough to get rid of any stray wire that might have tangled in the grill, but you never knew. Most of the wire had remained attached on one end, anyhow, trailing onto the ground, tangled and twisted.

"Just having a look," Diego said, straightening up and rounding the truck. "You've got a cracked headlight. How'd that happen?"

"Why do you care?"

The screen door opened, and Ella stepped out onto the porch. "Wyatt? What's going on?"

"Where are the boys?" Wyatt asked.

"They're doing chores. We didn't have any plans, did we?"

"No." Wyatt had begun to make inroads with his sister, and he didn't want to torch them, so he took a couple of steps in her direction, lowering his voice. "I just wanted to make sure they wouldn't overhear. We've got some concerns we'd like to talk to Daryl and Tucker about."

"What kind of concerns?" she asked, eyes narrowing.

"I'd like to know that too," Tucker said. He spoke in a lazy drawl that rose Wyatt's hackles. There was something insolent about it. Wyatt knew Tucker didn't care for him, but his attitude just now seemed to taunt him.

"Someone knocked down a section of fencing at the ranch. The cattle got loose," he said tersely. "It's just the latest instance of vandalism—"

"Downed fencing isn't really vandalism," Tucker said. "I reckon the Triple J has a lot of fences to maintain. It was bound to get away from you at some point."

"This wasn't poor maintenance. Someone knocked it down intentionally."

"Got proof?"

"Yeah, actually," Diego said. "We had some surveillance cameras installed. One of them caught Daryl's truck on the property round about three in the morning."

Tucker shot a look at Daryl. "That so?"

"It is. The bumper stickers are clear as day on the video," Wyatt said, backing up to point them out. "Not smart, committing a crime with something so identifiable on your vehicle."

Daryl reddened. "Lots of people have bumper stickers!"

"But these exact two? On a red, rusty truck?" Diego tsked. "That's a little too coincidental to be believed."

"Wyatt?" Ella asked, sounding worried. "What are you suggesting?"

"I think Daryl has been vandalizing the Triple J."

"I didn't do anything," Daryl objected as Ella said, "But why would he do that? He used to work at the Triple J. He was so loyal that when Grandad laid him off, he came straight here, saying he wanted to work for me. He's always loved our family."

"Laid off?" Roberto said, stepping forward and shaking his head. "We didn't lay off Daryl. He quit."

"Oh, well... maybe I remembered wrong." Her brow creased, and she glanced toward the ranch hand. "Daryl?"

"I left because of the way he treated you, Ella," Daryl said. "It wasn't right, pushing you away from the ranch like that. I wanted to make sure you were okay, so I came and asked for a job."

Ella looked disconcerted. "I didn't realize... Thank you, Daryl, but you didn't need to do that. I have my husband and boys here. I'm perfectly happy."

"I think we can all agree that Ella and Wyatt's grandfather made some questionable choices," Diego said. "That doesn't make it okay to harass Wyatt. There's been graffiti with homophobic slurs, downed fencing in more than one place, the workshop trashed. And probably other things I don't even know about."

"I didn't do none of that," Daryl said loudly. "Y'all just want a scapegoat!"

"The video doesn't lie," Wyatt said.

"Maybe I just went for a joyride on the ranch," Daryl said, face growing red. "You don't have any proof I committed any crimes while I was there."

Tucker shook his head, sounding aggrieved. "Daryl, you idiot, that's still trespassing. Why would you admit that?"

"They said they had video—"

"Which we haven't seen," Tucker pointed out.

"Maybe we call the sheriff's office," Ella said tentatively. "Let the authorities decide what's a crime and what's not?"

"Okay by me," Roberto said.

Tucker held up his hands. "Hold on a minute. Surely, we can resolve this amongst ourselves. There's no need for the sheriff."

Wyatt didn't particularly want to call the sheriff, either. He feared their evidence was too shaky and nothing would come of it. He didn't have a whole lot of confidence in the lawmen who'd shrugged off his concerns when he reported the graffiti.

"I'd rather not call in the law," Wyatt said, "but I need some answers, and I need this shit to stop. I want to operate my ranch in peace."

Tucker sounded skeptical. "Someone's been messing with your property. Surely you won't just let it go."

Wyatt tried to get a read on him. He suspected Tucker was attempting to cover his bases. He didn't want to incriminate himself, but he didn't want Wyatt to call the sheriff either. He needed some assurance he wouldn't be selling his own ass down the river.

"I realize there's been bad blood with Joneses and Daltons," Wyatt said. "There's that stupid feud—"

Tucker snorted. "Sure, it's stupid to you 'cause you're the one holding the deed to the ranchland. To my ancestors, it's not so frivolous. We were cheated."

Wyatt fought the urge to roll his eyes. He'd hoped that Tucker hadn't bought into the feud. The idea that one of his ancestors won the ranch in a game of cards was farfetched. Even if it were true, it was ancient history, and there was nothing to be done about it.

"Be that as it may," Wyatt said, "We're family now. Ella is my sister, and you're her husband. I don't want to call the sheriff out to your home and raise a ruckus, but I do need assurances that my ranch and my property will be safe from interference. This has gone on long enough."

Tucker nodded. "Fair enough. I might be able to help with that."

"What are you saying?" Daryl asked, sounding concerned. "Mr. Dalton—"

Tucker spoke over him. "Daryl has talked some trash on y'all. He talked a big game about making the Triple J pay for wronging

Ella. I didn't mind none because the Daltons and the Joneses have never been best friends."

"That's not how it was," Daryl protested. "I work for Mr. Dalton. He's the one behind all this! He was angry that Ella was left out of the will."

Now, they were getting somewhere.

"Tucker, is that true?" Ella asked, anger creeping into her tone. "Are you involved in this?"

Tucker was unruffled. "Of course not. I didn't step foot on that ranch."

"That doesn't mean you weren't involved in the planning," Diego countered.

"This was all Daryl. He's been loyal to Ella since she was a girl, and he wanted to get even with Old Man Jones. I had no beef with that, but it doesn't mean I orchestrated it."

"What, so you just sat back and let him trespass and vandalize my property?"

"Hell, I didn't know if he'd even go through with it," Tucker said. "But if he did, it was no skin off my nose. He was right. Ella deserved a helluva lot more than to be cut out of the will."

Even if Tucker hadn't participated, it was pretty clear he'd condoned Daryl's actions, maybe even encouraged them. Ella seemed to agree. She came down off the porch, lips tight and eyes full of fire.

"Tucker, I made a choice! I chose you and this life. I wasn't surprised by that will, and I wasn't sorry. I've got no regrets."

"Doesn't make it right," Tucker insisted.

"So what?" she said. "Since when do two wrongs make a right?"

"Maybe we *should* call the sheriff," Diego said in a low voice. "Daryl and Tucker have said enough to get us somewhere."

"Maybe so," Roberto agreed.

Daryl had moved close enough to hear them. "If you call the sheriff on me, you'll get Tucker in trouble too. That'll be bad for Ella."

There was sincere concern on his face. It disturbed Wyatt. Daryl had been a ranch hand for the Triple J when Ella was a child, and he'd apparently left the ranch and sought out employment with her. There was loyalty, and then there was unhealthy fixation.

"All right, here's my offer," Wyatt said after thinking the matter through for a few minutes. "You can take it, or I can call the sheriff and let him sort out the mess." He jabbed a finger toward Daryl. "I want you to fire this man. Besides the fact he's been committing criminal acts and I don't want him around my nephews, I don't think it's healthy the way he's so focused on Ella."

"I'm just looking out for her," Daryl argued. "Nothing wrong with loyalty."

Tucker grimaced. "Done. He's fired. What else?"

"This is bullshit," Daryl cried, kicking the tire of his pickup, then yelping in pain and hopping on one foot. "I've been loyal to Ella." He looked to her. "You can't let them fire me."

"Sorry, Daryl—"

"You bitch!" He lunged, and Diego grabbed his arm, yanking him back and pinning him to the truck. "I did it for you! I was *loyal!*"

Wyatt joined him, helping restrain Daryl until he'd exhausted himself and panted out, "Okay, okay, sorry. I'm sorry."

"Don't move," Diego ordered before nodding his head toward Tucker and Ella. "Go on, Wyatt. I got this."

Wyatt walked a few steps closer to Tucker and Ella. "This vandalism stops here and now," Wyatt said. "If anything else happens, I'll call the sheriff immediately and tell him everything we learned here tonight. That means you don't cause me any trouble, and if you hear even a whisper about someone with a beef with the Triple J, you let me know. That goes for Daryl too."

"I can live with that," Tucker said. "Daryl, no more, you hear me? You're done."

"I was just trying to help," Daryl said miserably. "Didn't seem fair, you getting everything and her getting nothing," he said to Wyatt. "I was only leveling the playing field some."

He certainly seemed sincere. It was a shame he'd twisted honest concern and loyalty into something that justified criminal behavior.

"No more, Daryl," Diego practically growled. "Or you go to jail. Got it?"

"Yeah, I got it."

Wyatt looked to Ella. "I hope you know I don't agree with Grandad's actions."

"I made my choice," Ella said. "I was fine with that." She glared at her husband. "Tucker knows that I've never regretted it. Not until now anyway."

Tucker flinched, the first sign that he was flappable.

"Still, it's something that's been on my mind too," Wyatt said. "I hope you know I plan to put the boys in the will."

She opened and closed her mouth, clearly shocked. "That's not necessary."

"I don't have children, and I've got no plans for any," Wyatt said. "The Triple J will need someone to carry it on. I want it to be my nephews, if they're interested."

Tucker scoffed. "Oh, sure, now you care," he said derisively. "What assurance do we have that you'll ever make good on your word, huh? Your grandfather cut Ella out, just like his ancestors screwed over mine."

"Not this old story—"

"No, not with a goddamn poker game," Tucker snapped. "That's an old wives' tale. The true story is that a Dalton invested in that ranch, and they cut him out of the deal at the last minute. Jones men have no fucking honor."

"Tucker!" Ella sounded shocked. "You can't honestly believe that."

"It's the truth," he said shortly. "Your family doesn't care to remember because it makes them look bad."

"Look, maybe that's true, maybe it's not," Wyatt said. "It's way before our time, and none of us can say exactly what went down. But if you want the Daltons to have a piece of the ranch, this is your chance. I want the boys to have their share, and that goes for Ella too." He glanced at his sister. "If you want to join the ranch as a partner, we'll work something out—"

"No," she said, "really."

"I've got some plans for the ranch you could help with, if you're interested," Wyatt said. "Just think about it."

"I have a lot of things to think about tonight," she said tightly. "You mind if I bring the boys over and do some of that thinking at the ranch?"

"Ella—" Tucker started, and she held up a hand, looking angrier than he'd ever seen her.

"Don't. I need some time."

"I don't want the boys over there."

"Too damn bad!"

They devolved into an argument in hissed whispers, and Wyatt turned away to give them a little privacy. Roberto stood with Diego, keeping an eye on Daryl by his pickup a few feet away. After exchanging a few words, Diego headed over to him.

"I've got to make a phone call," he muttered. "Sorry. I think it's important."

"Sure, go ahead. I've got this covered."

"Are we done here?" Daryl asked as Diego paced a few feet away, lifting the phone to his ear. "If I'm fired, I'd like to go home and start looking for another job."

Wyatt refused to feel guilty for putting Daryl out of work. He'd probably find something with one ranch or another, and he'd be in worse shape if Wyatt pressed charges against him. He didn't really care about punishment, though—he just wanted his cattle safe, his men able to focus on their jobs, and no more bigoted slurs haunting him.

"Yeah. Don't be an idiot. Take this chance and stay out of my business," Wyatt said.

"Fine."

"If I ever see another bigoted slur, I'll come after you myself," Roberto warned him. "My son is gay, and he's a better man than you'll ever be."

Daryl took a step back under the force of Roberto's glower. "That wasn't me. I swear. I did some stuff, yeah, but not that. I don't care that he's a fag—"

"What did you just say?" Roberto growled.

"I don't care that he's gay," he corrected quickly. "I didn't write those words. That's not why I... I didn't do any real harm."

That was debatable. While the homophobic slurs spray-painted on the barn had troubled Wyatt the most, the other harassment had cost him in time, labor, and materials.

"The graffiti happened while Grandad was still sick," Wyatt said to Roberto. "Probably before Daryl got all wound up over the will."

"Randall," Roberto said, and Wyatt nodded in agreement.

The dickhead ranch hand who'd talked shit and left was the same man Wyatt had been sure did the graffiti originally, but the sheriff's office had said there was no proof. There still wasn't. It left a bad taste in Wyatt's mouth, but at least it seemed like Randall got it out of his system when he left. Good riddance to him.

"You can go, Daryl," Wyatt said. "For your sake, I hope we don't meet up again."

He turned, heading for Diego, not bothering to watch Daryl scurry to his truck. Behind him, he heard the engine start up and Roberto's voice as he continued to talk with Ella and Tucker. He was more concerned about the intense conversation Diego appeared to be having on the phone.

With the confrontation over, his adrenaline was crashing and Wyatt felt ready to sleep for days, but it sounded as if Diego had another crisis on his hands.

Diego's phone buzzed, and he realized he'd missed three calls from Julien, along with a text urging him to get back to him as soon as he could. Fearing something awful, he made his excuses and edged away from the crowd in front of Ella's house to return the call.

"Diego, thank fuck!" Julien exclaimed. "Where have you been?"

It wasn't like Julien to skip all the niceties. Diego's sense of unease grew stronger.

"What's wrong? Are you okay?"

"It's Mati," Julien said. "He's in the hospital."

Diego's heart plunged to his stomach. "Shit, is he okay?"

"I don't know. I mean, he's stable. I checked on him like you asked"—Diego had forgotten he'd asked Julien to do that; Matias had never replied to his texts and now he felt like an asshole for taking off the weekend without making sure he was okay—"and when I had trouble reaching him, I sent Zac over to your place."

Something else Diego should have done. Diego was closer to Julien, and had reached out to him on instinct, but Zac was in Miami. Diego didn't have his number, but he could have asked around.

Julien was still talking. "Matias wasn't there. Wasn't answering his phone. We started calling hospitals and jails. Fuck, Diego. He was in the hospital after an overdose. He had a seizure, had to be detoxed."

"*Mierda*," he muttered.

"He's recovering, but he's a mess, Zac says, and he's freaking out about your apartment. I guess Duke fired him after he blew off one too many shifts. Zac saw him come in once after that, and he was high as fuck and making a scene until Duke had him tossed out."

Diego couldn't believe what he was hearing. Matias was a favorite dancer with the regulars. He had an Instagram with a huge following full of sexy pictures. Hell, he'd even modeled a time or two. It would have taken a lot for Duke to fire him. Diego had never known Matias to struggle with drug use, but he must have gone into some sort of downward spiral. He knew Matias had been upset by his breakup, but Diego never would have left if he'd thought there was a chance Matias would self-implode like this.

"Zac is with him, right? At the hospital?"

"For now, and I think he'll be in a few days more, but Zac takes care of his grandmother, so he's got other responsibilities. I'm checking on flights from here."

"No, don't. I'll head back tonight. If I drive, I can be there in two days—"

Wyatt tapped his shoulder to get his attention. Diego had only half been aware of his presence beside him. He'd noticed Daryl's truck leaving, but not much else.

"We can get you a flight out tonight, if you want," Wyatt said.

Diego turned toward him, lowering the phone. "My car would be here. I'd have to come back."

Wyatt's smile quirked. "Now, you know my secret motive. I'm not ready to say goodbye."

Diego took a bracing breath. He wasn't ready either, even though he knew this day was fast approaching. He was supposed to have more time... more time to do what, exactly, he wasn't sure. It wasn't like he could store up sex with Wyatt for a rainy day, and it was pretty evident he would never get his fill. There was no getting this man out of his system.

He didn't know what he wanted to do yet, so he turned his attention back to the phone.

"You still there?" he asked Julien.

"Yeah. What are you thinking?"

"I'll head home as soon as I can. I should have been there for Matias, and I fucked off to Texas. This is my responsibility—"

"He's your friend, not your child," Julien said. "Don't be so hard on yourself."

"I knew he wasn't happy," Diego said. "I just ... thought he'd bounce back."

"Well, there's one more thing I haven't mentioned yet."

Diego wasn't sure how much more he could take. How else had he fucked up?

"What?"

"He hasn't been paying your rent. Zac said there was an eviction notice on your door when he went to look for him. And while we're on the topic, why doesn't Zac have your number? He said he couldn't call you."

That would be because we fucked when we first met, and I didn't want him to get clingy. God, I'm such a dickhead.

Diego closed his eyes, leaning his forehead on Wyatt's shoulder. Wyatt ran a soothing hand over his hair, and Diego took a moment to breathe him in.

"I guess that's all the more reason for me to get home," he said, ignoring Julien's question. "Thanks for following through when I dropped the ball."

"You didn't drop the ball. You passed it to me, and I completed the— Ugh. Enough with the sports metaphors. Let me know when you see him, okay?"

"I will. Thank you."

He disconnected and looked up. "I need to get back to the ranch. I've got to go home."

Wyatt's arms tightened around Diego briefly, giving away his tension, before they walked over to Roberto to tell him they needed to go. Diego gave a hurried explanation and hugged his father goodbye.

"I'll stay and help Ella load up," Roberto told them. "I'll put her and the boys in the bunkhouse, if that's all right?"

"Yeah, thanks," Wyatt said.

"You can stay with your sister, if you want," Diego said quietly as they turned toward Wyatt's pickup. "My father can drive me back."

"Like hell," Wyatt said. "I trust Roberto to take care of Ella. I need to be with you for as long as I can."

24

The drive back to the ranch was quiet, despite the fact that Wyatt knew he was running out of time to say all the things in his heart. The silence between them was weighted and tense, and Wyatt was sure Diego's head was whirling with worries for his friend.

It was absolutely not the right time to talk to him about their future. But if not now, when?

"I'm going to drive to Miami," Diego said abruptly. "It'll take a little longer, but I'm going to need my car since I'll have to work every night. I'm being evicted, so—"

"What?!" Wyatt exclaimed. He'd missed that little tidbit. "When did this happen?"

Diego sighed, ruffling his hands through his hair. "Matias was staying at my place. He agreed to cover the rent while I was here, but that obviously didn't happen."

"Jesus, when it rains it pours."

"You're not kidding. I should have checked in more with him. I got so caught up in everything here..."

"Don't be too hard on yourself. We've had a lot going on."

"Yeah, but this isn't my life. I was just living in a fucking fantasy."

Wyatt's heart twisted. "It felt pretty real to me."

"Well, sure. All this is your life," Diego said. "But I've blown off my job, my friends, my responsibilities. Everything that's important. I can't ignore the real world anymore."

Everything that's important. Apparently that didn't include Wyatt. He'd been the one living in a fantasy.

He turned down the bumpy drive and came to a jerky stop in front of the house. Throwing the pickup into park, he said, "It's late. Maybe you should stay the night and leave in the morning."

"I've got to get back ASAP," Diego said. "Mati needs me, and I've got to try to work out an extension to save my apartment."

"You could just pack up and move here." The words were out of Wyatt's mouth before he could stop them. "Mati, too. The ranch would be a good place to recover."

He looked over to see Diego's wide eyes.

"You lived here once. You could live here again. With me."

"Wyatt..."

His tone of voice told Wyatt all he needed to know. He tried to hide his hurt, but he knew he'd failed when Diego brushed a thumb over his cheek and kissed him gently. "My head's all over the place. I can't make that kind of decision right now."

Wyatt swallowed hard, throat aching. "That's fair. I just... I had to try."

"It won't be like before, okay? I'm not going to block your number or disappear for six years. We're leaving on a much better note, right? We made some good memories."

Diego was already retreating into his other life. Wyatt could see it happening, but he couldn't do anything to stop it.

It took a shockingly short amount of time to pack up his things. Diego had packed light, and though he'd had to buy a few clothes when he decided to extend his stay, it wasn't enough to fill more than two duffel bags.

Amazing he could feel so at home with so few of his belongings. But then, what was in Miami that he really needed? A closet full of more T-shirts? A flat-screen TV that he hadn't missed at all out here?

Matias, though. Diego shouldn't have left him for so long, and he should never have asked him to cover his rent. He'd been looking for a way to extend his stay even before his father offered his help. And he'd stayed longer than he ever should have.

Now, he couldn't get Wyatt's blue eyes, dark with pain, out of his head. They'd made good memories, he'd told him. But he wasn't sure those good memories were going to lessen the ache already starting up in his heart.

He shouldered his bags and headed out to his car. After loading them into his backseat, he waffled.

Should he just go? Wyatt might not want yet another goodbye. But Diego didn't want him to think he was running away, like he once had.

He needed to say goodbye to Rosie, too. The rest of the crew was gone, other than TJ, and Diego didn't think the guy would care that much if he didn't seek him out, which was probably good. He was reaching his limit.

Rosie and Wyatt. One more goodbye, he told himself as he stepped up onto the porch.

Rosie came outside before he reached the door, Wyatt behind her.

"Oh, honey," she said, pulling him into a tight hug. "Wyatt told me what happened. I sure hope your friend is all right."

"Me too, thanks."

She pulled back looking worried. "Are you sure you want to drive at night?"

"Yeah, I need to get back as soon as I can. I'll be careful."

"It's a bad idea," Wyatt said bluntly. He thrust an envelope forward. "Take this."

Rosie patted Diego's arm and wisely backed away.

"What's this?"

"A check—"

"I can't take your money."

"Don't be stubborn. I'll put in for a refund on your ticket to Bliss Island, all right? I can't make you use it to fly home instead of driving, but I think you should. You're tired, and it's a long-ass drive. If you agree, I'll drive your car to Miami for you. If I head out first thing in the morning, I can be there within a couple of days."

Diego's heart lurched. The promise of seeing Wyatt in just a few days was tempting. But, Wyatt had obligations. Injured cattle to tend and a wedding venue to get off the ground. It would be selfish to take him up on the offer.

"You can't leave right now," Diego said. "You've got the ranch to think about."

"Fuck the ranch," Wyatt said, shocking him. "You wanted me to put you first once, and I didn't. I won't make that mistake again. Whatever you need, you come first, Diego."

"Oh, baby..." he murmured, pulling Wyatt into a tight hug. "I shouldn't have asked you to choose. I wasn't worth giving up everything else in your life."

"Of course you were," Wyatt said, pulling back, eyes red-rimmed. No tears fell, but his jaw worked as he struggled with emotion. "You were everything, and I was stupid to let you go. I should have stopped you, or chased you, or anything but what I did. I should have fought for you." His voice dropped to a whisper. "I should have asked you to marry me right then and there."

Diego felt his own eyes burn. He'd needed to hear this from Wyatt once. But now? He saw things differently. "I was so selfish. I grew up here, but I didn't really understand what I was asking you to give up. I owe you an apology, too. You belong here. It's in your blood, Wyatt."

"And what about you?" Wyatt challenged. "You were raised here, just like me. You returned to ranching like a natural this summer. Maybe it's in your blood too."

Maybe it was. But Diego had cut off his nose to spite his face six years ago, and now he was a man with two worlds. He had Miami and his job and his friends, one of whom needed him. And he had Texas and his father and Wyatt, whom he really, *really* wanted. But he couldn't have Miami *and* the ranch. He was the one who had to choose, and he wasn't ready. Not yet.

He tried to hand the envelope back to Wyatt. "Thanks for this, but I'm still going to drive."

"But—"

"Only until I get tired," he said, before Wyatt could launch another argument. "I'll be safe. I'm totally wired now and couldn't rest if I tried."

Wyatt nodded but pushed the envelope back toward him. "Keep it. Use it for whatever you need. You've worked on the ranch more than enough to earn it anyway."

Diego considered arguing. He didn't want to take money Wyatt could put to better use, but he'd already rejected Wyatt's offer to drop everything and drive all the way to Miami. He didn't have it in him to refuse him anything else. "Okay. Thank you."

"Don't be a stranger," Wyatt said, his eyes gleaming under the porch light. "I want everything with you, but I'll take anything. Toss me a few crumbs now and again, all right?"

Pain knifed through Diego. "I will."

He wasn't sure it'd ever been so hard to say goodbye. When he'd left six years ago, he had anger to fuel him. Regret and longing were going to be more difficult company.

Overwhelmed by emotion and speechless, he pulled Wyatt into a tight hug, kissed him one more time, and spun away to get into the car before he gave in and accepted Wyatt's offers to turn their lives upside down.

25

Wyatt drove over to the bunkhouse after Diego left, checking to see how Ella and the boys were settling in—anything to avoid thinking about the man who'd just left.

Again.

He'd forgotten with time just how much it hurt to be left by Diego Flores. This time was different than the last. He got a proper goodbye kiss and a promise that Diego wouldn't cut him out of his life again. But it still hurt like hell to watch him go, not knowing when he might see him again.

What if he never comes back? What do I do then?

"Wyatt, this is amazing!" Ella exclaimed when he knocked on the door before entering. Roberto had already left them, and it looked as if they'd started to unpack. "I had no idea you were doing all this."

"Did Roberto tell you about our grand plans?"

"A wedding venue, he said. I take it this is one of the guest rooms," she said. "I feel like I should be paying you."

Wyatt motioned to one of several bare mattresses. Packages of bedding sat piled in a corner. "It's not entirely finished."

Ella picked up the bottom sheet she'd pulled out for the king-sized bed in the center of the room. Lifting her arms to shake it out and let it drift over the bed like a parachute, she said, "I'm not going to complain about brand-new sheets."

Diego might have been sleeping on one of these beds—most likely in the cabin, though—had he not gotten that call. Wyatt wished the best for Diego's friend, but he cursed the timing. They'd grown so much closer over the weekend. He'd felt Diego's walls coming down, had seen the softer, more emotional side of him that he remembered from their youth.

He hadn't said the words, but Wyatt had felt sure Diego loved him. The question wasn't: *Does Diego love Wyatt?* The question was: *Can love be enough?* With one thousand miles and entirely different jobs and schedules separating them, Wyatt didn't know if it could be.

"I can't believe how good the floors look," Ella said, jarring him from his thoughts.

"We had to refinish them," Wyatt said as he rounded the bed, helping Ella tuck the sheet in. "Rented a huge sander, filled in some old gouges, applied a new stain. I don't *ever* want to do it again."

She laughed. "Can't you buy some of that faux wood these days? Might have been easier."

"It was tempting," Wyatt said. "But this is more authentic."

Cheaper, too, even with the rental fee for the sander and stain. It was mostly labor, which he and Diego had undertaken together. When he looked around, he saw Diego all over this room. The floors, which he'd helped sand, the walls, which he'd helped paint after hanging drywall. The bathroom, where they'd fit in a quickie, still sweaty from work, which for some crazy reason had seemed sexy, rather than gross, at the time.

"The bathroom's not finished," Wyatt said, "but there's a working toilet. Not sure how long you'll be staying, but I've got a guy coming out to upgrade it. I'll have him do the bathroom on the other side first."

264

Ella pulled out the fluffy comforter to spread over the bed, while the boys started arguing over who should get the top bunk.

"Boys, there's two bunkbed sets," Wyatt called. "You can both sleep on top if you want."

"Yes!" Matthew exclaimed. "I want the one by the window!"

"I wanted that one," Ethan protested.

Ella rolled her eyes. "Play Rock-Paper-Scissors to decide," she ordered, "and no cheating!"

The boys whirled toward one another, slapping their fists into the palm of their hands, then throwing out their choice. Matthew's paper wrapped around Ethan's rock. "I win!"

"You always win," Ethan grumped, but thankfully, he accepted defeat.

Turning back to Ella, Wyatt asked, "What did you tell them?"

Her smile grew strained. "Just that we were having a sleepover at the ranch for a couple of days." Shaking her head, she said, "I don't know why Tucker did such a thing."

"Well, technically he didn't do it."

"He encouraged it," she said. "I wouldn't be surprised if he put the idea in Daryl's head. Why else would that man take such risks?"

Wyatt picked up a pillow, tossing it onto the bed that was now made up with sheets and a thick bronze-colored comforter. Unlike the honeymoon suite, which was outfitted with a pearl-colored satin comforter, these rooms were meant to evoke country comforts. The bedding came in warm, earth tones, and the decorations were more rustic.

"Struck me as odd that Daryl quit here right after you left, then followed you to the Daltons. Don't you think that's a bit..."

"What?"

Ella was a practical country woman, but in some ways, she was naïve. She'd married the first boy she ever dated, and she'd never been out of Texas as far as Wyatt knew. He didn't want to disturb her, so he shook his head. "Nothing."

She must have seen the revulsion in his face, though, because she drew back. "Ew, no. You don't think..."

"I don't know."

Her lips twisted. "Daryl was always nice, right? It wasn't just me..." She shuddered. "He never touched me."

"Didn't say he did, or even that he wanted to," Wyatt said, though he was relieved to hear it. "Maybe he genuinely was loyal to you. Maybe Grandad pushing you out like that disturbed him. It got pretty ugly."

"But you don't think that's the whole story."

"I don't, no," Wyatt said. "He was way too invested in your life."

"Maybe so," she mused. "I just thought he was friendly and sweet. Ugh, but as disturbing as that is, I find it more upsetting that my own husband was acting out against my family."

Wyatt sighed. "We weren't much of a family for a long time. I reckon he's never seen us that way."

"Still, I never wanted this. And I never *cared* that I wasn't in Grandad's will. You don't have to feel you need to make that right. The ranch was always going to you. I've known that forever."

Wyatt stepped back, tucking his hands into his pockets. He knew Ella was probably hurting over Tucker's secrets, but he couldn't really find a lot of space in him to care one way or the other about Tucker. He was too twisted up about Diego leaving to feel much of anything right now.

"I still want you to be involved with the ranch," Wyatt said. "But only if it's what you want. This wedding venue will take some effort to manage, and I've got a ranch to run, too. So, if you're interested..."

Her eyes widened. "Me? I don't know anything about weddings!"

"Well, you've had one, so you're one up on me."

"Guess that's true." Ella paused. "Roberto said Diego had to leave?"

Wyatt nodded once. "He did. Hey, how about we head over to the house for some food. I don't know about you all, but I missed dinner."

Ella seemed to see right through his abrupt change of subject, but she didn't push him. "I've missed Rosie's cooking. Hey, boys, you hungry?"

"I'm starving," Ethan exclaimed.

"Me too," Matthew said emphatically. "I'm hungrier than Ethan."

"Are not!"

"Are too!"

Ella sighed in exasperation, and Wyatt laughed. The boys made for a good distraction, even if less than happy circumstances led Ella to bringing them to the ranch. Despite Tucker's actions, he was Ella's husband and the boys' father. Wyatt hoped they could move forward from this. Tucker seemed to love Ella, and Wyatt hated to see another family torn apart by senseless Jones-Dalton feuding.

———

When Diego arrived at his apartment, Matias was ensconced on the sofa, swaddled in blankets and looking *rougher* than Diego had ever seen him. A large bruise discolored his right cheekbone, and there was a scabbed-over scrape on his forearm. Diego dropped his duffel bags by the door, tossed his keys in the bowl on the small entryway table, and knelt before him.

"Hi," Matias said. "Good trip?"

His smile looked like plastic, and there was no hiding the sadness in his falsely bright tone.

"It was long." Diego brushed his thumb lightly over the skin just under the worst of the bruising. "What happened here?"

"I fell. It's nothing."

Diego looked into his eyes. "It's not nothing," he said solemnly.

Matias burst into tears, his breath going ragged. "I'm sorry! I fucked up so bad, and I'm s-s-sorry..." His voice hitched with a sob as Diego drew him against his chest. He looked over Matias's shoulder, spotting Zac hovering at the threshold between the living room and kitchen.

"It's okay," Diego murmured. "You're gonna be okay."

"I p-p-promised ....rent," he managed, breathing still haywire, his body shuddering as he tried to choke down his tears. Diego rubbed his back and just held him a minute. Any anger he'd felt about Matias failing to pay his rent was long gone. He was far more worried about Matias's health and state of mind. He'd never in his life seen him like this. He was the sassy diva of Caliente, all snark and sexy innuendoes. Diego knew that those manic highs must also have some lows, but he'd never witnessed Matias fall apart. Even when he'd asked Diego if he could crash after his breakup with Craig, he'd seemed bummed, but not utterly heartbroken.

"I don't care about the rent."

"B-but—" Matias took a shuddery breath and pulled back in confusion. "You're gonna lose your apartment, and it's my fault."

"Right now, I'm more concerned about you. How are you feeling?"

Matias bit down on his full bottom lip, blinking hard to fight back another round of tears. "I feel fine. Almost like it never happened."

"He almost died," Zac said quietly. "He was mixing party drugs with way too much alcohol, and he was completely dehydrated—"

"Okay!" Matias interrupted. "I fucked up. Everybody knows that!" He turned beseeching eyes on Diego. "I partied and lost my job. I tried to pick up other shifts at other places, but everything started spiraling out of control. I know I'm the flaky friend, the one you can't count on." He sucked in a breath, tears continuing to trickle down his cheeks. "I'll get out of here as soon as I can. I clearly can't be trusted."

"Stop," Diego ordered. He gripped Matias's hand, squeezing it. "You made some mistakes, but you're still here, and we're still your friends. I should have checked in more, made sure you were doing okay with covering the rent, but mostly, I just want *you* to be okay."

"I just hate myself sometimes," Mati said in a low voice. "Why do I ruin everything?"

"Hey," Diego said softly. "You don't."

"Craig was like the steady hand I needed to keep me in line, you know? I kept rebelling against what he asked of me, but why? Without him..." He shook his head. "I just feel so lost, and so alone."

"You're not alone." Zac joined them, sitting on the edge of the sofa and putting his hand on Matias's leg. "We're here for you."

"You're really not mad about your apartment?" Matias asked Diego in a small voice.

Matias was going to worry himself sick until Diego reassured him.

"It's all going to work out," he said.

With twenty-plus hours in the car, Diego had plenty of time to make phone calls on his way to Miami. He'd talked with his apartment managers and secured a two-week extension. He'd been puzzled about why he hadn't received any calls from them, but it turned out he'd failed to update his phone number a couple of years before. They were reasonable, though. He had to pay the back rent in full by the deadline, or they'd start official eviction proceedings in court.

He'd also talked to his boss, Duke, at Caliente. That phone call had been even more difficult than the first.

"Do I know you?" Duke had said when Diego called him. "I think I vaguely remember someone named Diego, but... nope. Nothing's coming to me."

"I know it's been a while—"

"A while!" Duke snorted. "Six fucking weeks, Diego? You told me you were going to a funeral!"

"I was, I did," Diego said. "But ... I needed to stay a while. It's complicated."

"Well, feel free to fucking stay forever," he said. "I got plenty of bartenders."

I wish, Diego thought. It was ironic. He'd told Wyatt so many times that he would be leaving, that their relationship could only be temporary, but here he was, one thousand miles away, wishing for forever like a goddamn sap.

"I should have called and given you an update," Diego said. Forcing out the words, he added, "Sorry."

Groveling didn't come easily, but he needed shifts at Caliente if he was going to have any hope of paying his back rent on time. Matias needed a place to stay, and Diego really didn't want to deal with collection agencies or some sort of court case against him to collect the money. Better to get caught up, so he could focus on his next move.

Fortunately for him, one of Caliente's regular bartenders had quit the week before and Duke only busted his chops for another ten minutes before he told Diego he was on the schedule as of Wednesday night, and if he didn't show, he could kiss his job goodbye.

Diego checked the time on his phone now. He'd have time to shower and change if he hurried. He'd driven straight from Texas, with only breaks to sleep, and he was hardly in the mood to stand on his feet all night—especially after getting used to an entirely different schedule—but he didn't have much choice.

"I've actually got to go in to work soon," he told Matias. "If I can get enough shifts, and some good tips, I should be able to get the rent money together before it's too late. I'm working with the apartment managers, so try not to worry about it."

"Will you talk to Duke for me?" Matias asked. "I could help you pay the rent."

"Sure, I will, but not yet. You should take some time and recover—"

"I feel fine!"

"I'm not talking about your body, though that bruise might concern some of your fans." Matias lifted a hand to his face, grimacing in response to Diego's comment. "You need to let your heart recover too."

Matias sniffed, scowling. "Oh, fuck, you're gonna make me cry again, damn it."

Diego laughed softly. "Sorry."

He wouldn't admit it out loud, but his heart was in some distress of its own. Twenty-plus hours alone in a car was a *lot* of time to think—not necessarily a good thing when you were wallowing. Moments with Wyatt had kept replaying in Diego's head, especially their last conversations, when Wyatt bared his heart and offered to move Diego to the ranch, or even come to Miami to help him. It was like poking at a sore tooth. You knew it would ache each time you touched it, but you felt compelled to do it again and again, almost as if you needed the bloom of pain to remind you it was real.

Diego prodded the hurt in his heart once more, wishing he'd said *something* to Wyatt to make this separation easier, and pushed to his feet to go shower. While under the hot water, he ached to have Wyatt against him, their muscles straining. A dozen memories spooled through his mind. Wyatt's tightness, his rough voice after taking Diego's cock into his throat, his muffled cries of ecstasy as he bit down on his fist. His unbridled cries when they'd been out on the open range, free to be as loud as they wanted in the midst of nature.

He was too disheartened to get aroused, though. Shower fantasies had nothing on the real thing.

Fuck, I just got back, and I already miss him.

But that wasn't true. Diego had missed him every hour of his drive. He'd missed him before he even stepped off that porch. He'd started missing him the moment he knew he had to leave.

Stepping out of the shower, the folded-up envelope containing the check Wyatt had given him caught his eye. He didn't want his money, but he'd taken it. He could use it toward his rent, and ease some of his stress, or …

He could use it as it was originally intended.

———

Wyatt was dripping almost as much as the paint roller in his hand, sweat pouring off him even after he'd stripped down to his sleeveless undershirt, when a tap on his shoulder startled him.

He blinked, surprised to realize the sun was going down. He'd been painting for hours. He looked at the barn before him. There was only a small stretch left to do. In between their other ranch responsibilities, TJ and Colby had scraped the whole thing, made some repairs to loose and missing boards, and painted most of it. Wyatt was almost disappointed they'd made so much progress before he took over because burying himself in work had become his new favorite activity. Hours flew by, and he didn't have to think about anything. Didn't have to wonder if Diego was sliding back into his old life as easily as he'd merged into Wyatt's. Didn't have to imagine all the pretty, young, half-dressed gay men who might fling themselves into Diego's path at a Miami nightclub.

"Wyatt, it's dinnertime," Ella said. "Didn't you hear me calling?"

"No, I was too focused."

"That's one word for it," she said.

"Huh?"

"I know you miss him," she said gently. "Everyone knows you miss him. You don't have to be afraid to show it."

Wyatt turned back to the barn. "I'm so close. Think I'll just finish. Tell Rosie I'll warm up a plate later."

"Wyatt, you can't keep going like this," Ella said to his back. "I know what it's like to be hurting, but you can't bottle it all up inside you."

Wyatt disagreed. He kept working, because it was the only way he knew how to keep going. If he spent too much time thinking about how much he missed Diego, he'd fall the fuck apart. And since Diego had turned down his offer to drive up to Miami, to put him first, he was doing what he reckoned Diego wanted him to do: Getting on with living and running the ranch.

Almost two months ago, Wyatt had been convinced he couldn't manage the Triple J on his own, despite being raised to do just that. He'd been full of self-doubt, fear, and hopelessness.

He couldn't go back to being that guy. It was thanks to Diego he'd come to believe he was strong enough, smart enough to get the job done. He wanted Diego by his side, as his partner—and he still hoped like hell that day would come—but until then, he wasn't about to waste the hard work Diego had put in to get the ranch in a better position.

He would work, and he would keep it together, and he would hope. It was all he could do now.

"I'm fine," he murmured. "Just a little longer."

He kept working, and eventually Ella left. He lost himself in the repetition of movement, the burn in his muscles, the stiffness of his back and neck. Darkness fell, forcing him to stop, and he gazed at the barn, looking fresh and new. The trim still had to be done. He'd devour that task tomorrow.

It was only now, alone in the dark, that Wyatt allowed himself to pull out his phone and check his notifications. There was one new text.

Herding gay boys is almost as exhausting as herding cattle, Diego had texted, followed by a winky face emoticon. *I feel like all I do is work. How's the ranch?*

Wyatt soaked in each word, even though the text didn't say much. Each letter on the screen was proof that Diego hadn't forgotten Wyatt the second he was out of sight. He was working every night, Wyatt knew, trying to catch up his rent. And in addition to practically killing himself to meet his deadline, Diego was looking after Matias, too.

He had a lot on his plate without Wyatt being needy, so he'd done his best to detach himself and respond only when Diego called or texted. Wyatt was afraid if he let go of that restraint, he'd beg Diego for answers he wasn't ready to give.

Wyatt reread a few of Diego's messages, reassuring himself that Diego was maintaining contact. Diego was reaching out to him. He wasn't alone in wanting to maintain a connection. His heart ached and his eyes burned, and he allowed himself a minute to feel how much he missed him. Taking a deep breath, he texted him back: *All good at the ranch. Barn is nearly done.*

He wanted to say so much more. *I miss you. Let's be together, I don't care where or how. I love you.*

But he'd tried that already. He'd given Diego his heart, his words. All he could do now was wait until Diego was ready to do the same.

If he ever was.

Wyatt forced himself to put the phone back in his pocket without making any new pleas and packed up his painting supplies. He needed a shower and bed. The exhaustion setting in now that he'd stopped working assured him that he'd sleep like the dead after he scarfed some leftovers.

Which was just how he liked it. No time for thoughts, or memories, or fantasies of being with the man he loved.

Diego moved behind the bar, muscle memory at work as he mixed drinks for the crush of men pushing forward, shouting for his attention. Lights strobed around the club, music vibrated up from the floor and through his body, and admiring gazes lingered on his chest and biceps.

He flashed a smile at one of the club regulars, Levi, a pretty little thing decked out in a tiara and fake silver eyelashes. "Here's the shot, birthday boy."

The smile took effort. He was just going through the motions at Caliente, his heart no longer in it. He needed tips, but he'd never been less in the mood to flirt with his customers. It hadn't seemed disingenuous before—maybe because he was single and chose to hook up when it suited him—but now it felt as if he was leading them on. Diego had no interest in any of these guys, not even Levi, who'd coerced him into bed more than once. He'd liked the way Levi was down for anything and breathily obeyed Diego's every desire. He now realized that he'd been a bit controlling even before he'd hooked up with Wyatt. Their dynamic wasn't all about Wyatt's needs, but his too. They were a perfect match.

What I wouldn't give to have him waiting tonight.

Diego missed the fantastic sex. He'd gotten used to having Wyatt whenever he wanted him, however he wanted him. Now, his body ached for release, and no one else would do.

It went beyond sex, too. He missed Wyatt's drawl, his lazy smiles, his bright blue eyes. Missed sitting out on the porch as the sun set, talking over beers. Missed shooting the shit about ranch work, helping Wyatt solve problems. At least they'd finally put a stop to the vandalism before he left. That was one less worry, and Diego had plenty of them.

Matias rejected the idea of counseling and wanted to return to work, but Diego wasn't sure it was a good idea. Diego was nearing his deadline to pay his rent, and he wasn't bringing in as much in tips as he'd like—probably due to his thoughts lingering on Wyatt too much for him to charm his customers out of their cash. And Wyatt was too far away, not just physically, but emotionally. He answered Diego's texts and calls, but he didn't say much. He was quiet, closed off. It wasn't like him, and it worried Diego.

Wyatt had worn his heart on his sleeve, but Diego hadn't done the same. He'd been too overwhelmed the night he left to express how he was feeling. Now, Diego had so many things he wanted to say to Wyatt, but he wanted to say them in person, when he was free to take the next step.

He just hoped Wyatt would be more patient than Diego ever had been, and that he'd forgive Diego for needing some time to figure out what had been in front of him all along.

The only life he wanted was a life with Wyatt.

26

Wyatt was tired and covered in travel grime that was more cringeworthy than a good, honest work sweat had ever been when he arrived at Bliss Island. He'd almost canceled the trip half a dozen times. He'd wanted to make this trip with Diego —for business reasons, yes, but also as a romantic getaway where maybe he could coax Diego into opening his heart to a future with Wyatt.

That had gone belly up, but Caleb and Julien had been so helpful and kind that Wyatt couldn't bring himself to bail on them, even if he wasn't fit company for anybody.

Julien stood on the pier, smiling and waving, as Wyatt disembarked with his duffel thrown over one shoulder. Bliss Island was surprisingly small. Wyatt guessed everything really was bigger in Texas, because he had expected something more than a little rock within sight of the Maine coastline.

A cool mist had coated Wyatt with the sea, and now he felt crusted with sea salt, in addition to his own sweat. A brisk breeze flowed over his skin, bringing up goosebumps. It was several degrees cooler than in Texas, but it was mild enough Wyatt didn't bother with more than a long-sleeved denim shirt.

"I'm so glad you could make it!" Julien exclaimed. "Caleb is stuck on the phone with a client, but I'll give you a ride down to the house."

He jerked a thumb over his shoulder, and Wyatt noticed the golf cart behind him. He could see a paved road extending beyond the pier, winding between towering evergreen trees. From the boat, he'd been able to spot an expansive mansion in the center of the island, along with several other buildings and a lighthouse. The whole kit-n-kaboodle was about one-tenth the size of the ranch.

"Thanks," he said. "I could have walked."

Julien gave him a brief onceover. "I'm sure you could have." Despite the teasing words, his brow creased. "You look worn out. How was your flight?"

"Long," Wyatt said as he folded himself into the golf cart. "Had a couple of layovers."

"Ugh, airports," Julien said. "I'd be just as happy to never travel again."

He didn't seem surprised to see Wyatt arrive alone. He could only guess that Diego had updated Caleb and Julien on their change in plans.

Wyatt had already made up his mind to fly to Miami when he left here. He needed to see Diego and get some answers. He should probably be more patient; it'd only been two weeks. He knew some folks made relationships work long-distance for months or years before they merged their lives, and he was more than willing to do the same. Trouble was, he didn't know if they even *had* a relationship. It wasn't the time or distance between them that was killing him; it was the uncertainty.

Julien drove Wyatt toward the house, pointing out the horse stables as they passed it, as well as a popular riding path that cut through the woods.

"I saw a lighthouse on the other end of the island," Wyatt said, mostly just to make conversation.

"Oh, the lighthouse has a fun story," Julien said. "Bliss Island had its own romance long ago."

"How do you mean?"

"The lighthouse keeper and the original owner of the island were lovers," Julien said. "I've done some research, read some of the letters they exchanged. Love letters." He wiggled his eyebrows at Wyatt, making him smile. "It's not all happy, of course. The original owner of the island was married, had children. It wasn't until after his wife died that they were free to be together. It was top secret, even then. Not something you could do openly back then, but being on an isolated island helped."

"Huh, that's interesting," he said. "So they lived here together?"

"Sure did. Bliss Island has always been a place full of love and happy endings."

Wyatt might have found the story uplifting if he and Diego were here together as planned. It might have been enough to motivate him to make another foolish marriage proposal. He'd learned the hard way that big romantic gestures weren't Diego's style. He was too practical. When Wyatt got to Miami, he wouldn't make sweeping promises or ask Diego to uproot his life. He'd just kiss the daylights out of him, if allowed, and tell him that he wanted to be with him however it was possible. Even if it meant phone calls and video chats and occasional trips back and forth. He'd take whatever he could get, but he *needed* something. If Diego couldn't offer at least that much, Wyatt would have to pull away, even if it meant cutting out his own heart.

"You mind if I get a shower?" he asked as the mansion came into view. It was about the same width of the ranch house back home, but it was two stories tall and of an entirely different, more elegant design. A large porch wrapped around the sides of the house, and small balconies extended from the upper-story windows. Beyond it, he could just glimpse the navy-blue ocean sparkling under the sun.

"Sure, you can freshen up," Julien said. "Afterwards, Caleb should have time to walk you through a lot of the planning and project management processes he has in place. Then we'll do dinner. We don't have an event until day after tomorrow, so there's plenty of time to see everything before we're overrun with guests."

"Thank y'all for doin' this," Wyatt said.

Julien smiled. "It's our pleasure. Let me show you to your room."

The afternoon passed quickly as Wyatt holed up in Caleb's office and went over his systems for booking clients, for planning the events — which entailed far more planning than Wyatt intended the ranch to provide — and accounting. He helped Wyatt get an idea of the expense of catering such events, though prices might vary regionally, as well as the time involved in pulling a wedding together.

All in all, it was worth the trip on its own.

That evening, Caleb and Julien introduced him to the household staff as if he were a dear friend instead of a virtual stranger before taking him into the tavern for a drink.

"You don't have to wine and dine me," he told them. "I'm imposing enough on your time."

"You're a guest," Caleb said. "Besides, any friend of Diego's is a friend of ours."

Wyatt threw back the rest of his Jack and Coke. "Diego's not here, though. Y'all don't know me from Adam."

Caleb and Julien exchanged a loaded look. Julien shook his head. Caleb frowned. Then, as if the silent argument had never happened, they turned back to him.

"We've gotten to know you through all the emails and phone calls," Caleb said. "We're invested in your plans now."

"It's true, you can't get rid of us now," Julien said lightly.

They really were kind. Wyatt nodded. "I can't thank y'all enough for taking the time to meet with me. You've got a real nice place here."

"Just nice?" Caleb said, sounding offended.

Julien laughed. "Caleb's a bit of a snob, so forgive him. He thinks everyone should be in love with Bliss Island just because he is."

"I'm in love with you," Caleb corrected Julien. "Bliss Island is just a nice icing on the cake. I'd go anywhere for you."

"Awww." Julien kissed him, just a peck, but Wyatt could feel the affection between the two. Envy swirled in his gut. Julien added, "Luckily you get to have your Julien and eat your cake too."

Wyatt cleared his throat, pushing back his chair. "It was a long day. Think I'll turn in."

Caleb looked up, his blue eyes clearing of the lovey-dovey haze. "We're being rude. Sorry."

Wyatt waved it off. "No, it's fine. You know us ranchers. Early to bed, early to rise."

"Just how early do you get up?" Julien asked. "Because I can't do breakfast before eight."

Wyatt laughed. He'd definitely be awake before eight. "When does the sun rise around here?"

"Oh, God," Julien said.

"Don't worry about it. I can go for a walk, check out more of the island. I'll be fine."

Caleb stood up, walking him toward the tavern exit. When they stepped into the hall, he pointed out a set of double doors at the back of the house. "That's our private quarters. If you need anything, you can just knock. Or text one of us."

Wyatt tipped his head. "I'll be fine. Y'all have a good night."

He turned away just as Julien came barreling out the door. "Is he still—Oh, there you are. Wyatt, can I talk to you before you head upstairs?"

"What is it?"

Julien put a hand on his arm. "It's about Diego..."

His stomach clenched. Had Diego told Julien something about how he felt. Wyatt wasn't sure he wanted to know what was on Julien's mind. "It's late," he hedged. "Maybe tomorrow—"

"He's waiting for you on the beach," Julien blurted.

Wyatt's heart skipped. "What?"

"He was supposed to be here earlier," Julien said apologetically. "His flight was delayed, and—"

"Where?" Wyatt interrupted. "Show me."

Julien led him back into the tavern and toward some glass doors that opened onto the back porch. "There's steps that will lead you down the cliffside safely. He's down there waiting to talk to you."

Wyatt swallowed. "Is it good news?"

Julien smiled at him, his eyes soft. "Why don't you go find out?"

Diego paced on the beach, his heart thundering in his chest. This grand romantic gesture shit was nerve-racking as hell, but Wyatt deserved it. Wyatt deserved all the words and gestures his heart desired after being so patient with Diego.

He watched Wyatt picking his way down the steps to the beach. *This is it. Remember this moment. God, he's gorgeous—*

Wyatt crossed the beach in three long strides, jogging over dirt, and caught Diego in a kiss. They stumbled, and Diego grabbed the nape of Wyatt's neck, holding him close as he breathed him in. Something tense and uncomfortable inside him finally relaxed. He was still nervous, but coming here had been the right decision.

Diego had needed to return to Miami—not just for Matias, but for himself. He'd needed to know how it felt to be back on his old stomping grounds. Without leaving Wyatt, even for two weeks, he couldn't have known how deeply he needed him and the life they'd created together at the ranch.

"What are you doing here?" Wyatt asked, sounding more guarded than usual.

Diego caught his hand, squeezing it. "I promised to make this trip with you. I used the money you gave me for a ticket out of Miami."

Disappointment flickered across Wyatt's features. "Oh."

Shit, that came out wrong. He'd made it sound like an obligation, not a desire.

"I wanted to see you too, of course."

"Of course," Wyatt echoed dully. "But if all you want is another night or two of great sex, you can save it."

Diego flinched. "That's not all I want from you. Is that what you think?"

"I don't know what to think, because you never tell me anything. I love you. I always have. I've made foolish, desperate proposals and put my heart on the line, but it's never enough."

"It's more than enough," Diego insisted. "It's everything."

"You have a funny way of showing it."

Diego took a deep breath. "I wasn't ready then, but I am now."

Heart hammering erratically, he dropped to one knee in the wet sand. Even with his pulse rushing in his ears, he heard Wyatt gasp.

"What are you doing?"

"I'm putting my heart on the line this time. I'm proposing to you, Wyatt." His voice softened. "When we were six years old, we made a promise to marry. I want to keep that promise."

Wyatt choked up. "You said that was kid stuff."

"It was, but it meant something to you. And to me too," Diego admitted.

He'd convinced himself it was nothing but child's play when their relationship ended, unable to face the reality that he'd lost something precious. He didn't want to deny what was real for them. They'd loved each other ever since they knew how, and long before they understood it.

"I want to be with you, Wyatt. I need to sort my shit out before I can move to the ranch, but—"

"I would have left it for you."

"I know, sweetheart," Diego said. "I don't want you to leave it. I asked you to choose once, but this time, I'm choosing. I choose you, and I choose life at the ranch with you. It's where we both belong. Doing anything else would only break both our hearts. So, please, Wyatt, say you'll marry me. We can keep all the promises we make to one another, starting with this first one."

"On one condition."

"Anything."

"Tell me you love me," Wyatt said. "I need the words—"

Diego surged up, kissing him hard. Lips still clinging, he whispered against his mouth. "I love you so fucking much, Wyatt."

Wyatt's breath stuttered against his lips. "Love you too. So much."

Diego pressed their foreheads together, unwilling to break contact just yet. "Walking away from you was the biggest mistake I ever made. I don't want to go another six years without you. I don't want to go another day."

Wyatt's hands tightened on Diego's biceps, and there was a long pause that made his heart swoop with fear.

"I want a life with you," Wyatt said thickly. "But I don't want you to feel obligated to marry me. The marriage pact does mean something to me, but your happiness means more. If you'd rather do a long-distance relationship and stay in Miami—"

"Fuck no," Diego burst out. "I need you in the flesh."

Wyatt's lips twitched. "Just my flesh?"

"I need all of you," he corrected. "I love you, and I love the ranch. I always have. I lost sight of that in my anger, but... It's where I belong, too. So, I'll ask one more time. Wyatt Jones, will you marry me?"

A goofy smile overtook Wyatt's face, his eyes bright. "I thought you'd never ask. *Yes*, I'll marry you."

"Thank fuck," Diego said as Julien and Caleb broke into applause behind them. It was a little embarrassing to have someone witness his new, sappy attitude about love when he'd gone around bitching that happily-ever-afters were just a fairy tale, but it was also fitting they should be there. Diego had witnessed their engagement—their *real* one—so it only seemed right.

Wyatt laughed lightly. "I can't believe you did all this. I was set to go to Miami when I left here to shake some answers out of you."

Diego grinned. "So your patience does have a limit. Good to know."

"These are the sort of things it's handy to know in a marriage," Julien teased.

"Did you mean what you said about keeping the pact?" Wyatt asked.

"Of course I did."

"And you realize my twenty-sixth birthday's next week?"

Diego turned wide eyes on Caleb. "You can squeeze in another wedding this weekend, right?"

Wyatt laughed. "It's okay, seriously—"

"We can do it," Caleb said with a mischievous smile. "I'd consider it an honor."

Diego gripped Wyatt's shoulders, looking him dead in the eye. "I want us to keep our promises to one another, but if it's too soon for you, we can wait."

Wyatt shook his head. "Are you nuts? It's about six years too late. I'll marry you anytime, anywhere, including right here, this weekend."

Wyatt and Diego got married on a slightly overcast day on Bliss Island, with Caleb officiating and Caleb's mother and Julien serving as witnesses, while a huge Texas crowd watched via a video call through Caleb's tablet. Roberto, Mama, Rosie, and the ranch hands were all in attendance, as were Ella and the boys, and Josefina and her family. They couldn't possibly all squish into the viewing screen, but they did their best.

Diego and Wyatt had gone to the mainland for a marriage certificate and done a little shopping to prepare for their big day. Wyatt purchased a white cowboy hat and a nice Western dress shirt, while Diego opted for a more traditional suit that made him look super sexy and sophisticated. Wyatt couldn't wait to tear it off him later. They'd decided, together, not to bother with rings and instead picked up some twine they'd tie around one another's finger for the ceremony. Ranch work and jewelry didn't mix.

Wyatt still couldn't believe that Diego had come all the way to Bliss Island for him, much less to propose and marry him within twenty-four hours. He'd gotten everything he'd wanted, but he still had to pause every now and question whether it was real.

The slight ache in his ass assured him it wasn't all a fantasy. Diego had thoroughly made love to him the night before, showering him with words of love now that he'd finally let down the last of his walls. "I love you," he'd whispered in Wyatt's ear as he sank into his body. "I love you," he'd groaned as he came.

Wyatt teased him afterward. "What did you say during sex? Did you drop the L bomb?"

Diego had rolled him under his body and pinned him. "Like you've never dropped an *I love you* while in bed with me?"

"Hmm. Don't think I have."

He glared. "You have."

"I don't remember."

"Wyatt," he growled.

Wyatt had laughed, amused at how much it bugged Diego that he pretended not to remember that spontaneous, embarrassing "I love you" that had escaped him back at the ranch. "Oh, I remember now. I was talking to your dick. I love him more than words can say—"

Diego used his dick to shut up Wyatt, even though he was nowhere near ready to go again. Wyatt had allowed Diego to pin him down and stuff his mouth with flesh, sucking until Diego hardened again and shot down his throat.

"Who do you love?" Diego had asked when he was done.

"I love you," Wyatt said, smirking. "And whatever you stuff in my mouth."

Wyatt shook the sexy but less than appropriate memories from his head as he took Diego's hands at the front of a tiny chapel. There were just five people in the room, counting them, but he was aware of their family back home watching as they each gave their vows.

Wyatt went first. "I persuaded you to make a marriage pact with me before I even knew what love was," Wyatt said. "Or maybe that's the way it seemed. But looking back, I think maybe I understood love better then than I do now. I didn't question my heart or doubt the future. I looked at you, and I just knew: You were the one I wanted to spend my life with. I know I've made mistakes, and it's cost us time, but I want to spend the rest of my life making it up to you. I want you to be the partner I've always wanted." He bit his lip, nervous to add this next part. "Grandad always told me that I couldn't do it alone, and he was halfway right. I can do it alone, but my life is so much richer when I have you. I don't ask for anything, other than your love and support, as we build a life together."

Diego's jaw was clenched so hard he looked ready to deck

someone, but Wyatt knew he was struggling to maintain his composure. He took a deep breath when Caleb instructed him to share his own vows. Wyatt had been surprised when Diego suggested they write their own, but he'd been happy to define their marriage on their own terms.

"I gave up on this day a long time ago."

There were audible sniffles coming from the video. Wyatt smiled encouragingly when Diego faltered. *Go on,* he mouthed, nodding.

"I saw the world in black and white, and right and wrong. And I, of course, was always right." There were a few chuckles in the room. "I regret that I didn't have more faith in your heart, because you've got one of the biggest hearts I've ever come across. But I don't regret our time apart, because it helped us grow up. I believe that I'm a better man for you now than I could have been six years ago, and I want to be the best version of myself for you every day for the rest of our lives."

Julien stepped forward, handing Wyatt a bit of twine. He wound it around Diego's finger, tying it neatly. "With this string, I thee wed," he said with a wink.

Diego snorted as he tied his bit of twine around Wyatt's finger. "How appropriate we're tying each other up right now."

"Hey now, this is a wedding," Josefina teased from the video call. "Save your bedroom talk for later."

Among cheers and laughter, Caleb said the final words of the ceremony. "You may now kiss your husband."

Wyatt dipped his head, smiling into a kiss.

He'd finally wrangled his groom. Or maybe he was the one who'd been wrangled. Ah, hell, it didn't matter. They were tied together forever, and nothing had ever felt more right.

EPILOGUE

A breeze rustled through the leaves of a massive oak tree where Wyatt and Diego had once climbed as children. Beneath it stood a simple arbor — built by the Triple J ranch hands — two thick beams, connected by a third, with bunches of flowers affixed down each side.

Twenty folding chairs stretched across the carpet of lush grass bursting from the ground in early spring. Holding the ceremony in March was a gamble, with less predictable weather, but they'd had a stretch of mild days, so Wyatt wasn't too worried. Bliss Ranch was ready for its first wedding, and it was fitting that it should be for one of its own.

A banjo player began plucking his strings, picking out a melody, as Wyatt stepped up to the end of the aisle that was formed between the chairs. Up front, Diego stood beside his father, both of them in tuxes.

Wyatt turned, holding out his arm. "Ready to become Mrs. Flores?"

Mama grasped his arm, her smile blooming across her face. "Honey, I've been ready for a long time."

Diego had been less than impressed when their parents

announced their own engagement the day he and Wyatt got married. Wyatt had laughed at his shocked expression.

"Our parents are getting married, and we just got married," Diego said. "It's kind of like incest."

"It's not incest," Mama had said, looking horrified, and Wyatt had turned his face into Diego's shoulder, losing it as Diego hastily apologized.

"How come you're not surprised?" Diego had asked accusingly. "I swear, my father talks to you more than me."

Wyatt rolled his eyes. "Yeah, he mentioned it, but it was pretty obvious. I'm not sure how you missed him sneaking off the ranch at night to go to town."

"I was preoccupied with another man," Diego had grumbled, and Wyatt's heart had melted all over again. He'd kissed Diego's pout away, and he'd warmed up to the idea, which was especially good, considering he was Roberto's best man.

Mama, dressed in an off-white ivory sundress — too practical for sweeping trains, yet too formal for an average day — stepped forward with him while their guests rose to their feet. Today was Bliss Ranch's inaugural ceremony, a soft opening for the wedding venue that was already receiving some bookings for the months to come. They'd postponed the opening until spring and spent all winter marketing the venue, offering Opening Season specials to encourage couples who'd gotten behind in their planning or had another venue fall through to book with them. Caleb had thoroughly educated Wyatt on what to expect, so he knew couples usually planned their weddings one to two years in advance, and it would take time to build up the event side of the ranch.

Mama and Roberto had suggested that Wyatt and Diego hold a ceremony, since they'd basically eloped on Bliss Island, and maybe one day they would. But they'd already celebrated their union — on Bliss and again at the ranch — far too impatient to await the opening of the event venue to be together the way they'd always wanted. Bad enough that Diego had to return to

Miami for a short stretch to pack up his apartment and say his goodbyes to his friends—all except for Matias, anyway, who sat in the front row dabbing at his eyes. Wyatt hadn't been able to leave the ranch for the three weeks it took Diego to arrange his affairs —thankfully his apartment managers agreed to release him from the lease early—but Wyatt had insisted on flying in to help him and Matias pack up and drive Diego's car and a moving truck to Texas.

By then, Matias had recovered some of his spunk and was the sassiest, brattiest man Wyatt had ever met. Hot, yes, but so annoying. Especially when bored on a cattle ranch with no useful skills. But the fresh air seemed to be doing him some good, and with each month that passed, he smiled a little more freely, so Wyatt was more than happy to host him. He just foisted him off on his ranch hands if he got to be too much of a handful.

Wyatt released his mother when they reached the front of the aisle, and she took Roberto's hands, joining him front and center to exchange vows. Wyatt retreated after giving her away. Ella stood up with Mama, and Tucker and the boys sat in the audience. Tucker had given Wyatt a sincere apology and offered to pay for the damages Daryl had inflicted, but Wyatt was happy enough to accept his handshake and his promise that they would move forward as family, not enemies. Ella had accepted his apologies too, but she'd made it clear he was on thin ice until further notice.

Wyatt and Diego's eyes met several times as the vows were said, remembering their own little marriage, still so new.

"I now pronounce you husband and wife," the officiant announced. "You may kiss the bride."

Wyatt clapped along with the rest of the guests as Mama and Roberto kissed chastely, Mama blushing pink. She turned, hugging Diego, and then Ella, before she and Roberto moved down the aisle, headed for the reception they'd set up in the barn.

Wyatt grinned as they stepped into the cavernous space

draped with silky material and twinkling lights. Rustic elegance, he thought with a tip of the head to Caleb. It looked gorgeous.

"Can I have the first dance?" Diego asked.

Wyatt brushed a kiss over his cheek. "Darlin', you can have all of them."

After a long evening of dancing and more than a few beers, Wyatt and Diego were alone in the reception space, bagging trash. Papá and Mama Jones—*Mama Flores?*—had snuck off to enjoy the honeymoon suite, while the rest of the party guests had enjoyed themselves a few hours longer.

At nearly one a.m., Diego was beginning to appreciate just how hard Caleb Taylor must work. They didn't even do the planning for this shindig, and Diego was exhausted. After returning from Bliss Island, Wyatt had attempted to reel Ella into managing the event, but she had her own farm to worry about, and in the end, Wyatt's mother had stepped up to manage the Bliss side of the Triple J Ranch. She had moved into the ranch house with Roberto, but he was building a small bungalow out past the bunkhouse a ways, where they'd have more privacy.

That meant she'd mostly planned her own wedding, but she hadn't seemed to mind.

Wyatt cleared his throat. Diego looked up, and nearly dropped the trash bag in his hand.

His husband was stark naked, a coil of rope looped over his shoulder. Seeing that frayed rope against his smooth skin sent goosebumps racing over Diego's flesh.

"No more work," Wyatt said with a grin. "It's play time."

Diego chuckled. "And what are you doing with that?"

They both knew of the two of them, it was Wyatt who would enjoy being tied down. Diego hadn't given much thought to bondage, but he sure as hell would be now. If he ever tied Wyatt up, he wouldn't be using the coarse rope they had on the ranch, though. He'd have to buy proper gear that wouldn't tear up Wyatt's perfect skin. Fuck, he'd look gorgeous all trussed up and begging to come.

Diego tossed the trash bag to the side, hands itching to slide over all that bared skin. Wyatt's strength showed in the play of his muscle as he strolled closer.

"What I should have done when you first came to the ranch," Wyatt said with a wink.

He threw out the rope, then coiled it up, positioning the large loop—which had already been tied with a Honda knot—all while naked. Diego appreciated his form *and* his form as Wyatt raised his arm and rotated his wrist, swinging the lasso around his head three times before letting it loose.

It dropped over Diego's head and one shoulder, and Wyatt tugged. Diego stepped forward, so as not to end up with a noose around his neck, and Wyatt grinned smugly.

"Well, you caught me," he said, humoring him. As a target that wasn't moving, he hadn't been much a challenge for Wyatt. "What are you gonna do with me?"

Wyatt crossed the space between them, still holding the rope. Leaning in close, he murmured, "I think I'll keep you."

He kissed Diego, and when he stepped back Diego pulled the rope over his head and dropped it over Wyatt instead. The lasso slid down over both his shoulders, and Diego took the remaining length of rope from his hand and wound it around him loosely.

His cowboy raised an eyebrow. "Turning the tables on me?"

"Something like that," Diego said, guiding him onto one of the banquet chairs in the barn. He stepped up close, jerking open his jeans and pushing his cock, still covered by his cotton boxer briefs, against Wyatt's mouth. He could fuck his mouth while he admired that rough rope decorating his body, but Diego had other ideas. He reached into his back pocket, retrieved the sachet of lube he kept on him at all times, and then stepped back to strip off his clothes.

He returned to Wyatt, pressing the blunt head of his cock against his lips. Wyatt opened eagerly, tongue sending a shock of electricity sparking over the tip of Diego's dick. He bucked, pushing into Wyatt's mouth—which was exactly what Wyatt had wanted, no doubt. But that was okay, he was content to let Wyatt play his games. Diego poured lube over two fingers and reached behind himself as Wyatt moaned around his cock.

He pressed his fingers into himself, prepping himself quickly. It wasn't until he swiped lube over Wyatt's bare cock that he seemed to catch on to the plan. He made a surprised sound, his eyes darkening with desire. Diego didn't bottom often, and he'd never bottomed while playing the role of dominant top.

"You're not the only one who can play cowboy," he murmured, taking Wyatt's mouth in a sensuous kiss. "I'm gonna ride you good."

Wyatt huffed, more breath than laugh, but he was amused by Diego's corniness. He wasn't quite sure why he was being so ridiculous, except he felt downright giddy. Asking Wyatt to marry him was the best decision he'd ever made. They made one another happy, and the ranch was doing great. It still wasn't everything it'd been before its decline, but it was steady and in the black now, with no more instances of harassment or vandalism. The wedding venue would supplement it—and hopefully one day be a significant source of income—but that would take time build up, and that was okay. They didn't need a lot, just enough to pay the bills and keep a roof over their heads.

Diego didn't mind getting dirty and working hard. Wyatt had offered him the opportunity to work events instead, but that wasn't really the life he wanted. He wanted the life he and Wyatt envisioned before their relationship was derailed.

And he finally had it.

He reached behind him, fingers feeling for the hard length of

Wyatt's cock. He grasped it, making Wyatt's breath catch, and guided it to his slick hole. It stretched him, burning a little too intensely. He'd rushed the prep and unlike Wyatt he didn't really enjoy pain with his pleasure, but he breathed through it and his body adjusted. Slowly, he impaled himself on Wyatt's cock, letting it fill him until his ass was flush with Wyatt's lap.

Wyatt grasped his sides, the lasso symbolic but not a true restraint, which was good. That rope was rough, and probably wasn't terribly comfortable even loosely draped over him, but Wyatt left it, seeming content to feel up Diego while he began to ride him. Wyatt's hands slid over his stomach, evading his needy cock, and twisted his nipples, sending tingles ricocheting between them and his balls.

He gasped for breath. Riding was hard work. "If you're gonna use your hands, be useful and grab my dick."

Wyatt obliged, stroking him as Diego powered himself up and down, both of them moaning and panting their way toward the inevitable crash into orgasm.

"Fuck, fuck, fuck," Wyatt said. "So close, D. Need you to come."

"Yeah," Diego said, arching his body, straining his muscles to get Wyatt right where he needed him, cockhead grinding against his prostate. "I'm there. I'm right there."

His body tensed up before pleasure fired through him like a solar flare and he came with a harsh cry. Wyatt clutched at him, hips bucking as he pushed as far inside Diego as he could, jerking as he shot inside his body. They'd given up condoms shortly after getting married, and Diego couldn't get over how great it felt to have Wyatt inside him, and vice versa, with no barriers between their flesh.

"Damn," Diego said, breathing hard. "Think we have a barn kink?"

Wyatt laughed as Diego worked himself free and stood on

shaky legs. "We got some kind of kink for one another. But we better clean up, or Mama is gonna have our hides tomorrow."

"That'd be a cruel end to the honeymoon," Diego agreed as helped Wyatt pull off the coils of rope and toss them aside.

"Let's finish this up so we can get some sleep," Wyatt said. "We've got an early morning ahead."

Didn't they always? But Diego didn't mind. He fell in love with Wyatt more every day. He started his day with Wyatt, and he ended his day with Wyatt, just how it should be.

Side by side, just like they started.

Just like they'd end.

Together.

—fin—

ABOUT THE RANCH

Researching this novel was an endeavor, considering that I've never been on a ranch. To create the Triple J Ranch and its day-to-day life, I read about Texas ranches and watched YouTube videos about working with cattle from ATVs, cutting hay, hooking up cow cake feeders to trailers, and so much more. I also spoke frequently with a Texas rancher, Maude Allen, whom I cannot thank enough for answering my many, many questions. Any inaccurate depiction of ranch life is solely my mistake.

The story in *Wrangling a Groom* that the Triple J Ranch might have been won in a game of cards—thus driving the feud between the Daltons and the Joneses—was inspired by an old folk tale regarding a real ranch, the 6666 Ranch (also known as the Four Sixes). In that case, the rumor was that it was won with a hand containing four sixes. However, the original owner and his descendants say the four sixes represent the brand placed on the first herd of cattle at the ranch.

There are no other similarities between the two ranches. The Four Sixes is a massive ranch, and Wyatt Jones's ranch is a more modest operation at nine thousand acres.

The name Jones was chosen partly because it's a fairly

common name in the region, and there have been Texas ranchers by that name. The name Dalton was chosen at random, probably subconsciously, because my husband comes from a line of Daltons —the criminal ones!—in Kansas.

Cow Creek, Texas, is entirely fictional, as is Riggs, Texas, but I imagined the ranch and its surroundings to be somewhere south of San Angelo, Texas, a good three hours or more from the largest cities in Texas.

THANK YOU FOR READING!

Thank you for reading *Wrangling a Groom*! If you can spare a few minutes to write a review, even a few words can help an indie author like me. If you haven't yet read Caleb and Julien's love story, you can find it in Book 1 of Marital Bliss, *Surprise Groom*. I can't say for certain where the series will lead me next. I do have plans to write a story for Matias, as well as other characters who have appeared in the series, so keep an eye out for future titles!

I have to acknowledge my beta readers, Susan and Anita, for working with me on a tight deadline, as well as my editors, Jill Wexler and Posy Roberts. I'm also extremely grateful to Maude Allen, who lives on a Texas ranch and answered my many questions.

I offer monthly giveaways in my newsletter, bonus content and more. Sign up at http://www.tinyurl.com/djandcompany

I also encourage you to join my FB group for fun teasers and other extras: DJ and Company

You can connect with me on social media in other ways, as well!

Queer Romance Freebie Fan Club - http://www.facebook.com/groups/queerromance

facebook.com/AuthorDJJamison

twitter.com/DJ_Jamison_

bookbub.com/authors/dj-jamison

goodreads.com/DJ_Jamison

ABOUT THE AUTHOR

DJ Jamison writes a variety of queer characters, from gay to bisexual to asexual, with a focus on telling love stories that are more about common ground than lust at first sight. DJ grew up in the Midwest in a working-class family, and those influences can be found in her writing through characters coping with real-life problems: money troubles, workplace drama, family conflicts and, of course, falling in love. DJ spent more than a decade in the newspaper industry before chasing her first dream to write fiction. She spent a lifetime reading before that and continues to avidly devour her fellow authors' books each night. She lives in Kansas with her husband, two sons, two fish, one snake, and a sadistic cat named Birdie.

BOOKS BY DJ JAMISON

Ashe Sentinel Connections

Changing Focus

Source of Protection

Rewriting His Love Life

Winter Blom

Hard Press

Chance for Christmas

Hearts and Health

Heart Trouble

Bedside Manner

Urgent Care

Room for Recovery

Surprise Delivery

Orderly Affair

Operation Makeover

Rapid Response

Marital Bliss

Surprise Groom

Wrangling a Groom

Real Estate Relations

Full Disclosure

Buyer's Remorse

My Anti-Series

My Anti-Valentine

My Anti-Boyfriend

My Anti-Marriage

The Espinoza Boys

Earning Edie (m/f)

Catching Jaime (m/m)

Standalones

Love by Number

Yours for the Holiday

All I Want is You